TWICE BITTEN

NEW MOON SERIES BOOK ONE

BELLE HARPER

Copyright © 2020 by Belle Harper

First Publication: April 30th, 2020

Cover Art by Mibl Art

Second round of Editing by Meghan Leigh Daigle

Formatting by Belle Harper

All rights reserved.

No part of this book may be reproduced in any form or by any electronic or mechanical means, including information storage and retrieval systems, without written permission from the author, except for the use of brief quotations in a book review.

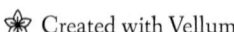 Created with Vellum

Mum and Dad.
Thank you for all your love and support. You mean the world to me, I love you both xx

CHAPTER ONE

LEXI

I lifted my bag up over my shoulder, the fraying strap held together with only a few stitches. The other strap had been gone a long time, but this bag had lasted almost ten years, holding textbooks and clothes. All I needed was for it to hold on another ten minutes as I made a run for it.

I wasn't stupid. I had been called to the school office. The new English teacher, Mr. Becker, had told me that someone was here to see me. He was one of those weird teachers, you know, that spoke like they knew the Queen of England but dressed like they came straight from Woodstock and just put on a blazer to blend in. But I ignored that as he had been very helpful. At least now I was starting to make a decent grade.

But I knew better. No one should be here to see me—I have no family, no friends. The only person it could be was the cops or even worse, my case manager. How could she have found me? I had crossed two state lines to get as far away as I could from her and my last foster home.

I looked to see if security still lingered around the front doors to the school. This wasn't a great school, and the security was lazy and uncaring. It was all clear as I suspected, but I had to run past the office to get outside the building. I held the strap tight to my chest and sprinted. I glanced into the office window as I flew past. I saw a uniformed officer standing next to a much shorter woman, who wore her blonde hair up in a bun. She turned toward me, and as soon as her eyes met mine, I picked up speed. She wasn't my case manager, but I knew she was one. *Fuck that. I am not going back into the system.*

I held my hands out in front of me as I slammed into the huge door. With a shove, it slammed against the brick wall outside, just as I heard a male shout my name. The cold air hit my face, but I kept running. It had been raining, just my luck.

With my heart racing, I knew the only place I could go to was the club where I worked. Maybe if I got there early, I could start my shift, get some cash, and make a run for it.

Ugh, this cop seemed to have a superpower, and he didn't stop chasing me. Fucking hell, this one didn't eat donuts and took his job way too seriously. *I turn eighteen in less than two months, fucker. Leave me alone.*

My throat was dry as my heart hammered in my chest. I was so close. If I went down that alley, I could double around and jump the fence and head to the club. I used the rest of my energy to push harder, my legs burning at every move I made to lose this guy. The sound of my feet slapping against the wet pavement flooded my ears as it bounced off the brick buildings around me.

I saw the chain-link fence up ahead, and my breathing was ragged as I grabbed ahold of it and scrambled up, my wet shoes slipping on the wire. I was trying not to get my clothes caught as I jumped down, but it caught the pocket of my hoodie and I stumbled, trying to get away. I could see the cop, so I ripped the fabric away and ran through the backlot of an abandoned apartment complex that I sometimes stayed at. I could hear the rustle of metal as the cop started to climb the fence.

I ran through the broken door and around to the left where there was a corridor. I knew there was a room just a few doors down that had a broken window I could jump out of. My feet crunched against broken glass as I slid into the room and grabbed the door frame to stop my wet shoes from sliding, but before I could grab it, I landed on my ass. *Fuck.* I could feel the glass in my arm. I quickly stood and reached down for my bag, which was now on the floor. *Shit, the strap.*

I clutched my ruined bag under my arm and bolted to the window, pulling back the tattered brown velvet drapes. With one foot on the frame, I could hear the cop heading toward me, but I didn't hesitate. I jumped and landed on the graffiti-covered concrete below. Pain shot up my legs and through my body at the landing, but I wouldn't let the pain stop me.

I ran.

I saw the neon sign up ahead, flashing 'Open! Live Nude Girls.' The girls would hide me at The Landing Strip. I barreled past Mr. Big, the club security, and straight to the back, where I saw Charlotte and Destiny. I pulled up to stop and looked over at Charlotte's startled face. She had on a short, pleated tartan skirt and tight white shirt. Her bra was bright pink with jewels that sparkled, and her tits were practically falling out of the top. The perfect outfit for getting generous tips.

"Wow, girl, you just flew in here. What's happened?" Destiny wrapped her arm around my shoulder. She was the mother hen of the club and really looked after the girls here.

I dropped my bag to the floor, flopped back onto the worn black leather two-seater, and tried to catch my breath. A bottle of water was thrust under my nose. My hands shook from the adrenaline as I took it and almost inhaled that water. My throat felt dry, but the cool water made me feel less shaky. I shook my head when Destiny prodded again as to why I ran in here. I wasn't going to tell her the truth.

"I...I thought someone was chasing me." That seemed logical enough. I worked at a seedy strip club, and there were always creepy stalkers who lingered around. I watched as that ticked over in her mind, and she gave me a slow nod.

"Your bag is broken." She pointed to the now strapless bag, and I rolled up my sleeve to see the damage the glass did. "And you're bleeding. I'll get the first aid kit."

Charlotte just watched me with a scowl on her face. Her makeup was thick, and her fake dark lashes made her blue eyes pop. She wasn't the nicest person to be around, but she put on a good show. I ignored her as I screwed the lid back on the empty water bottle. I laid my head back, drew in a deep breath, and held it before I exhaled. I did that three times before Destiny was back with a small first aid kit.

"Oh, we don't have much in here." I looked down and noticed it was mostly stocked with tampons. I raised my arm up to see how bad it was and noticed that the blood was still trickling out. Crap, that was a pretty deep gash.

"I'll go clean it up in the bathroom. Thanks." I grabbed the first aid kit and locked myself in the small bathroom. There was a shower, sink, and toilet in here. It was always clean. That was one of the things I loved about working here—not only could I work all night and not have to worry about where I was sleeping, but I could shower and wash up and be ready for school the next morning. Well, I guess that was now all going to change.

I ran my arm under the water and took another look. It would heal fast, nothing too bad. I found a small bandage and wrapped it around my arm. It would soak up the blood, and hopefully, it would be better by the time I went on stage in a few hours.

I assessed the damage to my hoodie. It wasn't too bad. They had a sewing kit here, so I could patch it up at least. I changed out of the hoodie and tee and put on a black fitted tank top. My jeans didn't look so bad—since I wore black, you couldn't see all the stains or blood. They probably saved my ass from the glass on that floor.

I quickly touched up my makeup, giving myself a smoky eye look, when a loud bang shook the door. *Fuck, Charlotte, give me a minute.* I quickly finished as the banging started again. I unlocked the door, and it flew into me. I didn't get a chance to think as a thick hand wrapped around my wrist.

I looked down at the fingers that held me tightly, noticing that the hand was one that had seen some real work. This guy works with his hands—short, clean fingernails and a nice golden tan. I followed the arm up until I saw the dark blue of a shirt. My heart sank as I glanced across and saw a badge and name. *Keene.*

"I'm sorry, girl, but this officer thinks you work here. I told him we had never seen you before." I looked past the cop's shoulder, avoiding his face as I pinned Gerry, my now ex-boss, on the spot. He told me this would happen if I was caught here, that he would deny knowing me. He gave me a small smile before he turned away. He just threw me to the wolves, but I couldn't blame him.

How did this cop figure out I was here? I was sure he wasn't following me when I came inside.

"Come on, Alexis." The cop pulled me toward the door, and I felt the pull in my wound. I moved to grab my bag and hoodie, and held it tightly to my side. I let him walk me out of the building without putting up a fight, and I didn't say anything to anyone as I passed by. Gerry had been good to me for the last few months, and I didn't want to get him in trouble.

As we got outside, I saw a car waiting for me. Maybe if I acted like this was no big deal and that I was coming without any trouble, he would let go of my arm. I took a quick glance to the cop. Dang, he was hot for an older guy. *And a cop.*

His other hand reached out just above the bandage and held even tighter, like he knew I was going to run. Well, that would be a good guess since I just led him on a pretty good chase. Once we got to the car, the woman with the blonde hair stepped out from the front passenger seat and gave me a kind smile. I rolled my eyes and looked away. *Three fucking months.* I was doing so well on my own.

"Alexis Turner, you're a hard girl to catch. You gave Keene a good workout. But now it's time to come with me to my office. You're in a bit of trouble, young woman." She opened the rear door, and Keene pushed me into the car and slammed the door shut. I reached for the handle and pulled. I could see the smile on his face. Child lock. *Fucker*. I moved to the opposite door and tried.

A deep voice had me sitting back into the seat. "Don't even try it. Keene is right outside." I glared daggers at the man's head. His dark hair was cut short, and he wore a uniform. *Ugh, great, another cop.*

I threw myself into the chair behind the desk, expressing my hatred for being here. I clutched my bag tight in my lap and played with the hole in my hoodie.

"If you need us for anything, Shelly, just let us know." The petite woman in front of me shook her head. She looked so delicate, like a flower. But from her conversation in the car, she was no daisy... This chick had thorns.

"I'll be fine, Keene. Thank you both for your help." And with that, he closed the door and I was alone in the office with who I assumed was Shelly, my new case manager. Or a case manager who would send me back to my old one. Fuck, I didn't care, I was out of here as soon as I could leave. She moved some files around and looked up, smiling at me.

"Where are you from? What are you?" she asked. I just shrugged. I didn't really know how to answer that question, but I wasn't going to tell her shit. She had all the information she needed on me. She could tell me where I was from and what I was.

"Okay, well, why did you leave your last foster home? They miss you." That had my body tensing as my eyes flashed up to hers. *Yeah right, they miss the paycheck*. I gritted my teeth and didn't speak. There was no point. I would be sent back to them, and then I would run again. This was just a small bump in the road. Well, an annoying huge bump. I would have to go somewhere else. I only had a few months left of school, and I had really started to like Seattle.

"Okay, not one for questions? That's fine. I'll just fill in these forms to send you back. You're lucky nothing happened to you. I don't know what you are, but I'll figure it out." I sent her a puzzled look. *Yeah right, she knew what I was.* I was a runaway teen stripper trying to make enough money to feed and clothe herself to get through school. But I won't be forever. One day, I will be free of all of this.

"You can send me back, I don't give a fuck. I'll just leave again."

She moved toward me fast, and I sucked in a breath at the movement. "You will not run. You will stay there," she said in a strange voice. Her eyes stayed pinned on mine, and I swear, they looked darker than before.

I laughed, and her brows furrowed. "Yeah right, stay there. Fuck that."

It looked like I had ruffed her feathers a little. I wanted to smile, but I didn't want her to see I was pleased with this. She watched me for a while as she leaned back in her chair. There was an uncomfortable silence until she pinned me with her eyes again. Yeah, I wasn't crazy, her eyes were a dark shade of blue now. *Could it be the lights?*

"Give me your bag," she said in that strange voice again. I gripped it tighter to my chest. No way was I giving her my bag. She tilted her head to the side and flicked her pen a few times on the folders in front of her.

"I promise you, I'm here to help. I think you could really use some help right now. You are a smart girl. You didn't just run, you enrolled yourself into high school. Your grades are really good. Mr. Becker was concerned for you when he called me, and I think he was right to be."

Mr. Becker... My English teacher called her about me. What a fucking asshole. I thought he was trying to help me. He asked to meet my parents once, and I told him they both worked all the time. It was an excuse that had worked in the past. Hell, it worked when I enrolled myself six months ago. Only to have Mr. Becker be the one to call child services on me. God, I wanted to hit him so bad right now.

"I can see you are not happy with him. But I promise, he was only looking out for you. I have a special home upstate. I think you'll fit right in there. They are a nice couple, and I was going there tonight to drop someone else off. If it's not a good fit for you, you can call me and we can work something out."

I rolled my eyes and turned my body away. I would run first chance I got. I had only been with one nice foster family. They'd wanted to adopt me, but then the father was killed in a car accident after he drove me to school one morning. His wife blamed me because if I hadn't been there, he wouldn't have been on the road. After that, I was moved into another home. That was how I knew not to trust anyone. They both said they wanted me. I called her 'Mom,' and she got rid of me like I was trash. I was grieving too, and I needed her. They were my first real family. I would never let myself be in that situation again.

The only person I can count on is myself.

I was moved into the waiting room outside Shelly's office. I could see Keene was still there. Maybe Keene and Shelly had something going on. Maybe they were married? Makes sense—she was gorgeous, and he was too.

I heard a commotion and looked up to see the cop who drove me here holding onto someone. They were putting up a fight, and I smiled to myself. So I wasn't the only one who hated this shit. When I looked up again, I was met by the most amazing blue eyes, like sunshine on a crystal blue lake. How can that even be a color? His hair was so blond, it was almost silver. It was slicked back, but some had fallen loose, giving him a sexy messy look.

His hands were behind him, and I could hear the commotion from around the corner. Keene was gone.

"Sit here, kid, and don't fucking move." The cop pushed him into the chair opposite mine. There was more yelling as a big, older man with hair the same blond color as the hot guy in front of me came barreling through the cops and into the hallway.

"You can't take him, you blood-sucking bitch. Just try me! We will fucking kill you. He is ours, not yours." I could see the guy across from me slightly flinch. I turned my head to see Shelly exit her office. She had such a casual air about this whole situation, like there wasn't some overgrown man screaming at her tiny five-foot frame.

"As I have told you, Thomas, time and time again, if you don't stop using your nephew, I will take him. He was caught again this morning, doing your dirty work. I pulled strings to keep him here. If I let Keene and Stoker take him in and officially book him, he'll be gone for many, many years. I only hope he is smart enough to leave you all and never go back."

Oh man, this uncle was physically shaking. His fists were balled up, and he growled low as Keene and Stoker held him back. The way he was slightly unsteady on his feet and the way he smelled told me all I need to know about this guy. *Drug addict*. Was he going to hit Shelly? She was so tiny compared to him. *Animal*.

"Go, Uncle T. I'll come back." I looked over and saw the guy watching his uncle, who made a deep growling sound again in his chest. I sat back in my chair a little more to get farther away from him, but that was a bad move. He saw me, and his hazy eyes turned on me.

"What the fuck are you?" He sniffed at me, and his brows furrowed. *What the hell am I?*

"She is nothing to you, Thomas. Just go. I will speak to you tomorrow." The cops pulled him out of the hallway. Shelly straightened her skirt and continued on as if nothing had just happened.

"Why are you still cuffed?" she huffed, and the hot guy shrugged. Shelly let out a frustrated sound and muttered something as she walked out to where the cops just went, her heels clicking along the hallway.

There was an uncomfortable silence that hung between me and the mystery silver-haired guy. I wasn't here to make friends, and he wasn't, either. The sooner I could get to this new place, the faster I could work out where I was gonna run to next. Eventually, Shelly and Keene came back, and they uncuffed the guy. He pushed his hair back, and Shelly held out a brand-new backpack in front of him. I hadn't seen one of them in years. I got one when I first came into the system. It had a cute little stuffed pink bunny, a toothbrush, and toothpaste. I would take it for the toothbrush alone—mine was worse for wear.

"Raff, just take it." I heard her sigh as she placed it beside him. When she turned to me, she gave me a smile that was filled with pity, sadness, and something else. It had the hairs on the back of my neck rising.

"Alexis, I have one of the staff chasing down a female bag for you, but it's late and we don't really have much time before we need to leave." I shrugged. It was fine. I was used to not getting anything. Why would today be different than any other day?

"We will leave in twenty. If you want to take a quick restroom break, please do so as it's a few hours' drive and we'll be getting there late." I laid my head against the wall and closed my eyes. I needed today over with now.

CHAPTER TWO

LEXI

So, it turned out they couldn't find a female bag, so I got a boy one instead. I didn't understand why there was a difference anyway, but Shelly explained that a female one had the type of supplies the first aid kit back at The Landing Strip had, and a more girly set of pajamas. I was fine wearing boy's clothes. It was only to sleep in, but I really did need a new bag. Plus this way, I didn't need to spend money on one. I only had about eighty dollars left to my name. I wasn't stupid—that money was in the sock that I was wearing. I never left my money in my bag; it was on me at all times.

We had been driving for a while, and Keene was behind the wheel. The way he acted with Shelly was like we weren't there at all—which suited me fine, since I wasn't up for causal chitchat. We stopped and Shelly grabbed some burgers for us, before we continued the journey to this foster home upstate.

It was dark and late when we arrived. I was exhausted, but I wasn't about to fall asleep in the car. I was used to not sleeping much, but I think it was the little workout with Keene after school that had made me so sleepy. We drove down some streets in what looked like a cozy neighborhood. It was hard to see when we finally stopped outside the house. The porch light was on, and I could see a window with a light on inside.

"Alright, you two, come on. And be nice, they're good people and there are some younger kids here. Please don't wake them up by fighting this." I nodded. I didn't want to scare some kids, and I wasn't going to do anything. *Yet.*

I walked up to the porch and noticed the door was a nice shade of blue, and the trimmings around the windows all matched. Total suburban house. Shelly knocked lightly, and I could feel Raff standing behind me. Normally, I didn't let people get behind me—they might get the jump on you—but I didn't feel like that with him. He felt safe...for now at least. Keene was watching us, maybe to see if we would do a runner. I didn't want to go for another round, so I stood there waiting.

I didn't know where I was, and I was tired. This place had a warm bed and would give me a roof over my head for tonight. And it would be even better if there was a lock on the door so I could sleep a little deeper—preferably one that locked from the inside.

When the door cracked open, a man in his forties greeted us with a huge smile. He had short dark hair with a bit of gray mixed in, wore a dark tee, and was barefoot. Another man with a much larger build and longer dark hair opened the door wide and said, "Come in."

The house smelled nice when we stepped in, like someone had been baking.

"Oh, huh... Shelly?" I turned to see the shorter guy staring at me, his mouth slightly dropped open. Did she forget to tell him I was coming?

"Um... I—this... Sorry, I'm Jack. I just wasn't expecting a girl, we... Oh, Grayson," he called out to the other man, who had disappeared before we even got inside. Shelly put her hand up to stop Jack from talking anymore.

"Hold on, Jack, we spoke on the phone. I told you this one needs to be here, at least for now. Until we work out... Look, can I talk to you?" She moved away from me, and they both walked off into another room. Grayson was back with a cupcake in each hand, chocolate with vanilla frosting. He froze when he saw me.

"Oh, you're a girl."

Holy shit. Had I walked into a boys-only house? Had they never seen a girl before? Not once had a foster family I was with made cupcakes to greet the new kids, or even made them in general. He held it out to me, and I took it. I took a bite and wanted to moan, it was so good. Dang, if he baked cupcakes every day, I might need to stay a little longer. I listened to Jack and Shelly as their voices rose a few times before they returned with fake smiles plastered on their faces.

"Sorry about that, Alexis. I misheard when Shelly called. I thought she said Alex Turner and Raff King. We only have one room made up currently. We have two single beds in there, but I have an office we don't use, so we can change that around. But we'll have to do that tomorrow, sorry. It's a bit late now, and the pups will be getting up early."

"You have puppies?" I blurted without thinking. I loved animals. They were kind, loyal, and not judgmental. Everyone turned to me like I said something crazy. He just said pups. *Didn't he?*

"No, sorry. Jack calls the kids 'pups.' They're on the other side of the house from your room. I remember being a teen once, so we moved all the boys around so that you would both have the room down that end away from the chaos and early bedtimes."

I'd always shared, but shit. Did they want me to share with Raff tonight? I made a move to step away from Raff. His hair hung around his eyes, which were cast down to the floor. He didn't speak or make a move to claim his cupcake from Grayson.

"Raff, would you be okay on the couch tonight? I promise we'll have the office cleared out tomorrow." He made a sound that everyone must have taken as a yes. Shelly and Keene said their farewells, leaving me and Raff in the entrance and two very confused men staring at us.

"Come with me, Alexis, I will show you your room. Grayson, can you pull out the couch for Rafferty?" Huh. His actual name was Rafferty.

The light flicked on as I stepped into the room. It had blue-colored walls, two single beds with matching sheets and comforters, and a lamp on a bedside table between the two beds. I glanced around and saw a desk in the corner with a computer. There was a real computer here in my room? I must have given a funny look, as Jack started to apologize.

"Sorry, that it's blue. We never have girls here—you're the first. Maybe we can paint it to your liking if you don't like blue?" I looked to this guy. Was he serious?

"I turn eighteen in two months, so I won't be here long."

He smiled and nodded. "We don't mind. You're welcome to stay here until you finish out the school year." His smile was genuine, like he really meant it. But I knew about these types of promises. They could take it back at any moment.

He gathered up the bedding on the other single and grabbed a pillow, then he headed to the door. He turned and smiled. "Breakfast is at seven-thirty, and Grayson cooks up a big meal. I will knock on your door at seven so you have time to be ready before the boys all get there and eat everything. The bathroom and toilet are just to your left. If you need me, I'm down at the other end. Double doors."

And with that, he closed the door behind him, and I dropped my bag to the floor. I looked for a lock, but there was none. *Great.* I quickly got changed into the new pajamas, which was a large white T-shirt and green-checkered sleep pants. I opened my door, but the whole house was silent. I quickly ran out to pee, then ran back to my room. I closed the door and looked for something heavy to put in front of it. The desk would be good, but there was a whole desktop computer on top, and I didn't want to mess with it. So instead, I pushed the bed closest to the door and jammed it up against it. That should wake me up if someone tried to get in.

I laid my head down on the fluffy new pillow. The soft sheets smelled like strawberries as I wrapped my body up in them. They were so soft, and it didn't take long before sleep came.

CHAPTER THREE

LEXI

I didn't sleep well, but I never did. *Bad dreams.* The clock on the desk read four twenty-three am, and I decided it would be as good a time as any to see what I had with me, what I needed, and to figure out where the hell I was. I knew I was still in Washington state, but where exactly was unknown.

I was startled slightly when the soft knock sounded at the door. I looked over and watched as the clock switched over to a minute after seven.

"Alexis, breakfast will be ready in thirty. Soap and towels are in the bathroom. You won't be disturbed in there. The younger ones have been instructed not to come down to this end of the house."

I held the sheet up to my chest and looked around the room.

"Yes. Okay," I called out and listened as his footsteps went down the hallway. I grabbed some clean underwear and socks that I had set down for today and pushed the single bed back against the wall. Stepping out into the hallway, I could hear people talking down from where I came into the house last night. I took my things with me and made my way into the bathroom. There was no lock on this door, either. I groaned to myself. What was with these people? No locks at all? Well, I guess that make it easy for me to leave.

There was a towel sitting on the counter, along with a bottle of shampoo, conditioner, and a brand-new bar of soap. I looked around to see if there were any hidden cameras or something. You just never knew...

I couldn't find anything, so I quickly started the shower, and when it was warm enough, I stripped down. I took the bloody bandage off and saw the cut from yesterday was healed. The area had dried blood, so I jumped under the steady stream of hot water to clean it. I moaned as my sore and tired muscles relaxed. The water felt so good on my skin.

I started to wash my hair when I heard a sound. My body tensed, waiting for someone to come in. When I didn't hear it again, I quickly finished and dried myself off. I felt clean and smelled so much better, that was for sure. I put on my new underwear and socks, but unfortunately, I was back in my dirty, blood-stained jeans. I didn't have much else, so I put on my bra and the tank top I wore last night.

I bundled my dirty clothes into a ball and took them back to the bedroom. I swiftly made my bed, because that was one thing I couldn't stop myself from doing. After working in a hotel as maid for a few months, I couldn't just leave a bed unmade. It made the room look messy. I placed the dirty stuff on the end of the bed and pulled my hoodie out. The rip in the fabric still needed to be stitched up. Maybe Jack had a sewing kit I could use. There was a chill in the air, but I didn't want to wear it right now, as it didn't smell the best.

I walked down to where I could hear all the voices and smell breakfast. I rounded a corner and could see a large table, laden with all types of breakfast foods. There were two bench seats on either side, and three young boys were talking loudly with their mouths full.

"Oh sorry, Alexis," Jack said as he quickly avoided crashing into me. His hands were full with three glasses of what looked like orange juice. The smell in here was amazing, the bacon and eggs on the table tempting me forward. I had never had bacon and eggs for breakfast like this. A head popped out from a door, and Grayson smiled and waved a spatula in the air.

"Good morning, Alexis. I hope you slept well." He waited for me to answer, but I didn't know what to say, so I just nodded. This was not your average foster family. Or if it was, I had been sorely unlucky with my past ones.

"Take a seat. Do you want orange juice? Coffee?" Jack was pointing to a space at the end of the table.

I went over and sat down, and he placed a plate in front of me as I mumbled, "Orange juice." A little boy with beautiful, silky jet-black hair was seated beside me, and I smiled down at him. His big brown eyes were so expressive as he looked up at me. He was maybe six or seven. His little mouth dropped slightly.

"You're a girl," he stated, and I snorted a little. Gotta love the honesty of a child.

"Yes, and you're a boy," I replied, and he smiled and nodded. I realized then that the whole table had gone quiet. I thought it was because of me, but when I looked to where the other two boys were now focused, I could see Raff lingering by the doorway. He was dressed in what he wore yesterday—he must not have had a change of clothes, either—and his backpack was slung over his shoulder. I guess he wasn't sticking around long.

The boy next to me shrank in closer and sniffed. Was he crying? I patted his little hand that was wrapped tightly around my arm. Jack came bursting out the door and into the room. He stopped abruptly and watched the scene in front of him.

"Oh, boys. Sorry. I didn't even introduce Alexis to you all, and this is Raff. They'll be staying with us for a while, so make them feel welcome."

The little boy let go of my arm a little as Raff took a seat on the other end of the table from us. The two boys on the other side looked frightened. *Shit*. Raff was a little rough around the edges, in a sexy kind of way, but I didn't think he was scary looking. But I guess I was used to what real scary looked like, and most times, it was clean-cut and wearing a suit.

When Raff rolled up the sleeves on his navy long-sleeved top, I saw tattoos. Holy crap, he was covered in dark ink. I knew I was staring, but I couldn't help it. I looked up to his face and saw his jaw tick. He could obviously feel all of us looking at him.

I saw the hint of dark just above his collar. *Dang.* How many tattoos did he have? His eyes turned to mine and pinned me. I was frozen and gasped slightly. With the intensity I felt, I couldn't pull my eyes from his. How could someone have eyes that color? I could feel the heat on my neck creep up. I quickly looked down and took a sip of my orange juice to distract and cool myself off. Dang, I would need a cold shower after that stare down.

Jack and Grayson returned to the table just in time to join in the uncomfortable silence.

"Sorry we took so long. I hope you like bacon and eggs, Alexis? Raff?" I nodded, but I didn't dare look over at Raff. The little boy next to me shifted slightly, but he was still holding my arm. I tried to move away a little, but he seemed pretty scared of Raff.

"Let me introduce the boys. This is Joshua." Grayson pointed to the little boy clinging to me. "And the other two rascals are Harry and Jaxon." They looked like they could be brothers, real ones. Harry had dark red curls, a sprinkling of freckles across his nose, and big blue eyes, whereas Jaxon had a more auburn-colored curls and hazel eyes. They didn't smile, and you could see in their body language that they wanted to be as far away as they could from Raff.

When no one said anything, Jack leaned over and took Joshua's hand from my arm. Finally, I was able to get some bacon, eggs, and toast onto my plate. I could hear Joshua sniffle again.

"Are you okay?" I asked. He gave me a puzzled look and turned to Jack.

"She don't smell like no shi—" Jack's hand was over his mouth before he could finish. I slid away from them, and the sudden movement had my heart racing and my hands shaking. Was he going to say I smelled like shit? I know my jeans weren't the best, but I showered. Jack removed his hand just as fast as he put it there, and he looked like he was in shock that he had reacted that way

"Oh, Alexis. It's not what it looks like. He just... He forgot his manners, is all." I could see him look down to Joshua as he apologized, but that still made me uneasy. There was a tense silence in the room.

I looked out the window into the backyard, trying to distract myself from what just happened. The sky was gray, and there was a forest that backed onto their yard. The trees swayed gently, and it looked like it was going to rain again today. Grayson broke the silence first.

"Okay, boys, I think you've had enough. Grab your school bags and go pack your lunch. Your bus will be here soon."

All three of them jumped up and left the room. Jack looked to me, and I could see Raff was really tense. Or maybe he was tense all the time, and I was only noticing it now.

"He is young, Alexis, and I'm sorry if I scared you. So, Rafferty..." Jack turned to Raff. "The high school bus leaves here at ten past eight. Shelly told us that you can't afford to take any time off school. Grayson packed you some snacks if you want. I can take you to get some more clothes and things you may need after school. I have some books ready for you in my office—one of the parents gave them to us last night when we said we needed them for a new student. You'll have everything you need for today, at least." I saw Raff pull out his cell phone and ignore Jack. Jack didn't seem surprised by the way Raff ignored him.

"Shelly knew about Rafferty coming here early yesterday morning and had everything set up ready for today. But you were a surprise to her...to all of us, so she didn't get a chance to set everything up with the school yet. She will be doing that first thing this morning, but I told her we would take you shopping and get what you need. Get a chance to settle in here. Maybe we can get something nice for your room? Give it an Alexis touch?"

I just shrugged. A day off sounded fine to me.

CHAPTER FOUR

LEXI

Jack drove a new silver hatchback. It was clean and still had that new car smell.

"So, where are we?" I asked as he backed us out of his driveway. At least if I knew the town we were in, I could find a map and figure out the rest from there. Shelly wouldn't tell us where we were going last night. All she said was it was the foster home I needed to be in. I didn't know what she meant by that, but so far, these people were alright. Maybe too nice, which worried me more.

"We live in a small community called Kiba, which is about ten minutes from Port Willow, where your new high school will be. That's where we are off to do some shopping. There is a Walmart where we can grab some stuff from." I nodded. I was only going to get jeans, maybe a new hoodie if it was on sale. But otherwise, I would just stitch the one I was wearing. With it being the winter, it would have to do. I shuffled my bag between my legs, I wasn't going to leave it behind. Jack watched as I took it with me, and if he wanted to say something about it, he didn't. I wouldn't have cared anyway. I never leave my bag behind.

At Walmart, Jack grabbed a shopping cart and watched me as I readjusted my bag on my shoulders to equal the weight out. With so much jammed in there, it was never going to be easy to carry, but having two straps was a lot better.

Jack cleared his throat. "Would you like to go to the ladies' clothing first?" I shrugged.

"Let's go over. Maybe we can find you something you might like." I walked behind him as he pushed the cart through the aisles, but he kept checking over his shoulder at me…I guess to make sure I was still there. A guy, maybe in his mid-twenties, stared at me for the longest time. It made me uncomfortable, so I moved closer to Jack. This happened a lot with guys, so it wasn't new. *Fucking creeper.* The world was full of them, but the weird ones that sniffed at me were the worst.

Jack stopped suddenly, and I almost walked right into him. I looked around. We were in the underwear section. I stepped away from Jack.

"Sorry, I haven't shopped with a female before. Just pick what you would like and put them in the cart. I'll wait for you over there." He pointed over to a rack with umbrellas and quickly made his way over, making sure to put distance between the female section and himself.

I looked around at the different types of underwear—boy shorts, thongs, lace, and cotton. I picked up a pair of black cotton boy shorts and checked the price. It was on sale. That would do me nicely. Maybe if there was a cheap pair of socks…

I couldn't find any on sale in my size, so I pushed the cart to Jack and he glanced in. His hand went to his face as he rubbed the dark stubble on his jaw before he looked at me with his face scrunched up. "Ah…just one pair?"

I nodded. I wasn't spending my money on more than one, it's hard enough to carry around what I have. He hesitated for a minute.

"You know I'm paying, right? This shopping trip is for you... We get a generous allowance by a local benefactor to do so. The money is yours to spend, Alexis." My heart began to race. He gets an allowance from someone to buy me clothes? The other homes just gave me whatever they had, and everything was second-hand and usually full of holes. I never got to keep it.

"How much?" I asked. It took him a few seconds to register what I was asking.

"Oh, um... They give us whatever we need. Do you need me to set a budget? Would that make it easier?"

No, I just want the cash.

"Can I get it in cash?" I watched his face fall slightly.

"I'm sorry, Shelly told me that you...ah, don't stick around long in homes. I really want you to stick around. We all do. I can't give you the cash, but you can buy whatever you want."

Fuck them. I started to walk, and Jack followed me. I grabbed the first thing I saw and threw it into the cart.

"Did you want to try some things on? We have all day, and this is a very large shirt. Did you mean to pick this size?"

I looked back and saw him holding up what I thought was a maternity top. *Try it on... That's a good idea.*

"Yeah, I should try it on." There were changing rooms close by, and Jack stood outside and chatted to the worker. Turns out there were two exits to this changing room, so I left the top, doubled around, and walked as calmly as I could to the front of the store. Creeper guy was there still. He turned to me and watched as I walked out the sliding glass doors.

I pushed my hair behind my ear, looking up and down the street, and saw people going about their normal day. A little girl was holding her mom's hand as she crossed the street. A dad with a child on his shoulders laughing.

Ugh, too much. This was too perfect a place. Jack and Grayson were the same, it was just for show, an act. They couldn't really be this nice. No one ever was.

I ran toward the main street through the parking lot and found the nearest bus stop. It was too close for my liking, but there didn't seem to be any others close by. I sat on the bench and placed my bag between my feet. I reached in and picked up my favorite novel. *Pride and Prejudice*. Yeah, I liked to read. If you had nothing else, reading was the next best thing, and I loved this book. It was the first one I ever got. It looked rough, but that was because I'd read it so much. Plus, Mr. Darcy was hot.

When the bus pulled up after only a few minutes of waiting, I quickly looked behind the bus shelter to check if Jack was following me.

Fuck. Jack was looking for me, and he had a Walmart security guard with him. I ran up the steps and dropped my cash in, taking a seat as far to the back as I could, praying the bus would leave right now. *Come on, leave.* That was when Jack spotted me.

I got down as low as I could, but he had already seen where I was. He started running, but before he made it over, the bus had closed the doors and we were leaving. I sat up and watched as he quickly turned and ran toward his car. Fuck, I didn't think about that part. I honestly didn't think he would care that much to chase me. None of the other foster parents ever had. Okay, Plan B then. I would get off at the next stop and wait for him to pass. Then I'd be long gone before he realized I wasn't on the bus anymore.

I walked into the warm house, my shoulders slumped in defeat. It smelled amazing in here, and I couldn't stop my stomach from rumbling as I wrapped my arms tighter around my waist. It was late, the sun had been down for hours. I'd thought I did good. I'd made it to Port Angeles and spent the afternoon exploring until this fucking asshole cop found me. Said he sniffed me out, so I called him a dog. He just laughed and threw me in the back of his cruiser.

"Thank you, Nash," Grayson said as he shook the cop's hand. I had to say, for a cop, he was kinda young and cocky, but the asshole had one of those panty dropping smiles. I rolled my eyes. *Still an asshole, though.*

"Alexis, are you okay? Come into the dining room, I made you a plate. I'll heat it up." I looked around the living room and saw three sets of eyes follow me into the kitchen—the younger boys were all still up. Jack prompted me to take a seat at the table and to leave my bag on the floor.

"Here you go." He placed a hot meal of chicken and vegetables in front of me and took a seat beside me with a mug of black coffee. Dinner smelled amazing, so I picked up my fork and dug in. I hadn't eaten since breakfast, and was hungrier than I thought. I was used to skipping meals or just having one a day, but if there was food in front of me, I wouldn't let it go to waste.

"Would you like something to drink?" My eyes shifted to Jack. He hadn't scolded me, hadn't yelled. Shit, he hadn't said anything about me running away from him. I didn't say anything, and he got up suddenly. I flinched and wrapped my arms tightly around myself.

"Oh, Alexis, I'm... I was going to get you some water." I didn't look at him. I didn't need to see the pity in his eyes. *I already heard it.*

I could hear him tell Grayson what had just happened. I could feel the lump in my throat and my chest felt tight. I grabbed my bag and ran off to the room I was in last night. I turned on the light and noticed there was only one bed in there now. I looked to the doorway across from mine where the office was this morning and saw the faint glow of light coming from the gap at the bottom.

I closed the door behind me. There was now a lock on the bedroom door. I quickly locked it and ran to the window, pushing the drapes to the side. Huh, it had a lock on it also. I wondered if it was there last night. I tried it, but this one was different. I couldn't open the window. They'd locked me in.

In frustration, I threw myself on the bed. I noticed that my dirty clothes from this morning had been folded and put over on the nightstand next to the lamp. I smelled them, and they smelled so fresh, just like the sheets. Someone had washed them. It was nice to have clean clothes...but I didn't know what to think about this. It was private stuff they touched, but it was to clean them.

I needed a shower.

I opened the bedroom door and listened to see if anyone was around or looking for me before running over to the bathroom. I knocked and waited. When there was no answer, I pushed open the door, and my heart jumped a little in fright. Raff was standing there, the red towel tucked around his waist. I saw he was covered in tatts, not just his arm or neck. I was talking a whole body worth of art.

He had a huge skull on his stomach, words and roses ran up both pecs—that was what I could see earlier on his neck, the tip of a rose. I looked down to his legs. They were inked, too. How old was this guy? These would have taken years to get and a lot of money. I stood frozen, completely ogling him. I glanced up and saw he was watching me too. His eyes were heavy-lidded as he lazily took me all in.

He had a deep purple bruise under his left eye and a cut on his lip. My mouth dropped open. I was going to ask if he got into a fight, but that was pretty obvious.

His eyes burned into mine as he stalked toward me like he was hunting prey. I didn't move as I felt my insides heat up. His nostrils flared slightly as he brushed past me on his way out of the room, our eyes only breaking apart once he'd left. I wanted to reach out and touch the skull, feel his skin beneath my fingertips, but I made a fist to stop myself from doing something stupid. When I heard the click of his door closing, I quickly scrambled to close the bathroom door. Okay, now I could think straight. I was a little wound-up, and maybe slightly horny.

There was something about Raff that called to me. I didn't know if it was just two broken souls who understood each other, or the fact that I wanted to lick every tattoo he had...

I quickly shook my head as I put my clothes on the counter and glanced back to the door. Would he bust in on me? Huh... The door now had a lock.

I locked it and took the longest shower I'd ever had. And I totally didn't think about Rafferty King the whole time.

CHAPTER FIVE

LEXI

I woke up in a cold sweat. My chest was pounding as I tried to draw in breath. I'd had another nightmare. I had them a lot, but it was just as scary each time. I didn't think they could get any worse, but they did.

Jack knocked on my door. I was still a little jumpy after the nightmare, but I quickly got up. I needed another shower, but I just didn't feel up to it this morning. I quickly got dressed in a fresh tee and my now really dirty black skinny jeans. I found some deodorant in the bathroom so I sprayed it all over my jeans, hoping Joshua wouldn't notice I smelled like shit today—or anyone else for the matter. I applied some makeup, just a little eyeliner and mascara. I flicked my hair and tied it up into a messy bun, then pulled down a few extra strands to frame my face and soften the look. I didn't have some amazing hair color—it was just brown, boring and plain.

I took a deep breath and looked at myself. I was wearing all black. The eyeliner made my unusual eye color pop. People often asked me where I got them from, my mom or dad, but I had no idea. I didn't remember their eye color...or much of what they looked like. I tried my best to forget them. They weren't worth remembering.

My eyes were amber, but people said they were yellow copper, or sometimes kids thought I had yellow eyes like a cat. But they weren't that yellow. Just the way the light hit them sometimes made them appear more that shade. With my lip balm in my pocket, I left the bathroom, ready to be yelled at for the whole running away thing.

It smelled nice as I made my way down to the dining table. Raff was already eating down at one end of the table. The other end held three boys who couldn't get farther from him.

Joshua's little head perked up and turned to me. He gave me a shy smile and waved me over, so I sat down near him. I couldn't blame him for thinking I smelled like shit yesterday or pointing it out. I filled my plate with yummy things as Raff got up and stomped back to his room.

Well, I guessed that left more for me. Jack sat down and started talking to the boys about going to the mall after school. He mentioned that I forgot to buy some things, so they all have to help me. I looked at Jack, waiting for him to say something, anything about what I did yesterday, but he just smiled and nodded.

Ugh, I couldn't take this. They didn't say anything, like they were ignoring the elephant in the room. I just wanted to get the yelling over and done with.

When I was done with breakfast, I went back to my room to grab my bag. As I left my room, Grayson was standing next to my door, his shoulder on the wall, looking very casual.

"Today, I think it's best you just take your books. Nothing else." His head tilted toward my heavy bag.

I stared him down for a few minutes, and when he didn't move, I went back into the room and dumped my bag on my bed. I put my books back in and left the rest on the bed. I had made the bed, but now it looked like shit. I guess this was their way of telling me off for running. Well, I could assure them, after yesterday's attempt to run, I needed a better plan. Apparently, I didn't count on fosters who actually gave two shits about me.

I hated to admit it, but I was okay here, for now. If I could just finish high school, then I would be set. I could go anywhere...finally start my life.

A door slammed open, and I jumped, my heart going a few extra beats. I looked up through my lashes as I zipped up my bag and saw Raff. He had his bag over his shoulder and was glaring daggers at Grayson.

Grayson was a huge guy, but I would put money on Raff in a fight. Where Grayson was big and full of bulky muscle, Raff was smaller but lean. I bet he would be quick on his feet.

"New cologne?" Grayson asked. Raff just held himself taller. "I don't know if that was the right move, kid." Grayson shook his head. "If you have trouble, go see Galen Donovani. You didn't yesterday. I understand being new is going to bring out the worst in some, but you can trust Galen. He will help you."

Raff pushed to move past, and Grayson grabbed his shoulder. *Shit*. Maybe I should make that bet now. I think there was going to be a fight.

"Just think about it," Grayson said as he let him go, and Raff shouldered past him. I swung my bag over my shoulder and tried to push past Grayson the same way Raff just did, but it was like hitting a wall. Ugh, I think I broke my shoulder. Maybe I was wrong...maybe Grayson would be the safer bet. But Raff was a wildcard. *That's for sure.*

The bus pulled up, and I had been standing about a yard away from Raff for a good five minutes too long. He spent the whole time on his phone. I got that he wasn't up for talking, but still...it would be nice to know one person at school. I shoved my hands in my pockets and stared at the sky, then at my feet. Eventually, I looked over at Raff, noticing his hair looked even more silver in the daylight. It was pushed back and had some real style, and dang, it looked good. His lip was healed, and his eye was no longer the purple from last night, just a slight tinge of yellow coloring it now.

When the bus pulled up, I practically jumped on to get away from him—and maybe to stop my thoughts from going over how attractive he was. The whole bus watched in almost deafening silence as I made my way toward an empty seat where a girl sat. She seemed younger than me, and her hair was a pretty ash blonde color in two braids. She smiled at me and gestured with her head, so I sat down beside her. I guess they knew which one was the foster kids' house. Great, so much for a good start at a new school.

There were growling sounds coming from behind me. I looked around to see what it was, and a bunch of guys were staring, some even standing and looking to the front where Raff had just got on. Some bared their teeth. *What the fuck did Raff do yesterday?* He certainly had an interesting way of making friends. When the growls died down and the bus started moving, Raff took a seat up front. The guys behind were watching the back of his head, and some of them were sniffing...me? Wait, they were sniffing Raff.

At least they weren't sniffing me. I found it creepy when guys smelled me—it was weird to do that to anyone, especially a stranger.

"Hello, you must be Alexis Turner?" The older lady behind the desk smiled up at me. She wore a floral shirt and thick, pink-rimmed glasses. I was a little distracted by wondering where the hell you would even find that color frame that I forgot to answer her as she waited.

I nodded and put on my best fake smile—the one I gave adults when I wanted to look sweet and innocent. She gave me a smile in return that told me she bought it. She shifted some paperwork on her desk as I waited.

"Sorry, love, won't be a moment... I think it's in the back." I shrugged. I didn't care if I was late to my first class. I leaned against the counter as I watched her go into a back room and open up a filing cabinet. I turned and watched the students as they walked in the hallway through the glass doors of the office. There were stairs across from me, and I thought I saw Raff run up there earlier. I wondered if we had any classes together?

We were both seniors. Well, Shelly had said that on the car ride up here, which was about all I knew about him. He had an uncle who seemed to think he owned him and was obviously into drugs—that was easy to see. Yet Raff didn't seem that type at all. And yet he got into fights on his first day of school and made a lot of enemies in a very short amount of time.

My eyes turned, and I noticed all the female students were looking at someone. I glanced to where they were focused and saw a hot guy stroll through the crowd of students. They were parting for him like the Red Sea. He wore dark, fitted slacks and a black turtleneck. His jaw was smooth and defined, his eyes never strayed from where he was going, and his brown, almost curly locks framed his face in such a perfect carefree way. He had an air about him, and I, like the other girls, stared openly at him. *I was totally fucked.*

I bet this guy was Mr. Popular and had half the student body wanting a piece of him—male and female. There was no way to deny that the guy knew he was attractive and probably starred in many fantasies.

When his feet slowed and he stopped beside a tall blonde girl, I knew straightaway I wouldn't be his type. Not that I was wanting to be his type. No, it was better that I wasn't. I needed to hide under the radar, get schooling over and done with, and leave this place. I watched the tall blonde as she flicked her hair and puffed out her chest, which was already on display in the very tight red tank top she wore. But he took no notice of her flirting gesture. His eyes closed and when he opened them, they flashed straight to mine.

I sucked a sharp breath through my teeth. His head cocked

slightly to the side, and I turned to see the office lady still messing around in the back office. *Fuck, hurry up.* My cheeks were burning hot. I totally got caught staring at him, and he knew. Ugh, what did I just say about not drawing attention to myself? I can't even stick to my own rules. Even if I wanted more, it wasn't going to happen. After I stopped my racing heart, I chanced a glance to see if he was still there, but he was gone. I sighed and slumped my forehead against the counter.

"Here you are, dear." I looked up and took the paper from her outstretched hand. I looked down and went over my schedule... *Ugh, what?*

"This is wrong, I didn't take world history. I can't just jump into that now so close to graduating." She took the paper from me and typed something on her computer. She moved the monitor so I could see what she tapped with her long pink nail.

"It says it right here, world history." I looked closely. It did say that, but I never took it before, and they even had grades. How did that get messed up?

"There has to be a mistake. Can I change? Make it a free period instead?"

She shook her head, then pushed those pink glasses further up her nose. "I can't change your classes. The principal can, but he's busy this morning. Can you come back after school?" I shrugged, I guess I would have to.

I left the office and stood outside the glass doors. I glanced down at the map and found my way to my first class. There were a lot of stares as I passed other students in the hall. I subconsciously rubbed my mouth on the back of my sleeve. Did I have food on my face? Or were new students not very common? It wasn't a large high school, but I still thought I could blend in.

By the time I found my class, I had three tall guys following behind me. It might have been flattering for some girls, but not for me. I shot them my best *I'm gonna fuck your balls up if you don't leave me alone* look just before I stepped into the class. I took a spare seat in the back as I heard the teacher yell at the tall guys to leave before she slammed it shut. I slumped into the chair and grabbed my text for English.

"You seemed to have yourself a fan club." I spun to the girl seated beside me. She had on a pink shirt that looked like it actually needed to be ironed, a headband to push her ash blonde hair from her face, and a big grin.

"Ah...yeah. I don't want a fan club."

She laughed, then quickly sobered. "Oh, really? I've been here my whole life, and I have never seen the basketball team stalk a girl anywhere like that. Let alone a new girl."

Well, I guess this was my lucky day.

"I'm Ada." She held out her hand to shake. I hesitated at first, but then took it.

"Lexi. Nice to meet you."

"So, you're from Kiba? *Dang.* The Kiba boys won't like the Kenneally boys stalking you through the halls."

The what? I tried to answer her questions as quickly as I could while trying to listen to what the teacher said because I was not exactly some honor roll, genius student here. I had to work hard for the grades I had. But in the end, curiosity won out. I needed to know the social hierarchy of this school if I was going to survive here.

"Okay, tell me what that means." Ada scooted her chair and desk closer, and you could see her eyes gleam from wanting to tell this information to anyone willing to listen.

"Okay, well, I'm from Watson. It's the second biggest town around here." I nodded for her to continue. "Well, there are a few smaller towns in the area, and the boys who come from them are like super crazy over it all. Like, you know...their turf. No one gets it, but they take it seriously. The boys from Kiba don't associate with the ones from Kenneally or Rawlins. And same for the Rawlins and Kenneally boys. They get into fights a lot.

"So, I guess with you being from Kiba, the boys there might feel the same way about you. I've seen the Rawlins boys start a fight with one of the Kiba boys when he tried to date a girl from there.

"So, all in all, it's like a regular high school, but you know, with weird turf wars that have been going on for as long as even my parents remember. But Watson and Port Willow are the only ones that don't have these groups of hot guys."

Great. I just moved into a live remake of *West Side Story*.

CHAPTER SIX

LEXI

My second class of the day did not go as well as the first. I hated statistics as it was, but as I walked in, I tried to ignore all the stares. Yes, I was the new girl. *Get over it already*. But where some turned away, a few of the guys in class stared openly at me and talked loudly. Were they the Kiba boys? They weren't the guys on the bus, and I think most of them were freshmen. I moved to an empty desk and sat quickly. I pulled out my books and tried to read some of the text, just so I didn't have to see them. The room went quiet, and I glanced up.

Raff appeared in the doorway, and as soon as his eyes caught mine, he moved and took the seat in front of me. Great, now I could stare at his pretty neck. I could still see the hint of his tattoo creeping up there.

My eyes were drawn away when Raff's books ended up on the floor. There were two tall guys—the ones from earlier, who were stalking me. The taller one, with what looked to be a permanent scowl on his face, grabbed Raff by his long sleeve top and yanked him to standing. I backed up, dragging the desk with me. *Holy shit.* The teacher was in the classroom, and this guy was going to fight Raff? What the hell did he do yesterday?

"Scum like you should go back to your trailer park pack." His friend took a swing, but Raff moved and turned his body before hitting the guy in the face with his elbow. Holy fuck, they were fighting, in class, with a teacher present. The guy's nose made a crunch sound, and I cringed. It was broken for sure. The teacher finally yelled out to them to stop, but they either didn't hear it or they chose to ignore him. The taller guy was still holding onto Raff and shoved him, causing Raff to lose his balance, and the asshole took that opportunity to punch Raff in the stomach. Hard. Raff's whole body bent over from the impact. *Fuck.*

"What is your problem, asshole?" I smacked my desk loudly with my hands, and both guys flicked their gazes to me. Raff was more tense than before. He spun, and I could see the way his eyes glared in my direction. He was mad, but seriously, the teacher wasn't doing shit. The taller of the two leaned in toward me, his dirty blond hair cut short, and his eyes were almost a rusty brown. They were distracting, so I looked away as I stood. He didn't say anything, so I glanced over and watched as his nostrils flared. I held my breath and felt the hairs on the back of my neck rise. This guy screamed dangerous.

His gaze turned deadly as he turned back to Raff, his fist clenched tight, and he was shaking as his lip curled up in a snarl.

"You making a claim, boy? 'Cause you have no rights to." He growled as he shoved Raff away, and the teacher told them to take their seats. They both sat, but they didn't stop. Instead of paying attention to the teacher, they studied me all throughout class, just whispering together as their eyes kept coming back on me. It made me uncomfortable, and I shifted in my seat, trying to shake the feeling that they were planning something not too nice for me after class was done.

Had they never had a girl stand up to them before? *Fucking bullies.*

When the bell rang, I moved quickly so I could talk to Raff, but he left in a hurry. I guess he didn't like me standing up for him, but I couldn't just sit there and watch it. He could hate me all he wanted, but I would never sit back and do nothing while someone was being bullied.

I walked out of class and found the asshole there. In fact, he had all his friends with him—all five of them tall and intimidating. I felt so tiny as they boxed me in, and my heart started to race as my palms got real sweaty. I did not do well with this type of situation. I could feel my chest starting to constrict as a panic attack was coming on. I was stronger...I wouldn't let them see me like this.

"What are you? A pussy? Tell me you're a pussy... I would eat your—" The guy stumbled to the left, and I looked to see silver hair. *Raff.* He shoved another out of the way and growled lowly.

"Leave her the fuck alone." His voice was so deep that I felt it through my body, and it was so sexy.

"My father said you can't make a claim. You have no pack," one of the guys growled back, baring his teeth.

Okay, this shit was getting weird now. I moved to get away, and Raff stood taller, blocking my escape and ready to fight all five of them, even though he was much smaller than them. I could see their fists curled—this was not going to be an even fight—and I couldn't just leave him here after what he had done for me. All the kids in the hall moved away or stood to watch this all go down. I was only a couple of hours into my first day of school, I did not expect this.

"There is a claim," Raff spoke loudly, and I had zero idea what was going on. Claim? Pack? Did he mean the Kiba boys thing? Did Raff join one of these groups yesterday, and that was why he got into a fight?

"Raff, let's go," I called out to him. Begging him silently to leave. He didn't move, but his head cocked to the side to let me know he heard me. I heard loud booming voices bouncing off the hallway walls, and I turned to see three large men approach. *What's in the water around here?*

"Parker, that *is* enough. You have been warned to stay away from

Rafferty." I realized these were teachers. Holy crap. They came and broke it all up and told the guys to leave. I watched as Raff's clenched fists went to his sides, and he stalked past me, not even giving me a second glance. I went to economics and tried to avoid everyone, but that was proving hard.

The food in the cafeteria looked better than any other I'd seen before. I noticed that most the students went to an outside seating area rather than eat inside like at my old school. It was cold and damp today, so I wasn't going to leave the warm building to freeze.

I saw Raff had grabbed some lunch, and as he was leaving the building, some guys pushed him, so he stalked off in another direction. I hated seeing that shit. I wanted to do something, but I didn't know what. I looked around at the tables. I wasn't used to eating with others. Honestly, I would rather be on my own, but maybe being alone wasn't the best idea right now. This school was harder to nut out than others.

I looked for Ada, but I couldn't see her, so I turned and saw what must be the jock table. Okay, that was a regular clique. All the guys there looked like football players, some were like seriously ripped, and most of them had tattoos. *Holy crap.* What the hell was going on with all these seniors and tattoos?

I think I lingered for too long, as two of them turned and saw me. The one with the full sleeve of colorful tattoos caught my eye first. His lips were full, his dark brown hair styled in a messy look, and he looked almost bored at the table with all his friends. Like he wished he was somewhere else. *Me too.* The white T-shirt he wore was tight and showed that he worked out, because there was no way he could get that body without a gym and weights. There were so many hot guys in this school...and I wasn't complaining. Just, I wasn't expecting it.

When the guy next to him turned to speak to his friends, he

didn't. He kept his gaze on me. It felt like my body was drawn to him, like there was a strange connection between us. I wanted to know who he was, what he was thinking, what his lips felt like... When he blinked and looked away, I did too. The connection was lost, and it was almost disappointing. I looked up once again to see him, but found the whole table staring at me, and there were at least fourteen guys there. Seniors and some juniors.

Okay, that was my cue to leave. I took my salad wrap and bottle of water, and took off. I wandered the halls of the school for a little while, looking for a quiet place I could escape to, eating and taking sips along the way.

When I saw more seniors walk through the hallway, I quickly turned on my heel and walked the other way. I looked over my shoulder to see if they were still there, then groaned when one smiled and started to follow me.

Far out. This school was worse for stalkers than any other place I had been. When I got far enough away, I saw another group of tall guys, all staring at me. Yep, fuck this shit. I wasn't sticking around to find out what they wanted. I quickly turned a corner and slammed into Raff.

Oh fuck. He grabbed my shoulders and held me steady. My heart skipped a beat. I breathed him in, and he smelled amazing, like rain on a hot summer day. *What the hell?* How was that even a smell someone could have? *I loved that smell.* He was warm and solid beneath my hands. When he looked down to my hand that was still clenched on his tee, I let go and, in my embarrassment, I ran.

I didn't know why I ran, but I just wasn't ready for all this...whatever this was. I had to escape, but I didn't know if it was to get away from the school, this town, the foster family...or Raff. My heart was racing, and I didn't know what was going on with me. I was confused and emotional—he made me feel things, which was something I didn't let myself do.

When the bell rang, I gathered myself together and pushed all the emotions down again, took a deep breath, and walked to art class like nothing had happened.

The art teacher was an older woman who wore overalls with many years of paint splatter on them. I liked her already.

"Alexis, it's lovely to meet you. We're doing individual pieces, the theme is feelings, and the medium is acrylic. We have a spare spot here." She pointed to a chair on an empty table, but I wanted to groan. *Feelings*. Something I just didn't want to deal with at all, but I loved painting, so I was glad to be using acrylics.

There didn't seem to be many kids in this class, as I counted six as I walked in. I think I'd found my favorite class of the day. I was given some paper and pencils to sketch my piece and saw that most students were up to the painting stage and were setting up their canvas.

There was a loud bang and laughter as the door flew open, and two guys pushed someone inside. When he straightened himself up, I realized it was the guy from the cafeteria. The one with the colorful tattoos and a handsome face, and who stared at me with eyes I was mesmerized by. *Oh god*. He was looking at me again, but this time, he narrowed his eyes at me. I guess he didn't like me. Ugh, what was up with me being attracted to bad boys with issues? And yes, him not liking me was an issue, but I guess that meant I would be safe near him. Even though I felt this pull to him, he obviously didn't to me.

"Maverick," the teacher said in a raised voice. "Go get your work and stop distracting class. It's not like you to be late, that's your brother. Don't turn into him."

He moved about the room, and I tried to distract myself with what I was going to sketch, but I couldn't help but watch him out from the corner of my eye. Eventually, he sat with his back to me. I let out a deep breath and relaxed. Feelings...why of all the topics this was the one I had to do?

I had done nothing all class, but I felt drained from trying to convey an emotion. I packed the paper in my bag and returned the pencils to the teacher.

"Oh dear, you can take these with you." She gave me a kind smile. I took them and nodded. I didn't mind this type of charity, since it would be nice to have them later when I got back to the house. I might be able to find an emotion then, or at least fake it.

I made my way to my last class of the day, following my map. It wasn't too far, just up on the second level. I needed to speak to this teacher because I wasn't supposed to be taking world history. As I got up to the classroom, I could see all the students entering. Crap, I wanted to chat with him before class started. I ran in last and closed the door behind me. When I spun around, I saw *him*. Butterflies danced in my belly as I took him in.

It was the guy from this morning, the one the students parted for... Wait, he was my teacher?

CHAPTER SEVEN

GALEN

I received a call yesterday from the case worker, Shelly, who often sends wolf shifter kids to us up here. Usually they were under the age of ten, but she was sending a teen here for the first time. The packs didn't like the older ones, since they were harder to bring in and ended up a lone wolf without a pack more times than I could count. That was why it was best if they were younger when we got them, and before their first shift was always the best.

I was told about Rafferty because the Alpha of Pack Kiba was worried about him. The other packs were warned about a teen shifter and to leave him alone. I tried to keep an eye on him yesterday, but he was great at evading. I had heard from Grayson last night that Rafferty had come home covered in blood from a fight. I was hoping to help him, but when I found him this morning, he wouldn't speak to me.

Shelly also told me about a young woman who was also staying with Jack and Grayson Rawson. She'd told me she smelled almost like a shifter, but she had never scented one like her before, and she wasn't sure if she even was one. When she couldn't compel the young woman, Shelly knew she needed to be up here. Alexis was alone, living on the streets of Seattle while she worked at a strip club and put herself through school. The fact that she still cared enough about her education meant she was at least determined to have a better future.

But Alexis wasn't a shifter, that had been clear from Jack when he spoke to me last night. He said he could tell from her scent she wasn't one, but it was a confusing scent. At times, she gave off an almost-shifter smell, then at other times, she almost smelled like a vampire. But most the time, he said that she smelled like neither, so it was very confusing and bizarre. No one knew what she was.

She didn't know anything about the shifter world, and everyone was warned not to speak to her about it until we figured out what she was.

Females were never born as shifters—wolves and even bear shifters had the same curse. A shifter in their animal form had to bite the female and inject her with their venom, and that would turn her into a shifter. Then she could produce shifter sons, but never daughters. The only shifters I knew that weren't affect by this were the big cats—panther and tiger shifters. They still bore females, but at a much lower ratio to the males.

There weren't a lot of female wolf-shifters around, since most females died during the transformation process. It didn't happen very often that a woman was made a shifter, and often the female would be mated to a few strong males in the pack. Not always, but most of the time, this was how it worked with wolf-shifter packs.

I had worked for Pack Kiba for the last five years in exchange for settling here safely. The elders were happy with my presence and enjoyed my protection, as I have theirs. I could compel humans to forget seeing a wolf, like when the boys here at school would fight and shift into their wolf form. That was why I held a position at the school, as it was where most incidents happened, and I also enjoy teaching. The shifter kids didn't like me here, but that was in their nature to feel that way. Humans were different—they were drawn to my presence, but didn't know why.

The packs could have started an all-shifter high school, separating the humans from the shifters like other packs often did. The problem was that they couldn't make those connections with the females if they did that. They needed to build those relationships if they wanted to find a potential mate.

When I walked into school this morning, I didn't know what I was smelling. It was clean, sweet, and it drew me in like never before. I had walked toward it before I could stop myself. Then I saw her and knew this was what they were all talking about—her scent.

Alexis Turner.

I was all but frozen at the sight of her. She was beautiful, her hair a light golden brown that was up in a loose messy bun, little wisps of it falling around her amber eyes. I had never seen eyes like that in all my life. It might mean something, a hint at what she was, but what, I didn't know. I held my breath, but I couldn't help it, I wanted another hit of that sweetness. Her scent was strong, even through the glass doors. My fangs slid out, and my body hummed with the need to taste her.

That had never happened before, and I was embarrassed that I didn't have better control of myself. I quickly left to my office, where I took a shot of whisky and calmed myself. I had fed earlier, so I didn't need to feed again, but this response to her scent was worrying. Shelly had never mentioned having this reaction to her, but come to think of it, if she affected all vamps like this, she wouldn't be here right now. They would have taken her a long time ago. No, this was something that just affected me.

And now she was walking into my class. I knew she would be in my world history class. I had seen her transcripts and altered them so she would be here. I had wanted to keep her safe, but I was sure I wasn't prepared for this.

"Welcome, Alexis. Please take a seat." I held my breath. She looked like she was going to speak to me, but instead, she darted around and seated herself right in front of me. I wanted to quietly ask her to move to the back of the class, but I didn't want to call her out. I knew if I was that close to her, my fangs would descend again, and I didn't want to draw attention to the fact this petite young woman was affecting me. The shifter students would hear about it, that she was a sign of a weakness for me, and I didn't want to subject her to that.

I turned my back on the class and got everyone to open their books. I took a deep breath, but her scent permeated the room. At least I seemed to have control of myself now. I must have just been caught off guard this morning.

I heard the door slam open, and I knew that scent anywhere. I hissed low, just for him to hear. He was the only shifter in this class. Most avoided world history because I taught it, but not Ranger Lovell. He took this class because of me.

I turned to him, saw his big playful grin spread from ear to ear, and I rolled my eyes. He made me laugh and infuriated me at the same time, but he was forever smiling and joking.

"No need to get grumpy with me, Galen. You know you love me."

I wanted to smack him upside his head. He liked to push my buttons and in a teasing way, which was even more maddening.

"Take a seat at the back." I pointed to two spare seats back there, but Ranger had already spotted Alexis...and she had noticed him, too. When he walked over to her in what was known as the 'Ranger swagger,' she rolled her eyes at him and looked away. I wanted to laugh, as it was funny that he didn't affect her. The female students were usually falling all over themselves to be noticed by Ranger. He sat beside her and leaned over.

"Hey, pretty girl." His voice had a seductive tone about it, but she didn't look at him, and I could see the confusion on Ranger's face from the corner of my eye. Damn. I chuckled to myself. I think I could really like this girl.

"I saw my twin brother notice you at lunch today... You must be special because no girl has ever turned his head before. I was starting to think he was gay or something."

That had her expression changing, and not in the way Ranger

had intended. His smile was still there, like she was going to fall into his arms and profess her love for him.

"So what if he's gay or straight? Do you have a problem with that? Because I don't. I have a problem with you. There's *something* wrong with you. Fuck, I feel sorry for your brother, having to be related to such an asshole." She was loud, and the whole class watched on, some of the girls' faces falling in shock that she was speaking to Ranger like that. Not me though. I enjoyed watching him being taken down a notch and the fire within her.

"You're a fucking prick," she hissed under her breath. A normal human wouldn't have heard that from here, but I wasn't human, and Ranger knew that, too. He turned to me as if I was going to say something about her language.

"Ranger, move now." I couldn't compel shifters, but I could call his father and tell him what his pack had been doing to this poor girl today. The packs needed to back off, even though they were obviously affected by her scent. She didn't understand this, so having these huge grown ass men—because most were eighteen but had bodies that no eighteen-year-old human would normally have—chasing and stalking her around the school was not going to work. I had been told she was a runner, and this was going to have her running. I wanted her to stay here. I wanted to help her and protect her.

I could hear Ranger grumble about me being an asshole and to go fuck myself, but I just smiled and started class.

CHAPTER EIGHT

LEXI

I couldn't wait to leave for the day. As soon as the bell rang, I was up and out the door. I could hear the teacher, Mr. Donovani, call out my name, but I didn't turn around. I just kept going forward. He was the one Grayson had told Raff to speak to this morning if he got into any more trouble, which was even worse. This teacher would have known my background, and I didn't want to see him give me the same sad eyes I'd get when someone found out I was an orphan and foster kid. No, thank you. Not today.

I would have to talk to Jack or someone about being transferred from this class. But funnily enough, I learned a lot today. I found it really interesting, and I was a little disappointed that I never thought to take world history before. But then again, it could have been the teacher. He was so young to be a teacher. I really thought he was a student.

"Hey, pretty lady, wait up." Ugh, I ran. *Ranger*. Who the fuck calls their kid Ranger? Honestly, it was a dumbass name for a complete dumbass asshole. And the asshole had no idea how rude he was about his brother's sexuality. It shouldn't matter who turned his head. As long as he was being treated with respect and was loved, who cared? This was the twenty-first century, for fuck's sake.

I pushed my way past everyone and noticed some of those tall guys standing near the bus I needed to take. They weren't on there earlier. Were they waiting for Raff? Or me? I didn't want to wait around and find out. I pulled my hoodie over my head to keep the chill out and started walking away from the bus. I remembered the way back to the foster house from the drive in, so I would walk back, maybe clear my head… Or I could walk into town and take the bus back to Port Angeles. After the shitty day I just had, that sounded like the best thing to do—get away from this messed up school.

I started to walk toward the main township of Port Willow when I felt someone following me. My heart sped up a little, and when I glanced back, I caught the silver hair of Raff. I wasn't headed back to the foster's, so why the hell was he following me?

I stopped suddenly, and I heard his feet shuffle to a stop.

"Why are you following me?" I demanded, putting my hands on my hips and looking him right in the eyes. He didn't speak, he just stood there. After an awkward moment, he looked away, then brushed past me and continued walking into town.

"Fuck you then," I called after him and started to walk the other way, back toward the foster house. Fuck it, the food was nice and the room was warm. It was a nicer day today, as the sun had broken through the clouds for all of five minutes, but it didn't rain, and it was only going to get colder as the day turned to night. I really had to stop thinking of running away.

I only had, what…like just over two months left of high school, then I was done. I would turn eighteen, graduate, and figure out something from there. Save up, find somewhere to live, and eventually go to college. That was the plan, but I needed a new job since I wasn't working at The Landing Strip anymore. I was definitely not going back to working in a strip club anytime soon.

When I felt Raff behind me again, I rolled my eyes as I looked to the sky and the clouds above. *What the hell was his problem?*

I turned around and pinned him with my finger right into his chest. *His very hard chest.*

"Are you supposed to make sure I get back to the foster house? Is that why you're following me?" When he started to walk past me again, I reached out and grabbed his arm. He jumped and shook me off violently.

"Fuck off," he hissed. I looked up and saw his eyes were almost glowing. Then he stilled and shrunk away from me, like I'd just burned him with my touch. *What the hell happened to him?*

"I... Shit, I'm sorry. I shouldn't have touched you. That was wrong. If anyone knows that, it's me."

He stuffed his hands into his pockets, and after a few moments, he shrugged. His head hung low, his hair now fallen over his eyes. I could see dried blood on his neck, so I moved toward him, and he kept still as I slowly peeled down the edge of his top. There were nasty gashes, like some animal had just ripped his shoulder open with long claws, and my stomach dropped. *Fuck, this is bad.*

"How, what happened?" His eyes flashed to mine, the same pretty color I had come to know. This guy was a little rough around the edges, but what these assholes at school had been doing to him was not acceptable. He just shrugged and walked off, and I followed him. I wasn't his shadow, but now...I was worried.

Raff kept flicking his gaze back to me until we were walking up the driveway to the foster house. Jack opened the door with his hand on his chest, breathing rapidly.

"Oh, you're home," he panted, turning back into the house. "Grayson, they're home! Call off the search."

I stopped just outside the door as Grayson came running out. His hands went to his knees, and he started taking in deep breaths before he stood. "I'm sorry. I get worried easily. The bus just drove past, and it didn't stop. I panicked, thinking that something had happened to you both, and I called Jack to come home from work. Can you call me if you're going to walk home? *Please?* My heart is getting old. If you need a lift, just call me, I'll come get you."

I was a little stunned. Actually, I was more than stunned. I didn't know what to say. Grayson wasn't angry, he was worried. About us. Raff was watching the scene unfold just like me. I wanted to point out that I didn't have a phone, try to brush off the strange feeling in my chest over this. So, I did what I did best...I deflected.

"Raff got hurt," I said as I walked past Jack and Grayson into the house. It smelled amazing again. I heard Raff behind me as he stomped past, Jack following him and asking him questions. I stopped and looked at little Joshua laying on the carpet in the living room. His little legs were kicked up in the air, and his hands held his head up to watch a cartoon. His face lit up when he saw me, and I couldn't help but smile back. He was one of the lucky kids that got a good foster home straight up.

"Alexis, do you want to watch with me?"

I walked in and dumped my bag on the floor with a loud *thud*. I got down onto the floor and lay on my tummy next to him, kicking my legs in the air and using my hands to prop up my chin, and he giggled.

"I've never had a sister before. Do you like *Teen Titans*?"

I smiled. No one had called me their sister before. I'd never cared about staying around long enough to make friendships or relationships with foster siblings. But right now, with Joshua, I wanted that with him. I would be that big sister he never had. I decided that for the next few months, I would be here for him. He needed all the love and support he could get. That was something I had never had, even when my parents were alive.

I bumped my shoulder into his. "I like having a little brother. I haven't seen this show. Is it good?" His little eyes lit up when I call him brother, and he threw his arms around my neck in a hug.

"Oh, yes, it's very funny, Alexis."

I hugged him back awkwardly with one arm. "You can call me Lexi. Only special people can call me that."

He pulled back and gave me a big kiss on the cheek. "You smell so nice, Lexi."

Grayson called out that the muffins were ready and that they were nice and hot. I'd never had a muffin fresh from the oven. Joshua and I sat together eating the muffins and watching his cartoons. They weren't too bad, the cartoons that was... The muffins were amazing. Grayson really knew how to cook.

I had been in my room for the last hour just thinking, something I should really stop doing. I was worried about Raff, and I was worried about school. I didn't want to be part of whatever the assholes at school were playing at. The weird stalking shit, it needed to end, and it would tomorrow. I let them have today, since I didn't want to draw attention, but tomorrow...fuck them.

I heard Raff's door open. I rolled over, trying to stop myself from getting up. He was fine, Jack said he was when Raff didn't show at dinner. I rolled over again, then again, until I gave up and flipped the covers off. I had on a tank top and the sleep pants I got from Shelly, and I had thrown my bra off hours ago.

I took the elastic band from my wrist and pulled my hair up into a messy bun. Then I slowly padded barefoot across my dimly lit bedroom and unlocked the door. The lock was loud. *Shit.*

I could see the bathroom light was on and the door wide open. I snuck down the hall to see...you know, to make sure he was fine. I didn't know why I cared so much about him. Okay, that was a lie.

I peered in and could see Raff slumped over the basin. He was topless and only wearing tight black boxers. I bit my lip to stop myself from speaking. I could see all of his tattoos. He was covered in ink head to toe, and they even went all the way under his boxers. I wondered if everything was covered in tattoos. Oh man, my mind was going places it probably shouldn't right now.

Is he crying?

Bandages covered his shoulder. That at least answered my question, so I could go sleep now. I went to sneak back, but it was too late. His eyes flicked up to the mirror, and he saw me. I froze as air escaped my lungs, and my heart sped up, just from that look alone.

He turned, his whole body on display. Well, not all of it. I couldn't help but sweep my eyes over his chest. I tried not to look at his boxers and what was hidden beneath them, but when I got to his legs, I could see a large white dressing on his upper right thigh.

My mouth dropped open. "What the hell, Raff?"

CHAPTER NINE

RAFFERTY

I could smell her before she even opened her bedroom door. That lock that Jack had put there at my request was loud. I knew Alexis didn't feel safe here, but for me, I'd never felt safer in my life—and I was in another pack's territory. Living with five other shifters, I shouldn't feel safe.

But I knew from living even with my own pack, a lock made you feel a little safer. It wouldn't stop anyone, most of all a shifter. But you could hear someone breaking down your door and give yourself a chance at least.

Jack put one on her window, which I wasn't impressed by at first and I protested, but when I heard her go to her window last night, I realized she would have run off again. I didn't want her to run. I wanted to keep her safe. *My wolf wanted to keep her.*

I tried to do that today, but it didn't go as planned. There were three different wolf packs at Port Willow High. How they all functioned in one school surprised me, but for the last two days, they had one common enemy—*me*.

I was considered a rogue wolf around here.

I knew this would happen before I got here. I knew it would be hard. They only place young pups in other packs, not one that was almost of age. *Fuck*, I should have let Shelly do this years ago when she first met me. I would be eighteen in three weeks, but Shelly had told me that Grayson and Jack would let me live here for as long as I wanted. My aging out of the system, the fact that I was from the Russet Pack just outside Seattle...none of that mattered to them.

I thought that being here was a better option than jail. *Hell*, jail was better than living with my pack, so this was a huge upgrade. But being here had been a lot more to take in than I had thought. I could deal with assholes, I had my whole life. All my uncles were assholes. Being fucked up on drugs all the time had turned them feral and violent.

No, it was the perfect family unit that I'd walked into that was hard to take in. Two caring parents, three kids who were dressed and well fed. Treated to cupcakes, muffins...bacon and egg breakfasts. And then *her*. I had never felt so strongly about someone, and it scared me.

I leaned my head against the basin. I could sense her coming toward the bathroom, and I wanted to hide my leg from her. She'd been so worried about my neck, and I'd snapped at her. I didn't mean to. I almost shifted when she grabbed me. I didn't want to act that way around her, and I felt so ashamed when I told her to fuck off.

I'd been told we had to hide our shifter sides from her until the elders of the packs worked out what she was. She was no shifter, that was for sure. But I'd never smelled anything like her, and it drove my wolf crazy. *Fuck, it drove all the wolves here crazy.*

When she lingered at the door of the bathroom, I couldn't help myself. I wanted to see her face. Did she hate me? I knew I wasn't making it easy for her to like me. I didn't make it easy for anyone to like me. If I did, I was sure my uncles would take that from me, just like they took my mom. I never made friends, dated, or had a girlfriend. All the things normal teenagers did, I didn't. I wouldn't give them anything they could use against me again.

I saw her eyes, the most unusual amber color—almost gold, it was like they glowed in the florescent light.

I wanted to tell her I was sorry for earlier. I wanted to explain that I didn't mean to snap at her. It was the venom from one of the Kenneally Pack members when they thought it would be funny to bite me before the end of school. The asshole knew I would have this reaction.

If a shifter injects venom into another shifter, it causes them to become more aggressive, like it messes with their hormones or something. It lasted in your system for about twelve hours, but it was out of my system now. I'd been slowly becoming immune to it over the years. My uncles used to bite me every day as a game when I first shifted. They were sick fucks. *I was only eleven.*

I turned and faced her. I knew I couldn't tell her about the shifter world and what she just walked into. She didn't know we existed, not yet anyway. But maybe if she saw, she would understand why I acted the way I did... *Maybe.*

I could smell a hint of her arousal in the air as her eyes drifted down my chest. I wanted to take a deep breath, but instead, I held it and waited to see what she would do.

"What the hell, Raff?" Her voice was loud, almost angry. She just stood there, looking at my leg. I didn't know what I expected her to do, but that wasn't it. She moved in close, and I had to breathe. I couldn't help it—I smelled her arousal in the air, but it was laced with fear. It was too much. She called to my wolf, and I didn't know why. I darted around her and straight to my room where I closed the door with a loud bang. I pressed my back against the door, taking deep breaths, trying to get her scent out of my mind. I rested my head against my door as I listened to her.

I didn't have a lock. I didn't need one here, but that meant she could come into my room anytime. I wanted her to come in here. I was hard and aching, and I rubbed my cock through my boxers.

I'd never wanted someone until Alexis.

Alexis was still in her sleepwear as I ate my breakfast quickly. Grayson was eying me, but I didn't care. He didn't understand. Fuck, I didn't even understand myself, but my wolf did. I got up and put my plate in the kitchen, then checked to see if I was being followed.

When I couldn't hear anyone, I quietly opened up her bedroom door and slipped in. Her room held her scent, and I took a deep breath, like I was an addict chasing my next hit. Her clothes were laid out on her bed. She'd made it this morning before I got a chance to roll in it. *Fuck.*

I rubbed my cheek and neck over her clothes, especially the hoodie, which seemed to be the only one she had. I stood back then took a deep breath. *Mine.* That was what I could now smell. I marked her clothes, now maybe the assholes at school would back off from her.

I took her pillow and rubbed it on myself—it wasn't as strong as rubbing myself in her sheets, but it was better than nothing. I could hear Grayson, his voice deep as he asked Alexis if she was finished. I quickly put her pillow back, opened the door, and slipped out the room as if nothing happened. Only a moment later, as I walked toward the bathroom, Alexis turned the corner. I didn't look at her, *I couldn't.* I was ashamed of what I'd done. But I would do it again, over and over.

I spotted Grayson at the door as I brushed my teeth, and he gestured to me with his thumb to meet him in the living room. I rolled my eyes at him, and he growled a warning at me.

"What?" I demanded when I saw him standing in the living room, looking out the window.

"Don't what me, boy, that's rude. You say excuse me." He took a deep breath like he was calming himself down. "Now, I know what you're doing, and I don't know why, but you have to stop. It's only going to make things worse for you. I'm trying to protect you and Alexis, and this is not the way to go about it." He ran his hand down his face as his eyes closed, then he took a deep breath.

I wasn't going to apologize for what I did. And when I didn't say anything, he continued, "It's hard when you can't just be yourself at home. When was the last time you shifted and took a run?"

I tried to think back, but it was the day I got busted with my uncle's drugs. I'd run that morning, but that was it. I refused to let the guys at school bully me into shifting. I was stronger than that—even though my wolf had been screaming to bust out at them and protect me. But I held him back, I wouldn't give in. I wasn't some weak wolf, and they knew it.

"Look, come with me tonight after school, I'll run with you. It'll be good for both of us." I just shrugged and threw my bag over my shoulder, then made my way out of the house into the crisp spring air.

Alexis finally came and stood beside me. She stood a little closer today, and I couldn't help the way my heart sped up a little at that. I left my phone in my pocket, not that I'd actually been on it yesterday. I was pretending to be doing something while I watched her from the corner of my eye. The wind picked up and blew the cool air toward me, and I could smell our mixed scent.

That made me smile a little, something I hadn't done in forever.

CHAPTER TEN

LEXI

Day two of school was...different, and so was day three. I hadn't seen much of Raff. It was as if he was avoiding me after the bathroom incident.

But I also didn't see that annoying Ranger at school, either, and everyone left me well enough alone. Day one, I'd had half the males in school as my stalkers, as well as day two, but I was now the school pariah, and no one wanted to talk to me. Well, except for Ada, which was fine by me.

But this was different. Today there were stares...a lot of them. At least no one came close to me. It was nice, but it was also not right. I had a bad feeling, and I was waiting for some epic prank to happen.

I had a locker, but I never used it. I was taking all my books from class to class. As much as my teachers protested, I didn't trust anyone in this school to keep my things in a locker. I didn't use the one in my last school, either. If I had, I wouldn't have had everything I do with me now—it would still be in that locker after I ran.

I was grateful it was finally the weekend. I slept in and woke up to the smell of breakfast and muffins. My stomach rumbled as I slowly peeled myself out of bed. I looked over to the computer in my room. I hadn't used it yet, and I had a project that I needed to do some online studying for...but that could wait until after breakfast. I was starting to really love these breakfasts. I'd already put on a little bit of weight since I'd been here.

"Lexi." Josh ran to me and wrapped his hands around my waist and placed his head on my stomach. I hugged him back. I loved this. Every morning, he'd been giving me hugs. The other two boys seemed scared of me. I could understand their feelings toward me, so I wasn't offended. I was once like that...and I guess I still was, but not with Josh. He was my little buddy. I guessed in some way, I was living the childhood I never had through him and being everything I wished I had when I was six.

"Lexi, I have left a plate for you in the kitchen. I made some muffins that the boys all ate. Did you want to help me make some more later?" I looked up as Grayson walked out the kitchen, wiping his hands on a towel. Did that guy ever leave the kitchen? He was forever baking. But he was forever smiling in there too.

"You can't call her Lexi, only special people can call her that," Josh almost growled at Grayson. That kind of surprised me. He was always so sweet, and now he sounded very angry. I peeled Josh off me, and Grayson had a look on his face I couldn't work out.

"It's okay, Grayson is a special person, too." I tried to defuse the situation, if it was one. Grayson just looked at Josh, his little head tilted to the floor, then he apologized to Grayson.

"Joshua, why don't you see if Harry or Jaxon want to go out and play?"

Josh nodded and ran down the hall toward their rooms. I hadn't been down that end of the house yet. Not because I wasn't allowed to or anything, I just didn't need to be down there, so I hadn't gone.

I knew the big double doors at the end held Grayson and Jack's room. And the three boys shared two bedrooms. Josh got his own room, but I was told that Joshua mostly ended up sleeping on the boys' floor at night because of nightmares. They set up a mattress on the floor for him, and I'd heard them talking yesterday about getting bunkbeds.

I had nightmares, and I never wished them on anyone. Mostly, they were things that had happened to me, just twisted to make them worse—if that was even possible. But the worst ones were of things that had happened to me that I kept buried deep inside for a reason. They would come out of the dark hole I'd put them in and find their way into my dreams. The worst nightmares were of when my parents were killed. I never wanted to relive that again, yet lucky me got to a few nights a week.

"Jack wants to take you shopping after breakfast. You really need some new clothes, Lexi. I know you don't want us to buy you any, I guessed that. But maybe if you let us do it this one time, you can pay us back with chores."

I arched my brow. "What kind of chores?"

Grayson chuckled deep in his chest. "Dishes? Every night for a week?"

Now I raised both brows. *Really?* That was not a lot of work for clothes.

He laughed. "Or you can just accept the clothes, and not wash dishes."

I couldn't stop the smile from forming on my face. I'd only been here four days, and right in this moment, I didn't want it to end. But nothing this good lasted forever. *Right?*

After a good two hours of shopping, I now had a cell phone—my first one ever. I could text and receive calls, and that was all I needed it for. I didn't have any social media since I had no need for it. I didn't need anything fancy.

I also got at least a week's worth of clothes, if not a month with

Jack shopping with me. Mostly jeans and hoodies. But also some T-shirts, tank tops, and some shorts since the weather was starting to warm up. Summer was getting closer, and so was my birthday.

Jack insisted I get a dress. "You know, in case you get invited to a party," was his excuse. I had a feeling that wasn't going to happen, given what had happened the last few days at school.

But in the end, I settled for a dark blue one which fell just above the knee. I wasn't sure at first, but it made me look...feminine. I felt like a woman in this dress. I knew that I probably wouldn't wear it anywhere, except the one event I'd thought of while I tried it on —graduation.

Jack said he needed to get some other things and took me to the housewares section. He just started picking up fluffy pink pillows and knitted blue throw rugs, showing them to me for approval. I was confused at first, until he asked me what color sheets I'd like. I just froze, and my tongue felt heavy... I didn't know what to say. I thought we were just getting clothes. But he wouldn't take no for an answer, and if I didn't tell him which ones I liked, he was going to buy every color.

The feeling in my chest returned, the warm one I didn't know was a feeling someone could have. I smiled and pointed to some dark purple sheets, and Jack just did his thing. Mixing and matching with me. I giggled at some of his terrible choices, and the lightness in my chest felt amazing in the moment.

When I got back to the house, Raff wasn't in his room or anywhere in the house. I wandered back toward the kitchen after putting some of my new things in my room. Jack said he would wash everything and set up my room for me later. Grayson was in the kitchen setting up the baking equipment.

"Did you want to learn how to make double chocolate muffins?" I hesitated at the door. I didn't know exactly why I was wandering the house. I'd spent most my time in my room. But now...I guess it was nice to speak to someone. I needed to work on my project for class, but here I was, standing in the kitchen with Grayson, who had the biggest smile on his face as he started to measure the flour.

"I... Okay." I stepped into the room, and his smile became infectious. I returned the smile as he showed me the recipe and how to sift the flour.

"You are a fast learner, Lexi. Are you sure you haven't baked before?" I looked at the disaster that was the countertop. I'd never cracked an egg before, and I may have had an accident with the first, and well, the second one, too. But Grayson just kept on smiling and showed me how. I was a seventeen-year-old learning how to crack an egg for the first time. This was stuff I should have learned with my mom, if she was the kind of mom that normal people had. Not me, my mom had liked the end of a needle more than feeding me. Which was why I avoided anyone who did drugs. I never wanted to end up like her or my dad.

"Ohh, something smells good. I can't wait to try one, Lexi. I bet they're just as good as they smell," Jack said, a smile beaming on his face as he walked into the kitchen, opened the refrigerator, and took out a bottle of water. I knew he was just being nice. But once again, I had that feeling deep in my gut that this wasn't real and it could be taken at any moment. I didn't want to open myself up for more heartache. This wasn't how people lived, this wasn't how *I* lived.

But in that moment, I closed my eyes as I listened to Jack speak about someone he saw while we were out earlier—just regular couple talk—and I dreamed that this was real...and all mine. They were my dads, I had three little brothers, and I watched *Teen Titans* after school each day with Josh. They asked me about my day, they cooked me nice meals, and took me shopping for dresses, all while I talked about the cute boy I had a crush on. I had a normal life, like in the movies I had seen.

The slamming of the front door had my eyes flashing open and brought me back to reality. It was stupid to dream.

Just a dream until the nightmare returned.

CHAPTER ELEVEN

LEXI

I woke up in the early hours of Monday morning to the sound of crying. It was muffled, but then I heard it grow louder outside my room. I threw my sheet off and slowly padded on the cool wooden floorboards to my door. I pressed my ear to the wood and listened. Someone was sobbing against my door.

"Josh?" I tentatively asked.

The sobbing stopped, and I heard him squeak out, "Lexi."

I quickly unlocked my door, and the hallway was lit up enough from the bathroom for me to see the blotchy red face of the beautiful little Josh sitting beside my door.

"Did you have a bad dream?" Why was he at my door? Why wasn't he with Harry or Jaxon? Or even Grayson or Jack? He nodded and sniffled, rubbing his nose against the back of his hand.

"Can I sleep in your room? I promise to be quiet... Just for tonight?" I heard the click of Raff's door open. His hair was messy and angled in strange directions. It was fascinating to see, as he seemed to always have it so put together. Seeing him like this gave him a softer look, like he was just as human as the next person. Plus, he was only wearing his boxers. Tight boxers. *Fuck.*

He looked down to Josh as I helped him stand, and Raff didn't say anything as I led Josh into my room and closed the door gently behind me. I didn't lock it, since Josh might not be able to get out if I did. But I felt...safe, especially with Raff on the other side of the hall. Somehow, I just knew in my gut that he was safe. That I was protected.

Josh curled up on the floor, but he couldn't sleep down there. He could share my bed. It was a single, but there was plenty of room. I picked him up, and he sleepily crawled in. I followed behind and covered us with the sheet, then I fell into a deep dreamless sleep.

Something had happened between Friday and Monday, and I didn't know what it was. Everything seemed the same when I got off the bus. But Ranger was back, and he didn't seem to get the memo that no one was speaking to me still.

"Hey, Alexis. Can I call you Lexi?"

I looked at him and blinked twice, as if I had all the time in the world to answer him, then replied in the most bored voice I could, "No, fuck off." This didn't seem to stop him. He wasn't going to give up as he kept pace along with me on my walk to class. I slipped into my classroom, and he kept on walking toward his class like it was nothing.

It was a pity because the guy was hot, and he knew it. My brain said *'stay away,'* but my body said *'touch me.'* It was frustrating, but I knew I was smart enough to avoid him—which was easier said than done. Lunchtime came, and I went to the cafeteria and grabbed a bottle of water and a salad wrap. They had pizza, which I was dying to have a slice of, but I needed something I could eat and walk with because there was no way I was eating in there.

"Alexis, come sit here. I saved you a spot." I turned and saw Ranger with a huge dopey grin on his face. The rest of the guys at the table all watched me from afar, but none so closely as Maverick. He didn't like me. I didn't know why, and yeah, I'd be lying if I said I didn't care. I did care, and that was unusual for me. I turned on my heel and left the loud room as quickly as I entered and slammed right into Galen—I mean, Mr. Donovani.

"I'm sorry," I said as I looked behind me. I could hear the door open from the cafeteria and saw Ranger step out and look to his left, then he slowly spun to face me. My teacher, the most beautiful male specimen I'd ever seen, was still holding my shoulder where he caught me.

"Oh, what do we have here?" Ranger drawled as he stepped toward us and cocked his head, like he caught us being inappropriate. I stepped back and put some space between Mr. Donovani and me. But even with the distance, I could feel my body sway toward his like it wanted to be touched by him again.

"Ranger, what are you doing?" Mr. Donovani asked as Ranger started heading toward us. One hand was in his jeans pocket, which made his saunter look so sexy. When he got closer, I could smell him. He smelled amazing for a guy, almost like wildflowers, which seemed like an unusual smell for someone so masculine.

"I was just seeing where Lexi was off to. I just didn't expect her to be running into your arms. But then again, I guess someone has to feel sorry for you...*Galen*."

My jaw dropped, and Ranger flicked his green eyes to me. *What the hell.* Mr. Donovani was our teacher, and he talked to him like that? Ranger had no respect for him, I could see that clearly.

"My name is Alexis, not Lexi, and where I go is none of your business."

I didn't want to stand around and listen to this shit anymore. I adjusted my bag on my shoulder, since the weight was becoming unbearable standing here, listening to this. I turned and walked away as if I knew where I was going. I didn't, but anywhere away from there was better.

I found a little alcove between two classrooms, dropped my bag, and hid. I opened my wrap and took a bite, and then I heard footsteps. I tried to be silent by holding my breath. It might just be a student going to their locker. When a dark shadow cast down on me, I squeezed my eyes shut.

"Let's go to my office." I looked up to see Mr. Donovani with a gentle smile on his face as he looked down at me. I knew I looked pathetic. I didn't move, I wasn't going to his office.

"I didn't do anything wrong."

When he got that I wasn't moving, he crouched down on the balls of his feet and placed his hand on top of my bag. "Alexis, I'm offering you my office so you can eat lunch. You can eat in there, away from guys like Ranger."

I shrugged like I didn't care, then he pulled my bag up and tossed it over his shoulder like it weighed nothing, and I stood up. Grateful that I wasn't carrying it, I followed him in silence to his office. I guessed this would be a good time to mention the whole needing to change out of his class thing.

The office was larger than I thought. He didn't have to share with another teacher, and the walls were lined with bookshelves. So many books, some very dusty, and it tickled my nose, it was so heavy in the air. His desk was placed close to the only window in the room, which looked over the back of the school where the national forest was maybe a football field away from the main building.

"Please, take a seat." He pointed to a wooden chair in front of his desk as he placed my bag beside it. He rounded the desk to the other side and took a seat on his leather chair, which squeaked slightly as he sat. He spun and looked out the window. My stomach rumbled, so I quickly started on my wrap again. The fresh tomato was so good.

"You can come here anytime you need to, Alexis. You can come eat lunch here every day. I keep the door unlocked, so even if I'm not here, you're more than welcome to come in and eat. Or if you need some space."

I swallowed, then looked up and found he was watching me. His hazel eyes caught in the light, and they were *so beautiful*. I need to snap out of it, my teacher was not beautiful. I nodded as they turned from beautiful to dark instantly.

"If you have any problems, you come straight to me." The words were spoken strangely, and he held my gaze. It was intense, until I waved my hand in the air and he snapped out of it.

"I can handle myself. And no offense, but you're like super young for a teacher, and the students here," one in particular, at least, "don't respect you. I don't know what good it would do coming to you. I can take care of myself, so I don't need some teacher to look after me." I took another bite as he sat back. I didn't blink, I refused to. His eyes didn't leave mine until he spun his chair to look out the window again. As I finished eating, the silence in the small room was charged, but he finally turned, a small smile on his face as he seemed to study me. I just gave him my best death stare, which I think made him smile more.

The bell rang, and it couldn't have come sooner. I got up and threw my wrapper into the waste basket. I dragged my bag up off the floor and swung it over my shoulder. I jerked the door open, but his voice caused me to freeze.

"I might look young...but I'm an old soul, Alexis."

CHAPTER TWELVE

RANGER

God, I hated Galen, that fucking pretentious prick. I'd been banned from school last week after he told my father what had gone down. I wasn't doing anything wrong—I did the same to all the girls at school. I just wanted to flirt a little... Okay, a lot, because god, she smelled so good. And yeah, she was driving all the shifters here a little crazy.

But that rogue wolf had messed with the wrong pack when he scented himself with her. Alexis didn't smell like him, not really. Only her clothes did.

I knew he'd done that to make a claim on her, as if the hundred-plus shifters at school weren't going to have a problem with that. She lived in Kiba territory, and he was not Pack Kiba, so it set my wolf off bad.

I was a little...volatile at times. My wolf was easily provoked, whereas Maverick was very much in charge of when he shifted.

Galen watched from his little office window as I challenged Rafferty in the forest that day she first came here. Maverick stood by and watched us. He wasn't happy with me taking matters into my own hands. He wanted me to wait until our father, the Alpha of Pack Kiba, had spoken to us over this rogue scum. And that was what made my father angry—that I challenged Rafferty over his fake claim on Alexis. He said that was not what an alpha would've done, and I was alpha-born. One day, I could be Alpha of Pack Kiba, but not until after I challenged my older brothers for it. Jett, Lyell, and Nash had more of a claim than me, and I had no intentions of being an alpha. I wanted to have fun, and I knew growing up with my father as alpha that he didn't have fun. *Ever!*

I'd known about her. I knew this strange girl was coming here. We were warned, but I wasn't prepared. None of the shifters were. Like, come on, Jack, warn us a little sooner that she was stunning, stubborn, and smelled like *mine*! Only problem was, all the wolves here felt the same pull to her.

I knew she wasn't a shifter... Well, not yet anyway. She had this amazing scent. It was like a mixture of bonfire, smoke, and marshmallows. There was no way to describe such a beautiful smell. She didn't like me, but she was turned on by me, that I could smell. I could work with that. Soon, she'd be falling into my arms and I could call her mine. And scum could fuck off to the scum pack he was from.

She wasn't turned on by some of the other shifters. Like Parker Tolson. He was a Kenneally and had been trying to make the point that since she was a foster, her living on Kiba land didn't make her automatically ours. My father disagreed. She was ours.

Their packs took fosters or lone wolves in just like ours, so they could've been lucky and had her sent to their pack. But she was sent to our pack. She was here because Galen was a Kiba Vampire. He worked for us, and his vampire connection in Seattle gave Alexis to Jack and Grayson.

So for that one reason only, I liked having Galen around. But also, because taunting him was fun. That was why I took world history. You didn't ever see another shifter in his class. Vampires had a smell that was not pleasant to a shifter, and the same went for him.

He told me that I stunk like wet dog after I told him he smelled like the ass of a two-dollar hooker.

It wasn't true, he didn't smell like that, but it was an unpleasant smell and hard to describe. Like his scent warned me away from him, whereas it did the opposite to humans. I made sure to bug him extra when I was in class by sitting as close to the front as I could.

"Don't, I can see it in your eyes." I turned slowly and winked at my twin brother, Maverick, ignoring his warning as I made my way to class. World history never was as good as it was today. I could see her lined up with all the humans, but even if I couldn't see her, I would've been able to smell her from here. Especially since she smelled like scum again today. That fucker better not have touched her.

I knew she ignored me at lunch and pretty much ran from me, but she couldn't get away from me here.

She looked up as she saw me approach, and her face shut down of any emotion. I gave her my biggest sexy grin that worked on all the girls here. One in front of her giggled and waved shyly to me, but I ignored her as I moved to where Alexis stood.

"Alexis, we didn't get to finish our conversation earlier." She turned those amber eyes on me. They were like flames and I was the moth.

"We weren't having a conversation, nor will we ever. Go to the back of the line." She jerked her thumb behind her, and I glanced back there. *Ugh.* Olivia was watching me from the end of the line, her eyes narrowed at me. Yeah, no way was I going near her. We might've hooked up at parties in the past, but that was to just an itch to scratch and she knew that.

She'd become a little crazy lately, wanting more. I'd broken it off with her, but it looked like she still didn't get the memo. I scanned back to the guy standing behind Alexis and growled lowly as I put my palm on his chest, shoved him back, and took his place in the line. She made a sound that told me she wasn't happy with what I'd just done. But I wasn't finished with her.

Her scent was so strong this close to her. I was glad Galen was an uptight prick who'd left the classroom locked. It was like he set this all up just for me. I took some of her silky, golden brown hair that was lying against her bag and ran my fingers through it. So soft. I brought it to my nose and inhaled the smell.

Her head jerked forward, and her silky strands fell from my fingers. She turned her face, no longer annoyed but very angry.

"What the fuck is wrong with you? Are you touching my hair?"

I shrugged. There was nothing wrong with me. No, all my body parts were working, and one part in particular was working very hard. "It was so soft, I wanted to pat it."

Fuck, I had no idea why I said that. It was like she was scrambling my brain. All my funny, flirty jokes just left and were replaced with nothing. Her eyes widened, and she made a huffing sound as she turned back around. She pulled all her hair to the front and held it in her hand so I couldn't touch it.

"So where are you from?" I asked, trying my best to recover from such a dumb comment. I straightened up and adjusted myself in my jeans. No answer.

"Okay... How about you ask me a question and I'll answer, then I ask you one and you answer?"

She turned around, her smile slightly wicked looking. But it looked like she was going to play my game. *Hell yeah*, this was so much further than any of the other shifters had gotten with her. I'd seen her on the first day with her snarky comments. And well, yes, I was supposed to leave her alone. She was off-limits to all of us, but since my father was the alpha, I could always get away with a little more.

"Were you dropped on your head as a baby?"

I heard the guy I had shoved make a snorting sound. Alexis tilted her head and raised her brows. Holy shit, she was a smartass and sexy.

I think I've found the one.

CHAPTER THIRTEEN

LEXI

I was pissed off at myself that I got distracted by Mr. Donovani at lunch and forgot to mention the class change. I walked home again after school, since it was nice way to clear my mind. Maybe his class wasn't so bad... If I could pass it, then why not?

Raff walked with me. We hadn't spoken a word to each other all weekend, and the only thing that was spoken between us was when he'd told me to "fuck off" last Friday.

I knew he didn't mean it in that way. He was hard to read, and I guess I liked that about him. He wasn't fake, and he didn't put on a show like the others did. Even just his presence made me feel safe, like I didn't always have to be on guard. I could relax a little.

A shiny black Range Rover sat out front when we got to the house. I saw Raff hesitate, so I stopped also. Did he know what this was?

"What is it?" I asked. Were they taking him back? Was he being moved to another foster home? No, they couldn't do that.

He gave me a small smile that I guess meant 'don't worry about me.' But how could I not? Now I was worried. I knew we weren't friends as such, but I felt like we had a bond. I didn't want him to leave. When Raff walked to the door and opened it, I quickly ran in after him. I could hear talking, and when I looked into the living room, I could see an older man, maybe in his fifties, was seated beside the cop who picked me up in Port Angeles. *Fuck.*

"Here they are, come on in and say hello to our...um, the Mayor of Kiba. This is Alaric Lovell, and you've met his son, Nash, already." Jack gestured to both men, who stood.

Raff looked at the carpet and didn't say anything. Yeah, he had the right idea.

"It's nice to meet you both. I've heard so much about you from my sons." I saw how uncomfortable Raff was, and the tension in the room was unbearable. I wanted to leave.

"Raff, you haven't been to see me yet. I've asked many times for you to come, but I've yet to see you."

Okay, that was creepy. Why the hell does some mayor need to see a foster kid? And Alaric seemed scary—he was really tall and build like brick wall. He towered over Raff, and it was really intimidating to watch. I couldn't stand it.

"Leave him alone. Can't you see you're scaring him?" His green eyes flashed to mine, and then I could see it—Ranger and Maverick looking back at me. *Lovell.* Well, I guessed this explained why they acted the way they did. The cop, Nash, came over and placed a hand on his father's shoulder.

"Father, take a seat. He's here now." Nash watched me as his father returned to his seat. Jack and Grayson were running around, getting some more cups and homemade lemonade.

Alaric pointed to the floor in front of him. "Sit, boy."

My mouth popped open. I couldn't believe this guy thought he could treat a person like this. Raff started to move forward, and I grabbed his hand to stop him. All eyes were on me.

"Excuse me, we might be fosters, or scum to your eyes, but that is not how you treat someone. He's not a dog, and he's not going to just sit like a *good boy.*"

I think everyone's mouths dropped open. Alaric's jaw twitched.

Nash's eyes gleamed, and I could see the hint of a smile on his lips. He was amused, but Jack looked really worried. *Shit*. Was he the guy who gave them the extra money to take in fosters and help them? Did I just bite the hand that fed us here? Well, fuck him if he was. He was about to learn a lesson here today.

I loosened my hold on Raff's hand, but he held on. He was holding my hand, and my heart skipped a beat. The room was silent as I looked up to Raff. His eyes were closed, and his head hung low. His silver hair was slightly mussed, and I wanted nothing more than to put it back into place in the way I knew he liked it. I squeezed his hand, and his eyes opened and flashed to mine. I thought he was going to say something when his lips parted, but his tongue darted out to wet them. I could feel myself getting turned on. I didn't even think that licking your lips was a sexy thing, but it turned out that it was.

Someone cleared their throat. My eyes flicked back to the men who were now standing in the room, watching us. *Fuck them*. I pulled on Raff's hand, and he followed me without question. He didn't let go of my hand, and when I led him into my room, he didn't protest. I slammed the door and locked it for good measure.

We stood there, holding hands. He was breathing deeply and watching our hands. I didn't know what had happened in his past or what was going on right now. But I thought for Raff, this, just holding his hand right now, was big. And I didn't want to let go.

The sexual tension was so thick in the air, even my breathing sped up. I could hear the men all talking loudly. They tried to follow us, but Grayson told them to leave us alone.

Our breathing was in sync, and my heart beat at a racing pace. I looked up into his eyes and noticed he wasn't much taller than me. Those amazing eyes now held mine. My chest was raising high with each breath, my nipples rubbing against the fabric of my black lace bra.

He took a deep inhale, and my skin prickled, I felt so alive. I wanted him to touch me, I wanted to feel his rough hands on my skin.

We just stood there, like time had frozen. When a loud banging came from my door, we both jumped and snapped out of it.

"Hey, you can't be in there together with the door locked," Grayson called out. Raff let go of my hand and unlocked the door. Grayson put a lot of force into opening it, slamming the door against the wall, then he just stood there, staring at us. He gave us a once over, then straightened up. "Door open, at all times." He nodded once and turned to leave.

The moment I just had with Raff was now gone as he walked out of my room.

CHAPTER FOURTEEN

LEXI

I didn't lock my room that night, since I was worried Joshua might come to me because of his nightmares. I had another nightmare again and woke up in a pool of sweat around two in the morning. I was hot and thirsty, so I quietly went to the kitchen to get a glass of water. I looked out the window to the backyard and saw it was raining. Not hard, but enough that you could feel the chill of the outside air coming through the cold glass. It was a dark night, with the clouds blocking out the moon's light, but I could see something in the forest. It was moving. My breath caught.

I moved closer to the window, and out of nowhere, a coyote came running toward the house. Then the sensor lights flicked on, and I could see it fully. It wasn't a coyote, it was a red wolf. *Holy shit!* My glass dropped from my hand and into the sink. It made a loud clanging sound that had the wolf outside stop in its tracks. It was raining harder now, and its wet fur hung limply on his body. When it saw me, I froze.

The light flicked on in the kitchen, and all I could see was my refection in the glass. I gasped as my hand flew to my chest.

"Lexi, are you okay?" The fright of Jack turning the light on made my heart pound.

I spun around with my hands still visibly shaking, so I tucked them under my armpits.

"I...I saw a wolf. A red one. In the backyard." I didn't think Jack would believe me, since there were no red wolves here in Washington. Well, I had been told that. And even if there were, they were like almost extinct, so to see one at all would be one in a million chance. Maybe it was a coyote after all?

"We get a lot of wolves around here, mostly gray. But somehow, we're lucky enough to have a red one live among us." I turned and looked out the window again. The outside light had turned off, and it was dark again, but there was no sign of the wolf. I nodded to Jack and left the kitchen to go back to my room. I couldn't sleep after that. The eyes of that wolf staring right at me, like he knew I was there. He'd sensed me.

I heard the sound of a door open and close, and I held my breath, trying to hear better. Was it Raff? Footsteps padded along the hallway, and I heard the sound of a light switch being turned on and the bathroom door close. Then it wasn't long before the shower started, and the sound of it lulled me to sleep.

The next day, Ada was waiting for me outside of class. "Hey, I was wondering if it would be okay that I asked Mrs. Jeffery if we could do our English lit project together? I don't really have many friends and none in her class. So, um...is it okay?"

We were told yesterday that we had to pair ourselves up like adults or she would pair us up today like children. Since I didn't know anyone else in that class, Ada was my best choice as a partner, even though she talked way too much. But I'd come to learn that was just who she was. I nodded.

"Oh, this will be great! Did you want to meet after school today?

We could go to my place or yours." I nodded. Maybe it would be nice to make a friend...a real one.

My morning was great, and when lunch rolled around, I ran straight to the cafeteria and grabbed a slice of pizza and a bottle of water. I made it out before it filled with students I didn't want to see—like Ranger, because I seemed to have been lucky so far that day and avoided him. I walked to Galen's office. Argh...I just couldn't bring myself to call him Mr. Donovani when I thought of him. I didn't think I'd ever be able to. I knocked on his door, and he called out to me.

I actually felt nervous for the first time. I guessed it was because I wished I wasn't his student right about now.

"I'm glad you're here. Come, take a seat." He spun in his chair and looked out his window again. I picked up my slice of pepperoni, and the cheese was a melty gooey dream as I took a bite. Oh god, that tasted good. I took another bite, wanting to eat it while it was still hot, and the pepperoni was spicy and so good. When I finished, I downed the water, my tongue a little on fire. But it was worth it for a hot meal in my belly.

"Good pizza, I take it?" I looked up, and Galen was smiling at me. I quickly wiped my sleeve across my face, trying to wipe off the mess I knew I had made of myself. It was almost like I'd forgotten he was there while I ate.

"It was." I sat there, not knowing what to do with myself. Was this something he did for new students regularly? Or was I the first one?

"I'll return, I just need to break something up." He stood abruptly and left, closing the door behind him.

"Okay..." I didn't know what else to say, and he'd left so quickly, I didn't get a chance to even really respond. I relaxed into the chair and took a real good look around the office and the shelves that were filled to the top with books. Some were stacked on the floor in a corner, but his office wasn't dirty. It was clean, yet also felt cluttered.

I reached over and pulled a book out from the shelf. It was old and beautiful. I pressed it to my nose and found it had that old book smell that I loved to scent when I was in the library. But the title wasn't in English. I carefully opened it and realized it was a Bible. It had a handwritten name in there, reading, 'Galen Donovani 1726.' Wow, was this like, his great-great-grandfather's or something, passed down to him. No wonder he liked history. That was so cool.

The office door slammed opened, and I jumped at the unexpected sound. I turned my head to see Ranger as he entered the room.

"Bullshit is what I tell you, he—Well, hello there, Lex."

I rolled my eyes as I carefully closed the Bible and placed it on Galen's desk. I turned and realized Galen had seen that. He tilted his head, and I shrugged. I didn't damage it, as I was always careful with books. I just loved books, and old ones were special. They'd been loved and some held memories, like this one did.

"My name is not Lex." I gave Ranger a look that said, 'come on, challenge me.' I was up for a fight. When I spun around a little more to see Ranger, I saw the arm with colorful tattoos and all black attire. Maverick was here, too. He didn't look at me.

"Okay, I think for lunch today you can sit in here and think about what your father said about fighting." Galen took the Bible from his desk and took a seat. Maverick hovered by the door after he closed it, and Ranger took it upon himself to sit on the armrest of the chair I was in. He was too close for comfort. I inched away, and I could see the smirk on Galen's face. Was he amused by my discomfort, or the fact that Ranger really wasn't my type? And that made him happy? Oh, I think I was overreading things here.

"Okay, Dad, I'll think about it. But you know as soon as I'm finished here, I'm gonna go back out there, and I'll do it again. I don't take orders from you."

Galen's smirk twitched and turned more into a 'you challenging me?' thing. It was intense, and I could feel the change in the room immediately. Ranger must have too, because he dropped it and turned his attention back on me again.

"So, I'm having a party this weekend. Actually, we have one like every weekend. But yeah, Saturday, I want you to come. It'll be fun. We have a heated pool. You can wear a bikini or not—" There was a loud slap sound, and my chair moved slightly. I looked up and found that Ranger was holding the back of his head and glaring daggers toward his brother. "Hey! That hurt, asshole. I was just saying that if she doesn't want to wear one, she could go naked. I wasn't saying—" The chair moved fully, and Ranger was on the floor. Galen just rolled his eyes at the twins like this was nothing new. Holy shit, Maverick was so not what I expected him to be. But it did shut Ranger up.

"I'm going to go now... Thank you, Galen." I picked my bag up and walked past them both on the floor. Maverick had his knee on Ranger's chest, pinning him to the floor.

"Are you coming?" I heard Ranger call out as I closed the door behind me and went looking for Ada so we could go to class together.

"Did you seriously get invited to a Lovell party? By Ranger personally? Oh my god, can we go together? Like, can you take someone? Like me? They usually allow a friend to come." I didn't know why she was so interested in these dumbass twins. Well, one was a dumbass and the other was a moody artistic type, which was exactly why I needed to stay away from them.

"No, I'm not going. I...I have a curfew," I lied, and for the first time, I felt bad that I did. I could see her visibly deflate. Shit, I wasn't doing a good job of having a friend for the first time. I just didn't want to go to some party, especially one that the Lovell twins would be at. Not to mention their scary dad, too.

"Do you still want to hang out and do our assignment tonight? I can take you to my place? I just have to ask Grayson first." I'd never invited someone over before. I'd never had a real friend before Ada, so this was all new to me. I'd avoided making any since I was forever moving around. No point before, but now...it was time to try.

Now I had a place. I had my own room, and Grayson would have muffins or cupcakes to eat.

I shot him a quick text, asking if it was okay, and he replied almost instantly that he was excited to meet my new friend. I felt that warm feeling in my chest again. When I nodded at her, she squealed.

"Oh wow, yes. I can drive us there so you don't need to catch no stinky ass bus." I nodded but didn't correct her by telling her that I walked home with Raff every day.

"Can we give Raff a lift?" Her eyebrows wiggled as she gave me a wicked grin, but I just rolled my eyes and smiled. "Come on."

CHAPTER FIFTEEN

LEXI

It was Friday. How I survived a whole week was beyond me. Poor Josh had a nightmare last night and came into my room, so I held and comforted him. I wished that helped me with my nightmares, but it didn't. I woke from one and scared him. I didn't want to do that to him, I wanted to protect him. Grayson was taking him to speak to his therapist today and told me that I should wake them next time he comes to my room. Grayson also told me that if I had a bad dream and wanted to talk to someone, that I could come wake them. They wanted to help me, too. I told them that wasn't going to happen, that I was fine.

They asked if I wanted to go speak to the therapist all the boys go to. Yeah, no thanks. Done that before, it didn't help. Nothing helped.

School was alive with excitement over who was going to Ranger's party tomorrow night. Ada found and cornered me in the cafeteria while I was getting my lunch before I made my escape to Galen's office. I'd been going every day since he offered. It wasn't that I needed somewhere really, but more like I wanted to be in there with him and spend time with him. He didn't speak much, but when he did, I listened. He was also very nice on the eyes.

"Are you sure Grayson won't let you out to go, even for a few hours? Please. Oh, please. And I know if you're invited, you get a plus one... I'm your plus one!" Ada jumped up and down in front of me, her blonde hair bouncing around and her big chocolate colored eyes begging me to change my mind.

"How do you know that?" She smiled and cocked her hip, a playful grin on her face.

"I asked one of the younger Kiba boys earlier, and he told me that it's fine to bring one friend." I rolled my eyes and shook my head, but kept smiling. This was what I'd learned was very Ada.

When Ada said she didn't have many close friends, I'd thought it was because she was shy. I'd started to realize there were just some traits that made her...well, her. She was a little pushy and talked a lot. She was on the debate team, which was perfect for her. But I liked her because she wasn't a wallflower. She spoke up when she saw something not right, like bullying, but also anyone breaking rules—which I think made most students wary of her.

Ranger had been much better toward me the last few days. He didn't say more than a hello, which was a complete change from what he'd been like at the start of the week. And everyone else kept ignoring me like they had since that second day. I still had a large number of eyes on me, just no one spoke to me, and so far, no huge prank had happened. Avoiding this party was for the best, just in case they were planning something.

"No, sorry, Ada."

Her smile dropped a little as she nodded. "That's okay. We can maybe do something, just you and me?"

I smiled and nodded. "Text me and we can arrange something." And with that, I took my pizza slice and bottle of water, and made my way as fast as I could to Galen's office.

"You really like the pizza here?" I turned to see Galen had entered his office. I was so preoccupied with thinking about my piece in art that I didn't even hear him come into the room.

My hand flew up to my chest. "You scared me." I giggled a little when he dazzled me with that smile. God, he had to stop the smiling...and I had to stop thinking of him like this. He was hot, there was no denying it. All the girls in school had crushes on him, and now I was one of them. It wasn't hard to have a crush on *Mr. Donovani*.

"Sorry, I didn't mean to scare you. I was in a small meeting."

I nodded. He'd been here most of the week, leaving here and there. This was the first time he wasn't here before me. I enjoyed the quiet, as it gave me a chance to really think about what I was doing with my life right now. Not that we spoke much when I was in here, so I did spend a lot of time in my thoughts.

"You should try the pizza, it's really good," I said, trying to make conversation. He never had lunch when I was in here, but he did drink his coffee in a steel travel mug. He sure loved his coffee, and he even took it with him to class sometimes. Maybe I should bring him a coffee one day, to say thanks and everything.

"No, I don't really like pizza."

I shrugged, at least it was one tick against his hotness. How did he not like pizza? Everyone loved pizza. His loss. *I loved it.* So filling and that cheese... God, the cheese was amazing.

He sat in his chair and took a sip of his coffee as he spun and looked out the window—the same thing he did every day. I pulled my book out of my bag. *Mr. Darcy, here I come.* Nothing better than a romance where letters were written to the heroine and she was courted by a gentleman. Nothing would ever happen like that again, since a text message wasn't the same as a handwritten letter. Nothing like that would happen at Ranger's party this weekend.

"Are you going to the Lovell's for the party tomorrow?"

I looked up. Galen was looking right at me. Did he know I was just thinking about that? His smile was tipped to one side, like he was smirking. It was boyish and cute, especially with his head full of beautiful, dark loose curls. He could pass for a young Mr. Darcy. *My*

Mr. Darcy. My breathing became quicker as he flashed his perfect white teeth in a smile.

I shook my head. "No, I don't even like the guy. He's a douche, and his brother is an asshole."

He chuckled just as I heard a throat being cleared, and I froze. I didn't realize the office door was still open.

"You wanted to see me." It was almost a growl more than words. I turned to find the dark green eyes of Maverick, glaring right at me. The air in the room felt like it'd been used up. I looked away to stare out the window. I didn't care if he heard what I just said. He could run to his brother and tell him, for all I cared. Fuck them both. *Why the fuck was he so hot?* Why did I wish he didn't hate me? Ugh...this was just too much for me. I needed to shut these feelings down. At least until art class, where I really needed them to work on my piece.

Just being in this room with Galen and Maverick was making me feel things I shouldn't be feeling. Maybe I needed to go to this party... No. No way. They were both assholes. Only, Maverick wore his asshole card on his sleeve, while Ranger hid it under false smiles and flirty teasing. As soon as you fell for it, then you would see the asshole inside.

The bell rang, signaling my cue to leave, and I quickly grabbed my stuff. But Maverick wouldn't move from the doorway. Instead, he tracked my every step as he watched me, and I glared right back.

"Move," I snapped, and his eyes lit up for a moment before he stepped aside. I wasn't going to back down from him. I would match him, blow for blow. I could feel him burning holes into my back as I left the office. He really hated me. Good, I didn't like him, either.

If only I can convince myself that.

I looked up and saw Raff walking toward me. His eyes held my gaze, and we didn't look away as we walked toward each other. I stopped suddenly, and he took a few steps closer, his eyes holding mine, never once glancing away. The energy bouncing between us was charged, and my fingers itched to touch him. My heart sped up and so did my breathing. I needed to get away from him, or I would do something I'd regret. So I ran...

Saturday was now my favorite day of the week. I'd never had the chance to just sleep in, and I was loving it. Especially after my nightmares kept me up half the night. My room was different now too—Jack had put new sheets on my bed, all my new clothes hung in the closet, and there was a fluffy purple pillow and the black throw rug that I had looked at. I needed to remember when shopping with Jack, he was a "touch it and it's bought' kind of guy. He'd also bought some string lights and hung them on the headboard. They twinkled and looked so cute.

The best part was when I got home after school last night, there was a new bookshelf with a couple of new books. Romance novels, but not ones I'd usually read. I loved my historical romance, and these were about werewolves falling in love with humans. But I was really enjoying the one I picked up.

I was sitting back on my bed, reading this intense fight scene, when there was a knock at the door. I called out that it was open.

"Oh my gosh, Grayson and Jack said you can go to the party. You didn't even ask them, silly." I jerked upright in surprise, my now forgotten book falling to the floor. Ada bounced into my room and plopped herself at the end of my bed, beaming ear to ear. She had a bag with her...and a suitcase. What the hell? I told her she could come over in the afternoon, but this looked like a sleepover. I didn't agree to that.

"Lexi, you aren't tied to this house, love. You can go to the party. You should've just asked...we knew about it. The Lovell's have a party twice a month. It'd be good for you to get out...meet some of your classmates." Jack smiled and nodded at me when I didn't answer, then closed the door behind him as he left.

"This is so great," Ada squealed in excitement. I turned back to Ada and shook my head. *No, this was not.*

"I don't want to go."

Her mouth dropped, then closed, then opened again. I could see the wheels turning in her head before she nodded.

"Okay...I'm sorry, I shouldn't have pushed you so much. I sometimes get fixated on something, and I don't consider others thoughts. My parents tell me this all the time, and I did it again... I don't want to do that with you. I'm really sorry, Lexi."

My chest felt light, and I was glad she wasn't pushing me anymore. I guessed maybe she was just as new to this friend thing as me. I had an urge to hug her. So I did, and she smelled nice. When I pulled away, she giggled.

"Did you still want to watch romantic comedies and eat ice cream and chocolate?"

I smiled. "Yeah, it's gonna be awesome."

CHAPTER SIXTEEN

LEXI

I decided I wanted to go to the party, *ugh*. I just couldn't stop running it over in my mind. I wanted to show Ranger and Maverick that I wasn't afraid of them. Well, mostly Maverick. Ranger, I still needed to avoid. Plus, we'd started watching *Twilight* on the iPad Ada brought with her, and I decided I'd seen this movie one too many times. Honestly, I wasn't a fan of Robert Pattinson. He just didn't do it for me or the character.

The suitcase Ada had brought was filled with clothes to try on for the party. Apparently, she'd come over with it just in case. She'd asked Jack about going as soon as he opened the door, trying to get a yes from the parentals by sucking up to them… only to find I'd never asked them in the first place. And they were more than happy for me to go.

Apparently, Ada owned more than just button-up shirts. She had a whole range of clothes suitable for this kind of party, but we were leaving early, and I wasn't getting into some pool. It was too cold to be swimming, and I couldn't even swim.

Ada promised she'd take me back to the house when I was ready to leave or by nine, and just being there would be great fun for both of us. I hoped so.

"Lexi, did you want to borrow one of my tops? I brought all this to share with you. That's what friends do, share clothes and secrets..." She winked at me and giggled.

I stared at the mess she'd made of my room—sequins and colorful tops and dresses were spread out everywhere. No way was I wearing those, it was too cold out. This was an outside party, and I wasn't going to freeze to look dressed up. I grabbed my black skinny jeans, which were starting to get a little tight now that I'd put on some much-needed weight. Cupcakes and muffins everyday did that to you, but I wasn't complaining. I now had some curves back.

"You're going to wear that? But you wear it every day," she groaned when I slipped my head into my favorite black hoodie, flicking my hair out as I pulled it down to my waist. So warm, but not as soft as it once was. The tear was now all sewn up, thanks to Grayson's help. You couldn't tell it was damaged at all unless you looked really closely.

"Don't you have like...a different one? In color?"

I shook my head and laughed. She laughed as I sat down on the edge of my bed and watched her try to pick something to wear.

"Okay...I have something that my big sister gave me. It's not my style." She pulled a black leather jacket out of her suitcase. "When I was packing for tonight, I saw it in my closet and just knew it was meant for you. I'll never wear it, and it'll go on living in there until my parents give it to Goodwill or something. I want you to have it. That's if you want it, of course." She placed the soft black leather jacket in my lap. It was fitted, with a silver zipper and buckles. I wasn't sure if it would even be my size, but I quickly threw my hoodie off and put my arms into the jacket. I instantly felt the warmth from the leather.

"Oh my god! See, I knew it! It was meant to be yours. This is like destiny." Then she cracked up laughing, slapping her thigh and trying to breathe through the bouts of laugher. I stood and moved around, liking how it melded to my body so perfectly. This jacket was made for me.

"What's so funny?"

She was now starting to calm the giggles and tried to breathe normally, but the giggles started up. She snorted, and that made her giggle more.

"My sister—" She giggled and snorted. "Her name is Destiny." And she cracked up laughing again. I couldn't help the rise in my chest and started to laugh at the silliness that was Ada. I had to remember to thank her sister for this jacket. Finally, her giggles slowed down.

"Okay, I'm good now. You look hot, I look hot." She pointed down to her blue jeans, sequined baby pink top, and black jacket. It looked great and really suited her.

"Let's do our makeup. I can do yours," she offered. I just blinked a few times before I realized she was serious.

"Ah, that's okay. I can do my own."

It took about an hour to get ready. After all the makeup was done, Ada had curled her beautiful blonde hair, then she offered to do mine. It was something I'd never done before, but it looked good on her and softened her look. So I shrugged and let her have at it.

My hair was a lot longer than Ada's, but it gave the same effect. I smiled and giggled as she twirled around and grabbed her iPhone.

"Selfie time." She pulled me close to her, and I could see us on the screen. She did the kiss pout and I copied her, then a few others. I was feeding off her energy, and I loved it. This was the best idea.

"Oh, I'll post this to Instagram. What's your username?" I raised my brows at her, and she laughed. "Oh man, we need to fix that." We walked out the bathroom and into the living room where all the boys were with Jack and Grayson, watching a movie.

"Oh wow, ladies. Your look stunning." Jack beamed while Grayson stood up and came over, and his smile was so genuine.

"Lexi, you look so beautiful. And, Ada, you too. I hope you both have a great night." He stood there, looking a little awkward, then Ada wrapped her arms around him.

"Thank you, Grayson. We're going now." When she released him, she walked over to the door. Joshy ran over and hugged me.

"Don't go, I'll miss you." I hugged him back as his words hit me right in the chest. I would do anything for this kid.

"I'll only be gone for a little while, and I promise I'll be back." He smiled and nodded before running back to watch the movie. Jack came over and stood beside Grayson, his arm wrapping around his waist. They were both smiling at me.

God, why was this hard? I took a deep breath, bent my head, and went for it. I wrapped my arms awkwardly around them both before moving away quickly.

"Bye," I called out as I rushed out the door. Ada was standing next to her blue sedan, and I looked up and down the street. I hadn't seen Raff all day, and I kind of wished he was seeing me right in this moment. As I slipped into her car, she giggled again.

"We're going to have so much fun! What should we listen to?" She played around with her radio, and a Rhianna song came on, then Ada started singing...off key.

We drove slowly up Kiba Court—the townsfolk really thought long and hard about what they were going to name the streets around here. It was a long street, and the houses were big and fancy. All these manicured lawns with huge houses—no, they were definitely mansions. Where the heck did they get the money for them? For a tiny town, there were a lot of millionaires.

"These are the houses most the Kiba boys all live at. Well, their parents' houses. I know the Lovell house is at the end, and it's the biggest. I've always wanted to go inside." I could see how excited she was, since she was bouncing a little in her seat. Maybe she was nervous? It was hard to read Ada, but I was starting to feel nervous, now that we were so close. I didn't expect them to have a mansion.

All these mansions were all surrounded by the forest—every single property backed onto it, just like Jack and Grayson's house. It was nice, and it felt protected by the trees, even though it was getting dark and the forest cast some long dark shadows.

I thought over what she'd said. The Kiba boys—the ones she was talking about when we first met—all lived on the same street? The ones that fight with the Rawlins boys and Kenneally boys for no real reason? I wondered if they lived on the same streets, too. When the huge white mansion came into view, I gasped.

"I can't wait to see inside. I heard there are like ten bedrooms, and they all have their own bathrooms. Can you imagine?" I didn't reply, since I didn't know what to say. This was where Ranger and Maverick lived? This was bigger than all the other mansions we'd just passed.

A little farther down on their property and to the right was a smaller house. It matched the large one, but looked more like a small cottage. The lights were on inside. I wondered if they had a gardener who lived there. That would be a huge job to do these lawns, and I didn't see Ranger being the one to mow the yard.

There were a lot of cars parked in the circular drive, and Ada made sure to keep her car just outside the front fence and parked on the cul-de-sac.

"Just so we don't get block in, and we can leave when you're ready or when the clock hits nine." I nodded, thankful she was thinking ahead and being so understanding about my wanting to be out of there by nine.

I was still in awe of this house, though. If being a mayor of a tiny town got you a house like this... Well, where do I sign up?

I closed the car door and saw two people walk toward us. When they came into view, I realized it was that cop, Nash, and groaned. Fuck my life. I forgot he was Ranger's brother.

"Why, hello there, Alexis. I heard you were coming." I didn't know where he'd heard that from. I'd sure made it very clear to Ranger and Maverick that I wasn't coming. The guy beside him was just as tall as Nash, but he had a darker complexion and short brown hair. He gave me a once-over before turning his attention to Ada, and I could feel her squirm beside me at his attention. His piercing gray eyes flicked back to mine, and he smiled. I wasn't sure what to make of him.

"This is Elijah, and we're on security tonight. Don't want no trouble coming in here. If you have any problems, please come to us."

I nodded. I guessed with a cop here, this would be a little safer than parties I'd been to in the past. I stepped around him. The night had really snuck up on us, and it was now almost dark. Lacing my arm with Ada, we took ourselves up the driveway to where we could see the lights and hear music and people talking at the back of the house.

When we rounded the corner, I realized I was out of my element. Girls and guys were in a huge pool, splashing and play fighting. There was a whole table filled with alcohol and some beer kegs.

"I'm not drinking, and neither are you. Don't take drinks from others, only pour your own," I warned Ada under my breath. She squeezed my hand and nodded.

"I wasn't going to, since I'm driving." I was glad she agreed. I wrapped my arms around my waist, feeling very out of place. And the eyes... So many guys were looking at me now.

I shouldn't have come here.

CHAPTER SEVENTEEN

MAVERICK

I knew she was here when I felt the change in the atmosphere. There was no other explanation for it. She said she wasn't coming. Nash had said that she was, and I didn't believe him.

I didn't want her here. I wanted her to leave. *Leave Kiba*. Ranger was obsessed with her. He wouldn't stop talking about her, and at dinner last night, it became very obvious that my father was taking his claims that he believed she was his mate very seriously. I didn't like that, because as much as Ranger thought she was his mate, I knew she was mine, too.

Though, I wouldn't do that to her. I'd decided long ago that I wouldn't take a mate, I refused to be part of it. She would never be a shifter, because I wouldn't change a woman. But that was what was expected of me, by my family and my pack.

I'd never told anyone about my plans to not take a mate, and now here she was, ruining my plans to protect her from all of this.

"Hey, she's here, I can smell her. Are you sure Ranger thinks she's his mate? 'Cause, dude...I can smell and feel that too. Like maybe she's my mate." I looked over to my best friend since childhood, Saint. He'd graduated last year and now worked for my father. He had recently cut his dark blond hair short, but it suited him and the hard line of his jaw. I'd always thought he'd be the first to get a girlfriend, but he was still single. I always wondered if he felt the same way I did about turning the women we love into shifters to continue our pack, but I never voiced it. I was worried if he didn't feel that way, that he might accidentally tell someone and it'd get back to my father.

It just wasn't right. So many women died during the transition that it was just horrific to hear the stories. Last year, there had been a failed transition with some packmates. That was all the pack called it —*failed*. The woman had died. That was a life that didn't need to be lost like that. It was bullshit, was what it was. And right now, I wanted to slap Saint for even thinking that of Alexis.

"She smells like that for everyone. So unless she has over a hundred mates, then it's just all messed up. We're not even supposed to smell our mates. That's just one of those old wolf tales." But with her...it didn't seem like an old wolf tale anymore.

He poured some more bourbon into my red cup as we watched her from the windows. She had those skinny jeans on again, but the leather jacket was different. Her hair was down and wavy. She was dressed up, and she looked so good. *Fuck*.

Her friend walked toward us. I moved away from the glass door, and she opened it and walked right into the house like she owned the place. One look at me, and she smiled and made her way over to me.

"Oh, hi! You'd know this place well. I need two cups and your nearest tap for water." I was a little stunned at this bossy little blonde-haired girl right in front of me, giving me orders. I looked over to Saint and found he was still watching Alexis. My eyes narrowed on him, my wolf starting to come to the surface, which wasn't good.

There was some clicking sound, and we both snapped out of it. We glared at the girl in front of us, who was snapping her fingers in my face.

"Oh, sorry. You and your friend need some water? Let me help you." Saint gave his megawatt smile, and the girl giggled. What was her name? Annie? Audrey? Ava? I couldn't remember, but she talked a lot and I tried to block her out at school.

She thanked Saint, who took her into the kitchen. I watched Alexis as she stood there with so many eyes on her, but she didn't seem to notice. Or she was really good at not giving a shit. That last thought almost had me smiling. When Saint and the girl returned, he strolled right past me, holding a cup of water, the girl chatting away as she held hers. He winked at me as he followed her outside.

All the shifters at school wanted to get to know Alexis, and Saint was acting exactly like them. Was it wrong that I wanted her to reject him? He was my closest friend, and I should want him to be happy, to find someone. Just not her. *Anyone but her.*

I was standing there, staring openly at her and hoping she would tell him to fuck off, that she wasn't interested in him. Even though I knew she didn't like me. I made sure of that...but still. A part of me, deep down, still wanted her to pick me.

To choose me.

She had to leave. *Now.*

CHAPTER EIGHTEEN

LEXI

Ada was headed toward me with a guy, who had a big smile for me, and I wanted to roll my eyes. He was holding two cups in his hands. Ugh, I hoped one wasn't mine.

"Hey, Lexi, this is Saint. He graduated last year." The guy looked the same as the rest of them—built, tight white tee showing off all his muscles...the dark blond hair was neat and gelled. He was cute. Okay, he was hot. I nodded hello to him as he passed the cup of water to me. I took it, then turned to a potted plant beside me and poured it out. I didn't trust anyone, and I wasn't joking about that. Ada didn't question anything, she just gave me her cup and I took a sip, then handed it back to her. I watched as he cocked his head at me, confusion written all over his face.

"I didn't do anything to it, it's just water. I swear." I shrugged. I didn't care. I learned that lesson long ago about taking a drink from someone I thought I could trust. Never wanted to repeat that again in my lifetime.

"So, you got to school here? What do you do for fun, Lexi?" I noticed the way he looked at me and that his questions were more directed at me than Ada. So I ignored him and started to talk to Ada about movies, hoping he would get the hint and leave.

When we'd finished our conversation about our English lit assignment, the water had run out and Saint hadn't gotten the hint to leave. No, he just asked a bunch of questions instead. Ada had spoken to him for the two of us, but I didn't have any interest in speaking with him. He seemed too interested in me, and I didn't like that. I told her I'd refill our water as I looked at the time on my cell. It was only just past eight, and I was bored already.

This party was nothing like the ones I had been to in the past. I watched the girls in the pool and the guys hanging around, laughing and joking. It was as if I was in a movie. The people here had money, and they looked like it too. Picture perfect. I turned and continued on my way to get water.

Inside the Lovell's house, it was white and sterile. I walked into the kitchen, which was huge with dark granite countertops. I ran my finger along the smooth surface until I reached the tap and refilled our red Solo cups. That was when I saw him from the corner of my eye. I jumped slightly, not expecting someone to be lurking around in here.

"Leave," was all Maverick said to me as he stepped out from around the corner. His dark jeans were low on his waist, his long-sleeved tee held the name of a band I didn't know, and his eyes...they were magical. Such pretty eyes wasted on an asshole like him.

"I was just getting water," I snapped back. Fuck, I wasn't doing anything to his precious kitchen. When I turned and started to walk out the door, he growled lowly.

"Leave the party. Leave Kiba." I clenched my fist as I turned to point at him, my finger hitting him directly in his chest. Shit, he was so close to me. He must have followed me, and I didn't even hear him. My skin prickled with nerves.

"Fuck you. I'll leave as soon as I can. I didn't want to be here...the party or Kiba. So don't worry, I'll be gone soon. Then you can be a broody asshole to some other *poor girl*."

God, he was such a dick. His expression didn't change, he just took a sip from his cup and stood there like he had all the time in the world for me to rant at him. I stormed off and found that Ada had moved closer to the pool. She was talking to some of the guys there, and Saint was no longer around.

When I got closer to her, an arm wrapped around my neck. I ducked down instantly and removed myself from whoever it was. I turned to see Ranger with a huge grin. He was wearing board shorts and was shirtless. He must've been enjoying the pool, as he was a little damp still.

"Don't touch me," I growled to him. I wasn't in the mood for his shit right now, especially after the lovely chat with his brother.

"I'm sorry, Lexi. I won't do it again." He rubbed the back of his neck as he looked to the party goers around me. Was he nervous? No, he was just looking to see if anyone saw me reject him so openly.

"Did you want something to eat? We have plenty of food over here." He started walking toward a table and pointing at the chips and other items there. As if on cue, my stomach growled. Dang traitor stomach. *Fuck it.* I followed him toward the food.

"If you want something else to drink, I can show you were we keep the juice? Or we do have bottled water."

I shook my head. "Tap water is fine." I took a handful of chips and started to eat them. It was hard to do that without putting my cup down.

"Here, let me." He held his hand out to take my cup, but I pulled it toward myself a little too fast, and it sloshed over the edge and onto my jeans.

"Oh man, I'm so sorry. I keep messing up. Did you want me to get a towel?" Gone was the jokester Ranger I had met so many times. He looked unsure of himself. His hands hovered in front, like he wasn't sure what to do. Huh...this was different.

"No, it's just water."

BELLE HARPER

I moved on and found some strawberries and ate a few of those. So good. I grabbed more food and ate, while Ranger tried to make small talk. I nodded to keep him distracted while I ate all the pineapple next. Holy crap, this stuff was fresh. The sour yet sweet taste burst in my mouth. *Fuck!* I want to take this home with me so I could have some later and share some with Joshy. *So good.*

"Did you want me to show you around my house?" That question had me realizing it was time to leave. I shook my head and looked for Ada. When I couldn't see her, I quickly walked away from Ranger. I turned to make sure he wasn't following me and saw that he was in the same spot, but it looked like he was talking to himself now. *Crazy...* I needed to keep away from him as well as his brother.

I found the edge of the property, and it was quiet over here. Even though I could still see the party close by, it was harder to see me over here in the dark. There was a small fallen log, so I took a seat and drank the rest of the water. The taste of the pineapple still lingered in my mouth. I would have to ask Grayson if we had money for it in the weekly shopping budget. I bet Josh would love it. And Harry and Jaxon...and Raff.

Suddenly, I heard the snap of a twig behind me, and all the hairs on my arms stood up. I slowly turned, my heart racing. I could see the glow of two eyes in the dark forest. A wolf stepped closer to me, and my breathing all but stopped. Maybe it would leave, maybe it wouldn't attack. It took one more step, and I could see it was a red wolf. Was it the same one from outside the kitchen window at Jack and Grayson's house?

"Good boy," I whispered, and his head tilted slightly at my shaky voice. The scream from a girl had me and the wolf turning to look at the party. One of the guys had thrown her into the pool. I took that as my chance to run. The red Solo cup dropped from my hand as I ran as fast as I could back toward the party. A few of the guys noticed me and rushed toward me. Out of breath, I pointed and whispered, "Wolf."

"Don't worry, we'll scare him off." I turned to see Ranger beside me, and he smiled just before he ran off for the trees, his cop brother hot on his heels. I saw three more run into the tree line and disappear. Holy crap, they were braver than me.

Then Ada found me. I was still shaking, and I wasn't sure if the wolf meant to harm me or not, but I was still a little rattled.

"Let's go home." She took my arm and started to lead me out of the party. My hands felt cold, and I looked down, rubbing them together, when she stopped suddenly. I saw the boots and dark denim jeans, and knew who was in front of me. I looked up to those green eyes.

"You shouldn't have done that. That's on you. This is your last warning from me. *Leave.*"

What the fuck did that mean? Something flashed in his eyes, like they almost glowed. But before I could work it out, it was gone, and all I could see was the harsh glare of his green eyes on me before he turned and stormed off.

"Fuck you, asshole," I called out after him. I was shaking now, I was so angry. Why couldn't he leave it? Did he follow me to tell me that again? I let out a deep breath and took Ada's arm to get out of there.

"What did you do to piss of Maverick Lovell? I've never seen him angry. Like ever, and I've known him since first grade."

Good to know it was just me that made him angry.

CHAPTER NINETEEN

LEXI

When Ada dropped me off, Jack was there to open the door for me. Which was good, since I didn't have a key to the house. I hadn't needed one, as Grayson was always there when I got home from school. I didn't even think about it when I left earlier, that they might be asleep or something when I got back.

"How was it? Was the party good? I remember going to the Lovell parties when I was younger." He had a wistful smile on his face, as if he was remembering some great times. Something I didn't have at all, but I didn't want to dampen his happy trip down memory lane.

"It was great. I'm tired now. So I'm going to bed." I quickly dashed past him and locked myself in my bedroom before he asked anymore questions.

What the hell happened tonight? I couldn't stop thinking of that wolf... What was the chance of seeing a red wolf twice in a week? Rare...very rare.

I dozed off for a while, in and out of sleep. I couldn't get the eyes of the wolf out of my head. I didn't think he wanted to hurt me. He didn't threaten me or make me feel like prey. I was uneasy because I didn't know what he'd do to me. It was a wild wolf.

I heard a huge thump and turned to my door. Was that from Raff's room? I hadn't seen his light on tonight when I got back, so I'd assumed he was asleep in his room. But now there was another thumping sound and a groan, and I started to wonder if he went out and now he was sneaking back in.

I hesitated, then I heard a sound like he was in pain. I unlocked my door and walked over to his. I hesitated again when I went to knock. There was no light on in his room. Did he hurt himself crawling through the window? I put my ear to the door. I could hear deep breathing, then a pained groan.

"Raff?" I whispered. I didn't want to wake the house up. It was dark, and everyone was in bed. When he didn't answer, I knocked lightly.

"Are you okay?" I heard shuffling and very heavy breathing, but he didn't answer. So I guessed he didn't want to speak to me. I started to walk away, when there was another groan of pain, and then I didn't care. I was going in there. I wouldn't be able to sleep with him injured. I needed to help him.

I opened his bedroom door and glanced around his dark room. The drapes were pulled to the side and the window open, letting in cold air and moonlight. I saw a dark lump on the floor.

"Are you drunk?" I felt on the wall for the light switch. When the room lit up, it took me a moment to adjust to the light, and I heard the same sound come from Raff. When I finally focused and I could see him...I gasped, my hand coming up to cover my mouth. He was covered in blood. His hair was stained red down one side, and his left eye was swollen shut.

I dropped to my knees in front of him, hovering my hands above his body, not knowing what to do.

"Tell me what to do, Raff. Who did this to you?" His breathing was harsh. Did he have broken ribs? I didn't know what to do for him, or how to help without hurting him.

"I'll get Jack—"

I stood up just as he groaned out, "No." My heart was racing, and I could feel my eyes glassing over. I bent down again, then stood. What should I do?

"Why not? You need to go to the hospital. Who did this to you?" His hand reached out toward me.

"Leave me...please," he whispered.

I didn't know what to do for him, so I closed his bedroom door and sat down on the ground beside him. I was not leaving him. He was always pushing me away. He had no one, like me. I was used to pushing others away, but I wouldn't do that to Raff.

"I can help you get cleaned up. Where are you bleeding?" His hands and face were all cut up. Fuck this was bad. *So, so bad.* I knew the guys at school really had it out for him, but this was too far. This was extreme, they could have killed him.

"Shower," was all he said as he tried to push himself to stand. I put my hand under his arm to help him get up. He swayed and groaned again as he leaned to his right, not putting any weight on his left leg.

I moved around him and put his arm around my shoulder to support the weight from that side, so he could use me as a crutch. We shuffled to the bedroom door, and I opened it quickly, then helped him out to the bathroom. Luckily, it was right next to his room, so we didn't have far to go. I turned the light on as we entered and closed the door so we didn't wake anyone.

"Did you need help?" I helped him lean against the counter, and I could feel the moment he saw his face. He flinched, and for the first time in a long time, my throat was tight and I wanted to cry for him, for us, for this shitty situation we were both in. He didn't deserve this. This was total bullshit—we were already outcasts. They didn't need to kick us down to remind us. I'd be going to school on Monday and letting my fists fly.

"Please..." he whispered as he tried to get his arm out of his hoodie. I felt how vulnerable he was in this moment. Like he'd never asked someone for help before. I took the cuff, and he pulled his arm out, then I moved to the other side and did the same. I grabbed the hem and found he wasn't wearing anything under, so I pulled it up and over his head.

"How...what, what did this?" After the first tear fell, I couldn't hold it in, and then I started shaking. He had huge open gashes, like someone had whipped him or scratched him with something, and blood was trickling out of them. What the hell caused this? I didn't understand. His tattoos were beautiful, but his back had been destroyed.

His hand found his jeans button, and with a shaky hand, he opened it and the fly. He slowly peeled his jeans down his body. I took a step back and turned the shower on, trying to ignore the fact that he was getting naked in front of me. I held my hand out, testing the water, not wanting it to be too hot. I could hear him stumble, so I quickly turned and caught him as he fell toward the shower, his jeans caught around his left ankle.

"Shit, I got you." I steadied him beside the shower and bent down, trying to not look at his cock as I pulled his foot out of his jeans. He wasn't wearing socks, and his feet were covered in dirt and some blood.

I stood up and looked at his body, hunched over. His breathing was heavy, and I could see he was in so much pain. He stumbled under the water and bent over, cursing as the water hit the open wounds on his back. My eyes blurred, and I quickly wiped the tears away. I needed to stay strong, so I could help him.

I grabbed some first aid stuff that was under the sink and a towel for him. I braced my hands on the counter, my breathing heavy and shaky. I was so hurt for him, as if I could feel his pain. I wanted to take it away, share the load.

I watched him from the mirror to make sure he didn't fall down and hurt himself more. I couldn't help but admire the beautiful body he had, but I could see he was struggling to wash the blood from his hair and hold himself up.

"Did... Do you want me to help wash it?" He stilled at my voice. Then I heard him say "Yes," but it was soft and laced with shame. He shouldn't feel like this. He shouldn't feel ashamed for admitting he needed help.

I moved over and opened the shower door, then reached into the shower for the shampoo. The over spray of the water was cool on my arms and wet my white tank top slightly. I poured the shampoo into my hand, and he turned his head, his right eye watching me. I could tell he felt exposed, like he didn't know how to act. This was not something he'd let others do for him—help him. I could tell, because it'd be how I acted if the roles were reversed. Hell, I'd never had to help someone like this before. This was new territory for us both.

I gave him a small smile, but he just looked so lost, and it was all I could do to keep myself from crying again. He tipped his head down, and I started to lather up his hair. I tried to be as gentle as I could, as I wasn't sure if he had a cut there or if the blood was from something else. When I felt it was clean, I moved back and he put his hair under the water. I watched as the shampoo ran down his body, over the hard plains of his abs... I quickly averted my eyes from following it any further.

He was just standing there, his hands resting on the tiles, his head dipped low. If it wasn't for the clean water spraying his body and running down the drain with a pink hue, I would say he looked like the perfect specimen of a man. The tattoos wrapped and weaved themselves all over, even down to his feet. *He was beautiful.*

My hands were still soapy, so I moved over to the sink and quickly rinsed them off, while he turned the shower off. I turned to help him get the towel, and he was now standing outside the shower, facing me in all his glory. My eyes wandered up and down his body, like I had no control over them. His cock was surrounded by the same unusual color as his hair. When I looked to his face, he gave me a sad smile. It almost broke me.

"Here." I quickly gave him the towel to wrap himself up in, and another to help him dry his hair. He let me do it for him, and it felt so...intimate. I quickly shook off the strange feeling at the pit of my stomach. Grabbing the first aid supplies, I gestured for him to come with me. I reached out, and he took my hand to balance himself as we moved slowly back to his room. I closed the door behind us and carefully sat him on the edge of his bed.

His good eye watched me as I rummaged through the supplies, finding some gauze and tape. I found an antiseptic cream, put some on my finger, and applied it to the worst of the wounds on his back. I applied it to his face, hands, and a few marks on his chest, then I used what gauze I had to cover the worse of the wounds on his back. He was so warm, and I found myself wanting to touch his bare skin more.

"Lay down, I'll pull your sheet up for you." He shuffled over, then lay on his side, groaning and hissing, the wet towel still around his waist. He moved his hips up and pulled it off as I pulled his sheet up and over him before I got another glimpse of his naked form.

"Raff, I'm really worried. We should tell Jack or Grayson. You might need to go to the hospital." I tried to sound calm, but inside, I was in a panic. He shook his head.

"Do you think you'll be in trouble? They've only done nice things for us, and I'm sure they'll understand. You're really hurt." When I started to move from him, he reached out and held my wrist.

"I'm okay... Thank you." He looked so weak like this. It was hard to watch him without feeling like I needed to do more.

But I respected his wishes. I nodded and turned out his light as I left him, even though my mind was screaming to stay with him.

CHAPTER TWENTY

RAFFERTY

The pain was something I could bare, but seeing and smelling the fear on Lexi's face was hard. No one had ever cared about me before, and it wasn't pity like I had seen in the eyes of so many others. This was real, she cared for me—I could sense her concern. She understood me in ways others never had. My wolf wanted her, and I craved to hug her. I hadn't hugged anyone since my mother died all those years before. but with Lexi...I wanted to so badly. My wolf wanted to nuzzle her, to claim her, and I wanted to as well.

She had been gone a little while, but the pain was not going to help me sleep any time soon. Also, I couldn't stop thinking about her or about the fight. I knew I wouldn't die. The assholes wouldn't kill me, since it wouldn't be fun for them if I was dead. At least they didn't inject their venom into me. I think that was more for Lexi's sake then anything else. Knowing that I was living with her, they wouldn't want me raging out on her.

I heard my door crack open and the soft padding of her footsteps. I knew it was her, her scent had my cock stirring and my body alert with her being so close. She'd seen me naked earlier, but I'd wanted her to see me so many times before, to show her how attracted I was to her. Just not that way—injured and weak. But I think she liked what she saw. I swear I smelt arousal from her as she looked at my cock, just a little through the fear she had for me. That was strong. But now she just smelled like herself, like roses. The ones my mom used to grow in our little garden.

I kept my eyes closed and my breathing even. I wanted her to think I was asleep and alright. I didn't want her telling Jack and Grayson. They would demand to know who did this, and I didn't want to tell them where I went. I wanted to protect her, and my wolf needed to keep her safe. I'd wanted to make sure no fuckwits tried to do anything to her... I felt very strongly for her, and I didn't know how to express those feelings. They were something I'd never felt, and I didn't want to fuck this up with her.

I felt a soft warm finger brushing the hair off my face, then she held the back of her fingers against my forehead. I think she was checking my temperature. Shifters always ran warm, but she seemed to as well. I wish I knew what she was. Maybe she was a shifter? Something different, special. It seemed like no one had done anything about finding out, and it was hard living with her and not showing off my shifter side.

I could hear her trying to move around quietly, then the door was closed. I thought she'd left, but when I felt her move to the floor beside my bed, my heart felt light and I got that nervous feeling in my stomach. *She was going to sit with me.* I couldn't mess this up, this was huge.

For her and me.

My sleep was restless. I couldn't believe I had fallen asleep at all, but I had. Lexi just being here made me feel so relaxed. She was a comfort I didn't know I needed.

I opened my eye to find the room was still dark, but I could see with the hint of light coming from the window. The moon was still high in the sky, and Lexi was asleep beside me. Her head was on her pillow, and she was breathing softly with her full pink lips slightly parted and her hair fanned out around her. She'd looked so beautiful tonight, and now she looked like a goddess.

I saw her blankets were with her also and realized she'd brought all that in. She didn't just come to sit with me for a while, she'd intended on sleeping in here with me.

Her left hand was resting lightly on her stomach, and I watched as her fingers twitched. That was when I saw her breathing become faster and shallow. Then she started to make sounds. Shit, she must've been having a nightmare. I'd heard her have them before. They would wake me up, and sometimes, I would wake before I even heard her. Like I knew it was going to happen before it did. I always wanted to go to her. To chase them away for her, but now...now I could do that for her.

Her head thrashed back and forth. "No," she called out, her hand reaching out to something. I reached out and took it in mine.

"Shhh...Shhh..." I rubbed my thumb back and forth on the palm of her hand, and her breathing slowed. She moved her body, turning it toward me and taking my hand in hers, then she hugged it tightly to her chest. It was an uncomfortable angle, but I wouldn't move or complain. I was so happy to have helped her. I watched as she fell deeper into sleep, wishing she was beside me on my bed. I'd wrap her in my arms, keep her safe, and protect her always.

"Rafferty? Alexis?" I heard my name, but I didn't want to move. I was so happy right now, even though I couldn't feel my arm anymore. It had fallen asleep, holding onto Lexi's hand, and she was still holding mine. I could feel her warmth.

"This isn't appropriate." I cracked open my eye and saw Jack standing in the doorway looking right at me, then he glanced down to Lexi.

I tried to move, to explain it wasn't what it looked like, but I pulled on my half healed back and groaned. Lexi gripped my hand tightly and sat up suddenly.

"Raff, are you okay. What hurts?" I closed my eyes for a moment to catch my breath. This was going to take me all day to heal from. The gashes on my back were deep.

"Raff, what happened? Let me see." Jack was beside me in a flash, then Grayson followed him in, his expression changing as he took in the scene—Lexi in my room, and Jack now hovering over my bare back, making sounds I didn't want to hear.

"Who did this? Tell me now. They'll be punished, Raff. This has gone on long enough. We need to address it now. We can't keep you safe if you don't tell us." I could hear the pleading in his voice, and I knew he meant what he said. I shook my head and tried to move away from him. They couldn't keep me safe. *No one could.*

"Raff...I brought you some lunch." I opened my eyes. My left eye was almost healed, and I could see with it again. I was in and out of sleep for a while, but when my eyes focused, I saw a smile greeting me. *Lexi.* All the breath left my lungs. That smile was for me, and I could feel the corner of my mouth lift in return. It made me feel light...happy.

I shuffled up to sitting, swinging my bare legs over the side of the bed and moving the sheets to cover my now semi hard cock. I'd put on some boxer briefs after Jack insisted. He said he felt more comfortable having Lexi in here with me only if I was semi clothed. I'd rolled my eyes, like anything would happen between us. That was only wishful thinking, and even if she did want me, my body wouldn't be able to do anything. I was too injured. But he was serious about the clothing, so I put some on.

The bed dipped a little as she sat beside me and passed me a plate with a salad sandwich. Her scent wrapped around me like a warm hug, making my skin feel hot and electric. I didn't look at her, worried she could tell how my body was reacting to her being this close. She leaned back, and I felt her gaze at my back.

"You're healing fast." I took a bite of the sandwich, trying to ignore what she said. But it was so hard, and I wanted to tell her. I wanted her to know the truth about me...about the world I lived in. I was angry that no one had told her yet. They'd said to give her time while they figured out what she was, but she needed to know now. Her scent called to too many shifters here, and I couldn't protect her on my own, as much as I wished I could. Three wolves did this to me last night, since I didn't have a pack that would have my back. I was on my own. I was a lone wolf.

"Raff...you don't have to tell them, but tell me. Who did this? Was it someone at school?" I could hear the concern in her voice, but I shook my head. I didn't want her to get involved. This was the first time I'd had a real confrontation with Pack Kiba.

Ranger only toyed with me at school, taunting me. This was the first time it went this far. Even though he wasn't the one to inflict the damage to my back, he was there. He watched on as his pack brothers ripped into me.

I shook my head. "It doesn't matter," I whispered. It wasn't as if anyone knowing would change this. Jack and Grayson were Pack Kiba, and the pack comes first. They couldn't really do anything except tell the alpha, and even then, it was like painting a bullseye on my back. I'd known I was tempting fate by being at the Lovell's party, but I still went.

I had to know, to see that she was okay. My wolf demanded it, since he didn't like being far away from her. But I think it would hurt her more to know she told them I was there and alerted them to my presence while I was distracted watching her. I thought for a moment last night that she was going to reach out to me. But she was afraid and didn't know who I was. She'd thought I was a wild wolf, and then it was too late. I wasn't quick enough to get away, and they knew those woods like the backs of their hands while I didn't. They caught up to me lightning fast.

When I finished my sandwich, we just sat there. I placed the plate beside me and held my hands together. I didn't want this to end, this feeling of comfort when she was with me. She moved a little, her shoulder now touching mine. I wanted to talk to her, but I didn't know what to say. Thankfully, it was comfortable, just sitting with her in the quiet.

Then I did something I'd never done before. My heart was pounding as I reached over and took her hand in mine. I felt a current of electricity though my hand, racing up my arm. That had to mean something, they way I was pulled to her... My wolf wanted to mark her as mine. I feared she would pull away from me, but she didn't. Instead, she laced her fingers with mine and rested her head on my shoulder as she took a deep breath. Her hair cascaded down my arm, and I could smell her so strongly. I rubbed my neck on her hair as she let out a small content sigh. I was marking her, but I couldn't help myself.

Lexi was everything.

CHAPTER TWENTY-ONE

LEXI

It was a feeling I'd never had before. Just being here with him, trusting him as he openly trusted me. He held my hand, and I could see the scars under his tattoos. So *many*. I could tell the tattoos were to cover them up, and not something that had happened after he got them. I didn't want to think about them anymore, so I laid my head on his shoulder, and the warmth from his body on my cheek was comforting.

I couldn't believe I actually fell asleep in here with him last night. And not only that, I had the best sleep of my life. I could feel his chest rising and falling, then he rested his head on mine, and I let out a deep breath. This was a feeling I liked. I didn't want to get used to it, but I also didn't want to walk away from it—whatever was happening between us.

When I heard Josh calling out to me, I slowly peeled myself from Raff's side. I'd promised to play outside with him.

"I'm coming, just hold on a moment." He kept calling my name, and I chuckled when his little head popped around the door frame.

"There you are, are we going to play now?" I could see his eyes flash between me and Raff. The boys were still wary of him, but Josh seemed to be warming up a little more as he waved to Raff. You could see he was a little nervous. When Raff didn't speak, I turned to him and saw he was watching me. I gestured with my eyebrows and nodded my head to Josh. The smile Raff gave me almost had me melting in a puddle. Fuck...he was so gorgeous. I'd told myself to not get involved with anyone, but now with Raff...all bets were off.

"Hi, Josh." His voice was light and happy, then he glanced back and gave me the same smile again. I knew then I wanted to be more than friends. This was bad...

My heart was racing and my breathing wild as I sat up in my bed. Another bad dream. I wanted to curse myself. I peeled the sheets down, since the blanket I'd put on top had made me too hot and I was in a pool of sweat. I pulled my sleep pants off, and was about to take my tank top off, when I heard my door click open. I froze, holding it to my body.

"Josh?" I whispered. I was in my panties and not wearing a bra under this tank. When I saw the large body round the door, I sucked in a breath.

"Raff." He stood there in the doorway, the light from the bathroom illuminating him and making him almost look like an angel with his silver hair as his halo. He nervously ran his hand through his hair and looked over to me. I couldn't see his face well, but I could feel his gaze on my bare legs. He was only wearing his boxers, the rest of his body on display for me.

"I... You were having a bad dream. I wanted to stop it, help you." I looked around the room to see what I could put on. I didn't want to put the sleep pants back on.

"Did you do that last night?" His head bobbed, and my heart speed up at that. He saw me have a nightmare, and he stopped it? I swallowed the lump forming in my throat.

He shivered, and I wondered if he was cold. I got up and walked to him, getting close enough that I could feel his warm breath on my cheek. Looking into his eyes, I could feel the attraction between us. It was so strong, like we were magnets, draw to each other. Needing each other. My breathing matched his as we stood there, staring into each other's eyes. I could tell he was aroused without even looking. I didn't want to break this contact, so instead, I reached out to his jaw and took it in my hand.

He had some stubble there, it was fine and fair like his hair, and felt rough against the tips of my fingers. I brushed my fingers along his jaw line until I got to his lips. His breathing sped up slightly, and his lips parted. I licked my lips. I wanted to kiss him, and I wanted him to kiss me.

I ran my fingers along his smooth bottom lip. When I pulled away, he licked where my fingers had been like he was tasting me. I saw the movement of his hand and looked down. His hands were both clenched by his side. I didn't know if that was because he was fighting this or something else was going through his mind.

"Raff," I all but panted. I was so worked up, so aroused. I wanted him to touch me. I wanted to touch him more, but somehow, I knew I had to wait for him. For him to be ready. I reached down to take his hand, and his fist loosened and held me tight. He was shaking. I looked up, and his eyes were squeezed shut. *Fuck.*

"Raff, what's wrong?" He shook his head, took a few deep breaths, then opened his eyes and looked down at me, his gaze hooded and dark. I walked him over to my bed, then stopped when I realized it was still damp from my sweat-inducing nightmare. But Raff didn't know and he sat down, right on the damp sheets. I cringed at the thought of him being on my sweat, but he just gave me a small smile and pulled me to sit with him. The air in the room had a small chill, but with him here, I felt so hot in just my tank top and panties. I wanted to take them off, bare myself to him, but I knew that wasn't right in this moment. This was just the beginning.

"Did you want to sleep...next to me?" He nodded and looked down to my bed. He could probably see the sheets were all a mess, but he surprised me when he stood and lifted the sheets and rearranged them. I slid under, and I could feel the dampness in the sheets, but it was gone when I felt his warm body move in beside me. He laid on his back and didn't touch me.

I rolled over to my side, facing him. He didn't turn to look at me, but he kept staring at the ceiling. I closed my eyes and breathed in his scent. He smelled so good.

I tried to fall asleep, but I couldn't. I wasn't sure what had happened, but he wasn't comfortable, and he didn't seem relaxed at all. I shifted a few times, trying to get myself comfortable.

"Shhh..." His hand pressed on my back, then he slowly started rubbing up and down. It was the only place we touched, and it was perfect. I started to relax finally, and my eyes grew heavy.

"Knock Knock. Lexi, time to get up." I was so warm in my cocoon, and my blankets felt heavy and so nice. I didn't want to get up. I wanted to sleep like this all day.

When I heard Jack knocking on Raff's bedroom door, I realized that my warm blanket was Raff. My eyes flew open, and I looked down to my waist. His inked arm was holding me to his warm, hard body, and there was one place that was very hard.

"Raff," I whispered. I could feel him stir and tried to turn in his arms, but he held my waist tighter as he took a deep inhale. Was he sniffing my hair? His hips moved, and I could feel his hard cock grind against my ass. *Holy shit.* He was really hard.

"Raff, we need to get up before we're caught." I felt his body stiffen behind me, and the instant he got up, I felt cold, missing him already. I rolled over and watched the surprised expression on his face as he looked at me. His bed hair looked so sexy, and I couldn't help but glance down at the bulge trying to escape those tight boxers.

When his eyes finally met mine, they widened.

"I..." He swallowed and looked around the room, then quickly moved his hands to cover his hardness. "I'm so sorry. I was asleep and..." I shook my head and tried to hide the giggle that was bubbling in my chest at him trying to explain his morning wood. This Raff was very different to the one I met a week ago, that was for sure.

"It's okay, it happens to everyone." I was feeling a bit that way this morning after feeling him grind himself against me. He just nodded and dashed out of my room without another word.

Breakfast wasn't as awkward as I thought. When I sat down, Raff sat closer to me, obviously over the weirdness from earlier. I smiled, and he returned it. The only weirdness that morning was Jack and Grayson. They eyed us a lot, and I had no idea why. Even Josh was looking at me funny. The crease in his brow was too cute as he angled his head at me.

"I know who did it...you know, who hurt Raff," Josh said. The other two boys pounced on him and held their hands over his mouth. Jack and Grayson were up fast, breaking it up.

"Did someone tell you?" Jack demanded. Josh's now watery eyes looked to Harry and Jaxon. Grayson pointed his finger at them.

"You have to tell us now," he growled out, and it was a scary sound. They both looked scared, and I was sure I did too. I didn't know he could be scary like that.

"I was playing with Jamie in the woods...he said...he said that it was Nash, Elijah, Austin, Saint, and Ranger."

I sucked in a sharp breath before I looked over at Raff. His eyes were on mine, and I could see the pain swirling in there. He didn't want anyone to know, but I could tell from that look on his face that it was all true.

Ranger... I was going to fucking kill him.

CHAPTER TWENTY-TWO

LEXI

I quickly got changed, no time for a shower, and I didn't even wait for Raff or the bus. I was going to confront Ranger and put my fist through his nose. My phone buzzed in my pocket, and I looked down to see it was Jack. I turned it off and waited for Ranger to come to school. When he didn't show, I was angry, but then I saw Raff get off the bus. The kids on there were always saying nasty shit to him, but I forgot. I should have been on there with him.

He saw me and walked over. He crowded me, but it wasn't intimating. In fact, it was comforting, like he was hugging me without even touching me.

"Don't do anything. Please, just leave it." I shook my head. No, I *couldn't* just leave it. That fucker was going to pay. Then the bell rang, and it was like our little bubble of warmth disappeared as we left to get to our first class.

The day started, and Ranger was nowhere to be seen. I asked Ada if she had seen him, but she hadn't. When I got to art and Maverick was there, I guessed Ranger was hiding.

"Where the fuck is he?" I demanded. Maverick slowly spun and gave me the most uninterested look he could. When he didn't answer, I shoved his shoulder to get his attention.

He growled low. "I'm not my brother's keeper. I have no idea where he is or what he's doing. But don't say I didn't warn you... because I did." Then he turned back to his painting. It was dark...so dark, with many dark shades of black and purple. *Moody.*

Finally, it was time for history class and Mr. Donovani... God, Galen was so other worldly. He was all dressed nicely in his suit, though it was a little retro—a blue suit jacket and trousers with a yellow skinny tie. It was just...so him. All the girls in class were just as affected by him as me, but at least I didn't look so doe eyed...or did I?

"Sorry I'm late, had an issue at home." I peered over and saw Ranger entering the class holding a late pass. He looked at me and smiled that stupid grin... I was going to punch that smug face. I could feel the tension building up in me, and his face dropped slightly.

Yeah, I know what you did.

The class dragged on for ages, but I was ready. I was going to confront Ranger and smash his nose in. As soon as the bell rang, Galen called me over to speak to him, but I didn't listen. I ran for the door and rounded the corner, waiting for Ranger to leave so I could confront him.

Bingo, I could see him as he left. He was the last one out as Galen locked the class up and went to his office, maybe to wait for me. It was lunch now, and I should be going to the cafeteria to get some food before all the good stuff was gone. But that could wait... I watched as Ranger turned his head and looked in my direction, like he knew I was there. I strolled out without a care in the world. The hallway was almost empty.

"Hey, Lexi. Are you okay?" I could see his nostrils flare, and his eye twitched.

I shook my head. "No, I'm not okay. Raff was attacked Saturday night..." I didn't say anything more, but he put his hands up in mock surrender.

"No, I don't know nothing about that." But his eyes never met mine. *Liar.* I shook my head as I got closer.

"You lying piece of shit." As I got up close, he breathed deep. God, he was one of those freaks too, the ones who were always smelling me. His eyes glowed, and I was stunned for a moment. *What the fuck?*

Then I swung at him. I caught his jaw with my fist, but his face hardly moved, and my hand screamed with pain. He was hard, and that fucking hurt. Tears welled in my eyes from the pain, but I pushed it aside. "You're a piece of shit. I don't want you to look at me or come near me again, you understand?" I stormed off as fast as I could, so he wouldn't see the tears falling. I thought I did some damage, but not to Ranger...to my hand. When he was out of sight, I rushed to the girls' bathroom and ran my knuckles under the cold water. They looked okay, but they throbbed and hurt like a bitch.

"Lexi? Are you in there?" My head swung to the doorway as Ada appeared.

"Holy shit, what happened? Ranger told me you were here." My heart stopped a moment. He told her I was here? She took my hand in hers and peered at the knuckles. I ran my good hand down my face to wipe the tears...and the makeup that had run. I looked in the mirror and winced at myself. I looked shocking. Ada passed me some paper towels, and I dried off my face. I looked in my bag and applied some make up to refresh myself, just a little eyeliner.

"What happened?" she asked again.

I thought back to my horrible shot at Ranger's nose and chuckled because honestly, I was a bad shot. "I punched Ranger." Her eyes flared open. When she didn't say anything, I kept going. "In the jaw... I was aiming for his nose. His face is too nice, I wanted to mess it up a little after what he did to Raff on Saturday night." Her mouth dropped, then she demanded I tell her everything.

So I did. Well, I told her everything she needed to know. Not about sleeping next to Raff and our almost kiss... Was it almost kiss?

We headed down to the cafeteria to get some food, but of course, all the pizza was gone. Then my name was called over the intercom.

"Alexis Turner, please report to Mr. Donovani's office."

Ada looked at me and shrugged. She didn't normally eat here, she'd told me she did all her school activities during lunch hours. She never asked where I ate lunch every day, so she must've assumed I was here. I grabbed a salad wrap and water, and made my way to his office. I had no idea what he wanted to talk to me about. Maybe he realized I really wasn't supposed to be in his class, and I was failing. I was going to tell him, just...I got distracted by his beautiful face every time.

On my way to Galen's office, I saw Raff making his way across to the tree line. I stopped to watch him, and that was when I saw Ranger coming from the right. Raff didn't see him coming, and I had to stop this. Maverick was following not too far behind Ranger, and I saw him wave off one of their friends who was following him. This was still two against one. I needed to protect Raff.

I ditched my bag and ran for the door. Once outside, the cooler air hitting my face made me more alert, and I ran. They were now gone, but I knew the general location of where they were. My chest burned as I made it just through the first line of trees, then I stopped, panting.

"I told you to stop. Father said this has gone too far, Ranger. As for you..." I turned toward the voice. That was Maverick and his dull uninterested voice, sounding like he didn't care if he broke up this fight or not. I didn't want to let them know I was here. Surprise was all I had going for me, and my hand throbbed in agreement. As I got closer, holding my breath, I could hear growls.

"I told you to stop marking yourself with her, but now...I can't stop him. He's just too far gone." I could see Maverick's head as I rounded a tree into a small clearing. His eyes flicked to mine, then back to what he was looking at. And then all the air in my chest whooshed out as all the hairs on the back of my neck stood up.

Two wolves were in the clearing...a red one and a larger gray. My stomach fell, and I felt sick. The red wolf. The same one from the party and the backyard.

The larger gray one snapped its jaw and went for the neck of the red one, and then they started fighting. My heart was hammering, and there was fur flying and snarls and a yelp. My hand hovered out, worried for the red wolf. He was so rare... I shuffled back. I needed to get away from this. *What was this?* I couldn't watch the red wolf be killed.

"Ranger, stop," Maverick said, and the gray wolf growled at him. Holy shit, Maverick was drawing its attention to us. Was he crazy?

"Rafferty, Ranger..." Both wolves turned as one, and their eyes fix on me. I felt like I wasn't in my body anymore.

Did he just call them Rafferty and Ranger?

I didn't wait to see, I just started running. I ran out of the tree line, and Galen was there. He was fast as he met me halfway back to the school building. Out of breath, I was trembling as he took my arms to steady me.

"What's wrong Lexi? What's happened?" I turned back, and saw Maverick headed toward us, his hands in his jean pockets. The way he walked was so casual, it didn't make sense with what had just happened. My heart was hammering out of my chest, but I pointed behind me... "Wolves."

Then Ranger appeared from the tree line. He was putting his T-shirt on as he strode toward us with that swagger of his, and I stumbled forward. What...how? Rafferty was hot on his heels, doing the fly up on his jeans, his hair all messy.

"What the fuck?"

CHAPTER TWENTY-THREE

RANGER

That asshole. He told her... That rogue scum, piece of shit told Lexi that I attacked him. I didn't and he knew that, but she seemed to think otherwise.

"I'm challenging your bullshit claim... Meet me in the clearing now." I smashed my shoulder into Raff's as I growled at him. He smelled like her...all over. She smelled like him too, so this wasn't just him scent marking. No, this was more. They had been together. I didn't even want to think about it. I wanted her... My wolf was vibrating, ready to take him down. She was mine, not his. He couldn't claim her. No one was allowed to.

Mav followed behind me as I made my way to the clearing, and he shook his head to let me know he wasn't happy with me. I turned back and flashed my teeth in warning.

"I don't give a shit what our father would say." I shook my head, trying to calm myself before I hit the clearing. I didn't want my wolf loose here in front of everyone. Plus, I loved these jeans.

Mav's hands went up in a 'do whatever, but you've been warned' gesture. The fucking asshole, always so calm and his wolf always under control. I fucking hated him for it sometimes, jealous of his control. As soon as I was in the clearing, I stripped, then felt the rippling all over my body and the flash of heat and pain before I changed.

I shook out my fur, growling lowly, and paced as I watched my brother lean against a tree. He was watching me, unaffected by my need to kill Rafferty King. I watched as his eyes rolled to where Rafferty appeared. That stupid hair of his, all neat and styled. I fucking hated it, and I fucking hated him. I growled, snapping my teeth at him.

The fucker never changed into wolf form to fight. He was like Mav—full of control. Which angered me more than it should. Saturday was the first time I'd seen his wolf form. I knew his scent, so I knew it was him, but I didn't touch him. I ran him off our land, away from Lexi. I didn't like that he lived with her, but hell...our father wouldn't listen to me about my need to claim her.

Rafferty stripped down, and I was pleased. He was finally going to fight me fair. He chose to claim her when he knew it wasn't right. He had no pack, no family, so he couldn't protect her. Saturday night proved that when my brother and pack brothers ripped into him. I told them not to bite with venom, since I knew he would be in the house with Lexi and I didn't want him to lose control in front of her and possibly injure her.

I watched as he changed, then snarled at him as we paced each other in a circle. I was waiting for the right moment. I was going to rip his throat out.

My brother rambled on about father, but I couldn't concentrate. I could smell Lexi all over him. His head turned just enough, and I went for it. He saw me coming, but didn't move fast enough as I sank my teeth in. He growled and whimpered as he shook free of me, then he lunged for my flank.

"Rafferty, Ranger..." I could smell fear...but it wasn't from Rafferty. We both turned at my brother's voice, and that was when I saw her. Lexi was pale, her hand over her throat as she gasped softly. The fear in her eyes made my heart fall. I'd done it again. I'd upset her... Then she ran. I turned to Rafferty, but he was already back in his human form.

Mav was already out of the woods and following Lexi. I could smell Galen nearby, and I felt better knowing he was possibly with her now, just because she felt safe with him. I still didn't like the guy. I grabbed my shirt and pushed Rafferty over as he tried to get his shoes on, then took off running. When I saw her face, my stomach dropped.

"Fuck." I heard Raff hiss out from behind me as I followed them, Galen holding onto Lexi. He would take her to his office. Well, I guess we didn't have to hid our wolf sides from her anymore.

I turned back to see Raff was following.

"This is all your fault. I'm not to blame. You fucked up... If you'd just told her it wasn't me that fucked your sorry ass up, then this wouldn't be happening right now." I was angry, but I also felt freer than ever. She'd seen us, so they'd have to tell her now. She couldn't be compelled, and if anyone had to tell her, Galen would do it right. He was good with words...even if he was a bloodsucker.

When I made it to his office, I could still smell the fear coming from Lexi. Her head swung in my direction, and I smiled, hoping she would be less fearful, but her eyes darted to behind me. *Raff.*

I felt him enter the room and stood close to the back wall as Galen closed the door behind him. She looked like a caged animal. Fuck, this was worse than what I had dreamed. I'd been waiting for this moment, and it wasn't anything like I'd hoped for. Her fear...

"Sit, all of you. Lexi, you can take my chair." She was hesitant at first, but she slowly moved over, watching us with each step, like we would jump over and attack her. My heart sank at that. She was supposed to be happy, to want me, to let me claim her...not be frightened of me.

I heard her sharp intake of breath, and we all looked to her. Her hand was on her neck.

"Raff...oh god." I turned to see where I'd bitten him. It wasn't that bad, but it was bleeding. Looked worse than what it was. But fuck...to her it would look really bad. This wasn't going in my favor at all. Mav the asshole just sat there on the floor...saying nothing, not even trying to defend me and looking disinterested, as always. He kept to himself and was a bit of a loner, but right now, I needed him in my corner, fighting for me. I wanted to claim Lexi as my mate. I wanted her to be with me, not the scum bleeding in the corner.

"Raff...you need to get that looked at." Her words were shaky, and he held his hand up to his throat.

"I'll be okay," he replied with a small smile. Argh...he would be healed soon enough. No need to worry about him.

"Raff..." she whispered, her voice filled with concern. I could see she trusted him fully, and that was when I knew. I knew in that moment that I had no chance of claiming her now without him. I had to fix this. I laid back in the chair, the heels of my palms pressed to my eyes, and I growled low. My wolf was agitated and feeling the unspoken rejection. Fuck, I keep fucking this up. None of my usual lines and moves worked on her. I was out of my depth here, and I was frustrated.

"We need to address the problem here. You boys didn't listen to the alpha, and now you've been caught. Lexi." Galen turned to her, his face full of concern. "I understand you'll have questions, and this is a safe space. They won't harm you *or* each other." He turned back to me and gave me a glare. I put my hands up to defend myself and opened my mouth to speak.

"No, don't. Save it for your father. This was you, Ranger." I sank down in the chair, feeling like a child being punished.

Galen turned to Lexi when she didn't speak up. "First question, were Ranger and Rafferty wolves?" I saw her swallow and nod.

When no one answered, I sat up straighter and smiled. Maybe this would show her I could be trusted, by answering her questions. I could do that, I was great at this...usually.

"Yeah, I was a wolf and so was Rafferty... Mav is one too, but you hardly see him shift... He's a little shy of showing us his—" A slap to the back of my head cut me off before I could finish.

"Ouch..." I rubbed my head, turning to the source. "That hurt, asshole." Mav was now standing behind me, glaring down at me, and I swore his eyes glowed. I must've pissed off his wolf, which made me chuckle.

Was that his weakness? I smiled to myself.

CHAPTER TWENTY-FOUR

LEXI

Wolves. I wasn't crazy, but I felt sick and scared. Rafferty was a wolf. Ranger had some stupid grin on his face like I might get up, clap my hands, and give him a round of applause for telling me that they turned into wolves.

"Like...what the fuck?" I didn't care if Galen was here and a teacher, this was crazy ass shit. I rubbed my eyes and opened them.

Still here...

This wasn't a dream. This was a nightmare, and not like the ones I had. This was a real living one. No...no this was just bullshit. They were fucking with me, that was why Ranger had that messed up grin on his face. They'd played me.

"Ha ha...yep. You got me. It's not April yet...but you fooled me." My voice cracked as I got up, but I wasn't going to sit around here, listening to this bullshit. Maverick was just messing with me out there, calling the wolves that were fighting by their names...that was it. Right?

But then I saw Raff's neck... That? How...how do I explain that to my mind? I felt cold and shaky.

"I can show you, if you like." Ranger stood up, and Galen told him no as he started stripping off his clothes. Maverick just stood back and leaned casually against the bookshelf, like this was just a lazy Sunday afternoon. How was he not affected by this? Oh yeah, he was one too.

Galen tried to shove Ranger back into the chair as his hand was on his fly, ready to show me everything.

"No, this is a great idea. If I shift in front of her, then she'll see that it's real. I'll even turn my back to her, so she doesn't have a look at the goods. Okay, *teach*?"

Galen stood there unmoving. There was a silence in the room, and all I could hear were my ragged breaths. Galen rolled his eyes as he took his hand from Ranger's bare shoulder, then Ranger smiled as he stood up and winked at me. He turned his back to me as he stripped bare, and I saw that his ass was whiter than the rest of his skin.

"Ready?" he asked over his shoulder, his eyes starting to glow. I stumbled back into the chair and pressed back into it as far as I could go. He didn't wait for me to speak, and I watched as Ranger changed in front of me, from a man to a gray wolf. My hand pressed tightly to my chest, trying to calm my breathing. This... What? I couldn't breathe, my throat was so tight.

"Lexi, are you okay? Just take deep breaths." Galen was now beside me, holding my hand as I stared out, not looking at the wolf in the room. Was I having a panic attack? I hadn't had one of those in forever. I closed my eyes, breathing deep. In and out. In and out.

"I shouldn't have let you do that, Ranger. That was my mistake for allowing it. I'm sorry, Lexi," Galen said as he rubbed my hand in his, and it was warm to my cold. When I opened my eyes, I was startled. The gray wolf was now sitting behind Galen, its eyes glowing, but now I saw it close up. Its eyes were green, just like Ranger's, but they were lit up. Its head cocked to the side with its tongue lolled out. Galen spun his head and hissed lowly at Ranger.

"Ranger, give her space." But Ranger didn't move, his ears just moved, and I could see his tail was wagging against the floor.

"I... How does this happen?" I asked. Galen cleared his throat before he stood up, letting go of my hand and resting against his desk in front of me.

"They're shifters. There are many kinds, but the ones in this area are all wolf shifters. There are bears, panthers... Well, there's a lot of different shifters. But the ones who live here, in this area and go to Port Willow High, are all wolves. They're all gray wolves. Except Rafferty. He's different."

My eyes sought out Raff, but he looked so ashamed and small over in the corner. "How?" I croaked out, my hand going to my throat again.

I saw him shuffle and sit a little higher. "I'm a red wolf," he practically whispered. Maverick was watching me from the corner of his eye. He warned me, he told me to leave. Why? Because of this? Because I wasn't supposed to know? My heart started to race. Were they going to kill me now? I knew their secret.

I jerked back when the warm weight of Ranger's wolf head laid in my lap, his eye peering up at me. I tried to back up further in the chair, my hands in the air. I didn't know what he wanted, but he was scaring me. Was the wolf different to him? Like, could he control it or...?

"Ranger," Galen groaned. I could tell he was getting frustrated with him. "He won't hurt you, Lexi. It's still Ranger, just in wolf form." Galen's face told me he wasn't happy with Ranger's move. I saw him glare at the wolf, who I swear was smiling at me. When I saw Raff getting up and the blood still on his neck, I remembered what he'd done. I shoved the furry head of Ranger off my lap.

"You fucking attacked him. Do. Not. Touch. Me," I growled out to Ranger. I stood up, swaying lightly. Galen moved to take my arm, but I flinched away. I walked around the desk, trying to put distance between myself and Ranger, and made my way over to Raff. He tensed slightly and closed his eyes.

"I just want to see your neck," I whispered. I didn't want him to be scared of me. I reach out for his hand, hanging limp by his side.

When I looked up, his eyes were on me, and I could feel our connection. I smiled gently as I moved the collar of his T-shirt to see how bad it really was, and he let me.

"They heal fast, so that'll be gone by tomorrow. When he turns eighteen or thereabouts, he'll heal almost instantly." I turned to Galen. *They heal fast?* I didn't miss that. I heal fast too. Wasn't that normal? Was I normal?

"So, you're a wolf?"

"Yes, but oh, um...I'm a shifter—born a human and shift into a wolf," Raff answered. I was a little confused...okay, a lot confused about all of this.

The bell rang, and it was like the air in the room changed. I looked around the office, trying to avoid looking at the huge wolf just sitting there beside Galen's desk. My bag? Where did I leave it? Galen pulled it up from the floor near the door and handed it to me.

"I grabbed it for you." I nodded as I swung it over my shoulder. On a shaky breath, I looked around the room at the guys...and wolf.

I needed to leave this place. *Now.*

CHAPTER TWENTY-FIVE

LEXI

Galen must have called Grayson and Jack, because they were waiting outside the school in their car for me. He knew I would run. They took me back to the house, and the ride back was quiet, which made me more nervous than ever. They usually just chatted away when they were together. At least the ride wasn't long, and then we were back at the house.

"Grayson will bring us in some tea and muffins," Jack said as he gestured to the living room, and I dropped my bag at my feet. I was stiff as I sat on the edge of the seat. "Coffee. White. No sugar," I called out. I wanted coffee, not tea. Tea was okay, but I needed something stronger, to wake me up from this.

"One coffee coming up." Jack fidgeted a few times and looked to the door. Was he expecting someone? *Oh shit.* Was someone coming to take me away? Was Jack keeping me here until they got here to take me away and kill me?

"What's going on?" I tried to act causal, like this was all normal. I would't tell them what I saw, I'd deny it all. They didn't need to worry about me running around and telling others that I saw a boy turn into a wolf. I'd be thrown into the loony bin for talking like that. Fuck no. No way. I wasn't stupid.

"We got a text from Galen, saying that we should meet you at the school. That you accidently discovered the shifter world." I looked around the room, because I needed an escape plan. Were they wolves too? Oh god, Jack and Grayson were wolves. They had to be.

"I can sense your fear. Don't worry, Lexi. There's nothing to be afraid of. We've been waiting to tell you, but I guess Ranger and Raff set that into motion a little earlier than planned."

My hands were shaking, so I put them under my armpits to try and hide the fear. Grayson walked back in the room, a hot cup of coffee in one hand and a plate with three muffins in the other. When he handed them over, my hand trembled as I took the mug, then he placed the plate of muffins beside me. He gave me a gentle smile.

"They're all for you." Then he backed up and took a seat on the floor. Jack followed him, and they sat beside each other, looking up to me. I felt less intimated by them at this angle, and my hand stopped trembling as I took a sip of the hot coffee. But my stomach was like a rock, I was too shit scared to stomach anything else.

"You're probably wondering, and yes, we're wolves. We're from Pack Kiba, and so is Ranger. We're gray wolves, as most usually are. Red wolf shifters, just like the ones in the wild, are rare as well. That's why we want to make sure Rafferty has a good life here, and hopefully one day, join our pack."

My hands were shaking again, and I had to used them both to steady the mug, trying not to spill hot coffee on my lap. I could see they were watching my hands now gripping the mug tightly.

"Are you going to kill me? Is that why I'm here? You said you don't normally take females. What do you want with me?" My voice broke at the end. The panic had now set in, but so had the anger, bubbling deep inside. I wasn't going to go down without a fight. They could try, but I wouldn't go easily.

Their eyes went wide...with shock? Confusion? They shook their heads, their hands waving in surrender.

"No, god no, Lexi. No one will hurt you, that's not what this is. We're not explaining this right, since we've never had to do it before. I'll try and start. Okay, if at any stage you have questions, put your hand up and I'll answer it." I swallowed the lump in my throat and nodded slowly.

This was not my life. This was not real.

"Lexi, shifters live in communities, like we have here in Kiba. Not all the residents are wolves, we let humans live here also, but a majority are shifters. There are two other packs that live nearby, Rawlins and Kenneally. Our leaders all work together in times of need, but otherwise, we're very territorial. We don't associate with the other packs. How are you doing so far? Understanding?"

I nodded. I was understanding as much as anyone could, as this was a lot to take in. I took a deep breath and put my hand up.

"The whole hating each other at school, that's because they're wolves and don't like each other?" They nodded, and Grayson said that was pretty much it, but that they didn't act like that as adults. They were just teens with crazy hormones. That strangely made sense to me.

"So, you would've probably noticed there are a lot of males. That's because we're cursed.... Well okay, the story goes that we're cursed to never have female children, only males. But we're blessed with a venom that changes females, to make them shifters and carry shifter offspring, which are always male. No matter how many times they try, they always have males. You may notice some bigger families, they were trying to 'break the curse.'"

Jack was good, and I was following along with what he was saying, but it sounded like a fairy tale. I just wanted to go hide and pretend this day was over.

"So, you being female here... That's new for us. Not because there's anything wrong with you, but you have...um. a scent." He gave me an apologetic look. *I smell?* "You don't smell human, but you don't smell like a shifter...not one that anyone has come across before. You draw in the shifter males with your scent. I don't know why, but I heard about your first day. The boys, we didn't warn them properly, and they got a little aggressive.

"Some believe you're their mate. That your scent calls to them, so they've asked to claim you. Our alpha, Ranger and Maverick's father, has stopped them all, along with the other alphas. So don't worry, no one will claim you. You won't be forced to be with any of them. That's not why you're here.

"We want to protect you. Some other packs are bad...and they would take you and hurt you. That's why Shelly brought you here, to us. We can protect you, and we'll find out what you are."

This was too much to take in at once. I nodded my head and put my empty mug on the coffee table. Then I took the plate of muffins and my bag to my room and closed the door, locking it behind me. I was hoping that they'd all stay away from me. I needed to think clearly about this. Jack had said they wouldn't hurt me, but I didn't want to take the chance. I paced my room, thinking over the events of the day.

When they were all sleeping, I would escape. I needed to get far away from here. My window had the lock on it, but I was sure I could figure out how to break it.

CHAPTER TWENTY-SIX

GALEN

I sat on the leather sofa between Nash and Jett. Nash was tense, and I would be, too. Alaric was pacing. He wasn't my father, but I knew he had a temper like all alphas did. He wasn't happy with how Nash had handled Rafferty Saturday night. I'd heard that argument all day Sunday. If I'd known that Lexi was going to be attending the party, I would've been here, or at least warned Alaric how Ranger had been acting before he left the boys to throw their party.

We were waiting on Ranger. He'd taken off once we'd all been summoned here, and everyone here knew why. Alaric had told him to wait until he'd figured out what Lexi was, that he was to leave her alone, but Ranger just couldn't help himself. I didn't blame him though. She pulled to me like no other, which had me questioning daily what she could be.

Alaric had also told Ranger to stop picking fights with Rafferty, but Ranger was wild and reckless. To be honest, Alaric wasn't as tough on him as he was with the others. Ranger toed the line more than any of the Lovell brothers.

"Come on. Now, boy." Alaric's voice boomed through the house.

I saw Lyell shift on his seat beside Maverick, who honestly looked like he couldn't care less that his father was agitated. But we all knew Maverick would have Ranger's back no matter what. Wherever Ranger was, Maverick was two steps behind, cleaning up his mess.

Lyell was more like his mother, and I enjoyed his company. He preferred books to sports, so we had a lot more in common than the other brothers, and we'd spent many hours in the library here talking about the works of our favorite authors.

I could feel Nash shift again. He was all business and always had his father's back, trying to prove himself as the next alpha. I'd known the Lovell family a long time, even their mother Laura, who I'd met many times before she passed.

But I've only lived here, with Pack Kiba, for the last five years—since her death. I lived on the Lovell estate, in the caretaker's residence. It was smaller than my last place, but it was cozy.

"Father, it was an accident. I didn't mean for it to happen. She just—" Ranger's mouth slammed shut, and he lowered his head at the loud growl from Alaric. Everyone in the room submitted to Alaric.

"You were told no more. You were told to leave her alone. You didn't obey my orders, so now she knows, and not on the terms I'd wished for. She's an unknown. We have many people searching to find out what she could be. She's shown no signs of shifting, so we believe she isn't a shifter. But today, you disobeyed an order. From your alpha. You went after the red wolf and started a fight. Why? Why would you do that?"

I was sure Alaric didn't actually want an answer. I think he was just frustrated that his son couldn't listen to a direct order, given by the alpha. Alaric turned and took a stack of thick folders out from his briefcase and placed them on the coffee table with a *thud*.

"It was because he marked her. He put a stronger claim on her, and I know she's mine. He's doing this to piss me off."

I could feel Nash shake his head beside me at Ranger's pleading to his father. Even I knew not to speak to the alpha like that, and I wasn't a wolf shifter.

The tension in the air was thick as Alaric slowly strode up to Ranger. Then his hand reached out and took Ranger by the back of the neck. He pushed him to the floor on his knees.

"Do. Not. Speak," Alaric snarled as he returned back to the folders and flipped one open. No one spoke, and I held my breath. I enjoyed working for Pack Kiba, but at times, I didn't enjoy the way Alaric treated his sons.

"We've looked into a lot of leads and haven't found the answers yet. This is her whole life. Here." He tapped on the papers in front of him. "Her mother and father were killed in a drug deal, and she was found a few weeks later by a neighbor after they complained about the smell coming from the apartment. She'd been living in a cupboard, taking herself to school and returning home every day."

My heart sank. I knew she had a bad past but this... Fuck. My heart ached for her. She was so strong, and yet she'd gone through so much trauma as a child. No child should have to go through that.

"Alaric, I think these are things best not spoken about. They're not who she is, and I don't think she'd be happy with everyone here knowing her past." I looked around the room, and everyone held the same expression—shock, pity, sadness. These were things she wouldn't want people to know about her for this exact reason.

"You're right, I'm sorry. Please don't let on that you know that. I'll skip over the other points." He flipped through the documents and spoke about her parents. Her mother was admitted to a mental hospital while she was pregnant with Lexi. Her father was a small-time drug dealer, and that was the only family she had. There was no other family they could find, which is why Lexi ended up in the system.

"So as you see, we're at a dead-end right now. I have a few of our men working on what other packs might know about the way she smells. We're trying to be as discreet as possible, but it's not helping with our investigations. We don't want to let on that we have her here, not until we know what she is at least.

"She's safe for now, as long as all the packs work together. So no more fighting with the red wolf. Jack and Grayson have told me that he means something to her. If he has claimed her and she doesn't understand, then that's a different story and I will handle that myself. Not you." He pointed to Ranger, who looked up just to see his father's glare. "Nor will any of you. Now, Ranger, come with me. I wish to speak to you in private." And with that, we were all dismissed.

I wished I didn't know so much about Lexi's life this way. I wanted her to trust me enough to tell me these things herself, but I needed to know more. I needed it to protect her. I wanted her safe, and if I had to read about all the bad things that had happened to her, I would do that to protect her. I knew she wouldn't be happy if she found out, but I would do what I had to.

I moved over and picked up some files and started to scan though them. I could feel Jett move in and look at some as well, so I raised my brow at him.

"I'm working on this too. Might as well get all the information so I can help her."

I flipped through the file of her foster homes...and learned she had run from every single one. There was a lot of them since she was a child, and some of the things I read made me livid. *Fuck.* I looked down at my phone for the time.

"I gotta go."

CHAPTER TWENTY-SEVEN

LEXI

It took Raff a long time to leave my door. He'd knocked and knocked, and then just sat out there for most of the night. I didn't want to see him. I couldn't. It was just too much. I was falling for him, but this shifter thing was huge. Like freaky, out of this world, crazy huge. I just couldn't deal with it. He turned into a wolf... Just thinking about it made my mind go crazy.

I was angry at myself for giving him a piece of my heart, something that could break. I was taking that back now though. They could all go fuck themselves.

The more I thought about it, the more I felt like crying and throwing things. How could he not tell me this, that he turned into a wolf? Well, I knew why he didn't, but still. Maybe he should've kept away from me or pushed me away more.

Fuck, this was just not what I'd planned. I should've left before this happened. I knew this place was too good to be true, but I was lulled into a false sense of normal, with parents who cared and a loving family home.

It was just past four in the morning, and the lock on my window was impossible to pick. I was pissed off about it, but that wasn't going to stop me. Opening my bedroom door, I could see the light was on in Raff's room. I remembered the whole 'they can smell you' part of the conversation earlier. Would he be able to smell me leave?

I moved quickly to the bathroom and locked the door. *Fuck, fuck, fuck.* He'd know if I left, and he wasn't going to let me just leave. He would follow me. Would I let him? My heart sank at the thought of leaving him, but this was what I needed to do. I couldn't bring him with me...he belonged here. Like Jack said—he was a rare red wolf. He could join their pack and live here. God, that just sounded so crazy.

I started the shower and pretended I was washing myself while I slowly pushed open the small bathroom window. I shoved my backpack out, hoping he wouldn't hear it hit the ground right next to his room. When I didn't hear anything at the bathroom door or from outside, I pushed myself up and out, the cold night air hitting my face.

It was a small window, but it was no trouble for me. I could slip out of one smaller. My shoulders burned as I slowly, quietly lowered myself down the other side. My feet barely made a sound as I slowly placed them on the ground. I could see my breath fog up the air in front of my face. It was a colder night than I'd expected, and I felt a chill run down my spine.

I looked around and saw Raff's window was closed, but I could see in, since he hadn't drawn the blinds. I couldn't stop myself from moving forward a little to see him. He was lying on his bed, wearing blue sweatpants. One knee was up, and his feet were bare. I scanned further and saw that he was topless...and all those tattoos were on display. He was beautiful. I felt a lump form in my throat at the thought of leaving him.

Why couldn't he just be...not a red wolf, just a normal guy? I wanted to go inside and tell him to come with me, that we could leave this crazy place together. Stop Ranger from hurting him. His arm was up and draped over his eyes, and I could see he had headphones on.

I let out a slow, shaky breath, the cold air burning my lungs and making my nose run. I reached out toward Raff and closed my hand in a goodbye. *He would be better without me.*

I wiped a lonely tear as I picked up my backpack, swung it over my shoulder, and slowly creeped around to the front of the house. I glanced back, just one last time. I felt a passing of guilt that I didn't say goodbye to Joshua. *Little Joshy.* I would write him a letter and tell him how sorry I was. I hoped he would understand it wasn't him. I just...I couldn't do this.

I crossed my arms against my chest and tucked my hands under my armpits. I could feel my nose starting to run more now. I sniffed a few times, and my eyes watered. *It's the cold*, I told myself as I wiped it on my sleeve. But as many times as I tried to tell myself, my heart told me it wasn't.

It was quiet out here. The only sounds were my feet on the pavement and the random calling of an owl. I scanned everywhere, looking for anything out of place. This definitely wasn't my first time walking alone at night. I knew what could hide in the shadows.

Suddenly, I heard a car...and it was getting closer. I turned to figure what direction it was coming from, since the sound was bouncing off the houses around me. The bright lights blinded me as it turned from a street up ahead and onto the street toward me. *Fuck.*

I stepped behind a fence and squatted low. The car was slow and the engine was loud as it rumbled down the street toward me. My heart started to race, thinking it was Jack or Grayson looking for me, but when the car got close enough, I saw it was black and not their silver car. When it continued on past me, my heart settled. I waited for it to be far enough away before I got up and started to walk much faster. I didn't like being out here, and now that I knew werewolves could smell me... Shit, they could be tracking me as well. Why I didn't think of that? My heart started to race again, and I started to run.

When I heard the engine purr down the street behind me, I realized this person must be looking for me. I glanced behind me, and the car picked up speed as it headed right toward me.

"Fuck," I hissed, trying to catch my breath. I hadn't run like this in a while, and my backpack weighed too much, but I didn't want to drop it. When the car pulled up in front of me, I skidded to a stop. Fuck the bag. I dropped it, my heart pounding in my ears, and ran toward someone's house. I could hide in their backyard, but shit, they could smell me, right?

An arm grabbed me and hauled me to a stop. The pain in my shoulder from the sudden stop pained me, and I let out a scream before my mouth was muffled by a hand. Then a voice close to my ear told me it was okay.

I turned back toward him, and he dropped his hand from my mouth "Galen?" He was staring down at me. *What the hell?* I shrugged him off, and he let me go as I took a step back, rubbing my shoulder. I looked at the black car, then back to him, still trying to catch my breath.

"What. The. Fuck?" I was angry as I looked around to see if there was anyone else with him. Why the hell was he out here looking for me?

"I had a feeling you really weren't okay this afternoon, so I came to find you."

My brows furrowed. He came to find me? My history teacher, the one who knew all about werewolves and was just like super okay with them? He didn't tell me about the weird creepy claiming thing that Jack spoke about, though.

"Just get in the car. I'll drive you to the bus stop myself." I tilted my head, and he cocked a brow. "That's where you were going, right?" I rolled my eyes. I felt stupid and frustrated at the same time.

Ugh. Why the fuck was he so good looking? It was distracting. I dropped my shoulders and relaxed my body. "Fine," I muttered.

He didn't say anything as he walked me back to his car, though he reached down and picked up my backpack on the way. He opened the passenger door, and I slipped in, feeling the warmth of the heater instantly. He gave me my bag, and I placed it on the floor. I sagged back against the seat once he'd closed the door and let out a deep breath. It had been a long day, and I was mentally and physically exhausted after that run. I'd been getting too lazy, so I needed to work out more if I was going to do that again.

We ended up outside of town at a truck stop. "Let me get you breakfast first, and we can chat." I was pissed off. He said he would take me to the bus stop, and this obviously wasn't a bus stop. But my stomach betrayed me, so I'd spend his money on food. I needed to save everything I had in my sock so I could get far, far away from here.

I ordered, and we sat in silence for a while. It was tense, not comfortable at all. Not like the times I had lunch in his office. I knew too much about this werewolf stuff, but I didn't know exactly what he wanted to chat about. He hadn't made a move to say anything, but I could guess it'd be about seeing a boy turn into a wolf in his office yesterday.

There were a lot more people in here than I'd expected, even though it was early. Another person walked in, the bell sounding their arrival. The waitress, an older lady, placed my food in front of me, and I thanked her before she walked off to greet the newcomer.

I looked down at the full plate—pancakes, bacon...eggs. It smelled so good, and the first thought that popped into my head was Jack and Grayson's house and how they cooked this every morning. Just this... it wasn't the same. There were no laughing and smiles, no cute little Josh...no Raff. I felt sick as I swallowed the lump in my throat and eyed Galen. I was mad and emotional—two things that didn't mix well.

"Why did you bring me here? I told you I'm fucking leaving this place."

The casual way Galen pushed the maple syrup toward my plate as he watched me with that penetrating gaze had me sitting up straighter. I didn't know why, but around him, I wanted to be...better. I wanted him to see me as an equal, not some stupid teenage girl who had a crush on their teacher.

"You need to eat, and you're not leaving." He took in my silence and sighed. "Look, I'm sorry. The boys shouldn't have shown you that way."

Sorry for what? That werewolves were real? Yeah...that was the best reason to be leaving Port Willow. This place was full of freaks. Next they were going to tell me there were vampires.

I poked my fried eggs with my fork. I wasn't hungry. No, that was a lie. I was, but I didn't want to eat all of this in front of him. He hadn't ordered anything, not even a coffee. *Huh...* When was the last time I saw him eat something? Anything? *Never.* I looked up at him, a tired expression on his face.

"Don't tell me...you sparkle?"

His brow rose, and I could see the hint of a smirk. He glanced over to a table full of diners before he leaned in so close, I could feel his breath on my face. "Is that your way of asking if I'm a vampire? I thought you'd be more direct than that, Lexi." He cocked his head, challenging me.

Was he saying yes? He didn't say no. What the hell? My heart started to race, and I could see him shift in his seat. His eyes widened slightly. *Oh fuck!*

"Yeah...well, I'm Team Jacob."

I didn't move. I refused to back down. I watched as his expression changed, and for the first time, I saw him smile. And holy fuck, that just made him go from sexy teacher to sex god in three seconds flat.

"Well, that's disappointing, but the boys will be happy to know that."

Fuck!

CHAPTER TWENTY-EIGHT

RAFFERTY

I was so tired. I laid in bed, thinking over what I should've said to Lexi when she found out. I should've come home with her. I shouldn't have listened to Galen and let her leave. I was stupid to listen to him. I thought she'd be happy to see me when I got back from school. I was hoping for another special night like the one we had last night.

Now she wouldn't speak to me, and I didn't know what to do. I needed her, and I wasn't there when she really needed me. Waking up in the morning with Lexi had been the best feeling in the world. I was embarrassed that I rubbed my cock against her ass, but I was half-asleep and had been wrapped up in her scent all night. I'd forgotten where I was in that moment, and I thought she would be upset with me. *Fuck*, we hadn't even kissed yet, but I already knew I never wanted to kiss anyone else in the world. Only Lexi.

Lexi had been in the shower for a long time, and I was worried. I knocked on the bathroom door, but she didn't answer. I didn't want to use my shifter hearing on her. I didn't want to upset her more by pushing her—I could tell she wouldn't like that. I wouldn't like it if someone didn't give me some space to think, and Grayson told me that she needed space.

I wanted to go lay in her bed and wait for her, and my wolf wanted to take in her scent, to roll in it. *Mark myself*. But I didn't want her to be upset or angry if she found me in there, so I returned to my bed and laid down. My eyes were gritty and tired, but I couldn't sleep even if I wanted to.

I'd never felt this way before, and I was lost. How did I go back to what we had? My wolf was more agitated than usual. I wanted to go for a run to let off some steam, but I couldn't leave her here, just in case she needed me. I hoped she did. Plus, I wanted to show her my wolf. He wanted her to stroke him, curl up with him...

There was a knock at my door, and my heart jumped into my throat.

"Rafferty?" It was Jack. I pulled my headphones out and sat up. The shower was still going. Had she been in there for an hour? I ran my hands over my face and through my hair as I called out for him to come in.

"I just got a call from Alaric. Galen has Lexi. She's safe right now, and he'll be bringing her back later. I just wanted to tell you, and let you know that none of this is your fault. I don't want you to think it was."

All the air whooshed out of my lungs, and I couldn't breathe. *She left me...*

"No, Raff, look at me." Jack was in front of me, squatting on the floor, his eyes searching mine. "This was a lot for her to take in. It has nothing to do with you and what you two have. Okay? I know you were getting close, we could smell that yesterday morning. We might be old, but we can still smell when you've both marked each other. Lexi is... Look, I know she cares about you. Her leaving isn't about you, it's about her. Okay? There is nothing you could've done. This is what she does, and I was prepared for that. I slept in the living room, expecting her to leave out the front door when she gave up on her window lock."

I didn't want to listen to him. She could have taken me, she should have. Instead, she left me.

"Who's in the shower?" Jack turned and walked toward the bathroom door.

"She went in there..." I heard Jack curse as he tried to unlock the door. About five minutes later, I heard Grayson and him outside, trying to get in through the window. I realized that I didn't even hear or see her slip outside. I was so lost in my head that my wolf didn't even sense her leave.

She was right there, and—

She didn't want me.

A few hours later, I could hear yelling in the house. I didn't go to school. I'd refused to go, and Grayson had said it was fine to stay home today. I didn't care if he thought it was fine or not, I wasn't going. I needed to wait for her, to see her.

There was some banging sounds, and I heard Lexi's door slam shut. I could smell her. She was back. My heart felt light, but my stomach plummeted as I remembered that she left without me. I could smell Galen, and Alaric was there. I opened my door and was met with a stare down from Nash. *Motherfucker.*

"What's going on?" I asked Galen. He looked concerned and tired. What had he done to her? I could sense my wolf growing angry, pacing, wanting to bust out and tear him up. Sensing my shift in mood, Galen looked up and shook his head. It was Alaric who answered me.

"She will be living with me now. She's here to pack up her belongings. It'll be easier to keep her safe there. She's not understanding this and has locked herself in her room." He looked back to the door and knocked again. I could smell the distress coming from Lexi, the fear, the anger.

"Fuck off, I'm not living with you or your fucked-up sons!" Nash looked to his father with a 'what did I do?' expression.

I couldn't help the smile that spread my lips as Alaric stood there with a dumbfounded look on his face. Lexi was one of a kind.

Jack, Alaric, Nash, and Galen were now all looking at me. I took a step back farther into my room when Alaric gestured with his hand to her door.

"You, boy, she likes you. My sons told me that you've tried to claim her, yes? She'll listen to you." I knew where he was going with this, but I wasn't going to get her to come out and leave with them. I shook my head, but then he growled at me, his voice demanding I submit. My wolf was submitting to his, even though I didn't want to. He was the alpha here, and my wolf could sense that.

I bit my tongue for as long as I could so I wouldn't do what they wanted. It wasn't right for them to do this to her. She might've run away from me, but she was leaving everything when she ran. And if that was her choice...

"I know what we'll do. We'll take Raff back to his old pack if Lexi doesn't come out of the room. We'll send him back to his loving, *caring* family, and I'll escort him there myself."

I could see a gleam in Nash's eye as he glared at me, and I felt like someone was sitting on my chest, I couldn't breathe as chills crawled up my spine. He couldn't do that, he wouldn't.

"Yes, that's right. Get your stuff, boy. I'll send you on your way now. She has thirty seconds to get her stuff and leave before I send you back to those addicts." Alaric smiled at me. He fucking smiled.

I could feel the fear coming from Lexi. I didn't just smell her, I swear I could feel it in my bones, in my mind. My wolf was vibrating so hard, I could lose control in a moment. I took another step back when Nash reached out and grabbed my arm, pulling me toward him. I growled lowly. My wolf so close to the edge, I'd shift right here if I didn't have such good control, but I could only control it for so long.

"Hey," Jack yelled at Nash.

"Get off me," I growled, just as Lexi's door clicked open.

Everyone turned as one, and I shoved Nash away from me. Lexi's face was red and splotchy, like she had been crying. I'd been so upset that she'd left me that I didn't think I would see her like this. She looked so small, so unsure of herself, and I stumbled toward her. They'd used me against her, and all her choices had been taken away. I'd go back to my pack if it meant she was happy. I'd do anything for her in this moment. She eyed everyone warily in the hallway. Jack gave her a sad smile that said, 'I'm sorry.' He had no choice in this—he and Grayson were very low ranking in the pack, and they wouldn't get a say, even if they tried.

"Good. Well, now you're ready. Nash." Alaric nodded to Nash as he brushed past him and walked into the living room. Jack followed Alaric.

Nash grabbed the top of Lexi's arm, and I saw the fire in her eyes as soon as he made contact with her. She wasn't small and weak. *She was fire.* Lexi turned to look at him straight on, and Nash looked like the cat that caught the mouse.

Lexi gave him a huge sarcastic grin, before she reached up to his shoulder and her knee met his balls. Even I winced when she smashed into him with such force. Nash let go of her and dropped down, cupping his junk with a huge yelp. Alaric started yelling about something, and Galen was trying to get Lexi to calm down. Her scent was strong, like we might now get a glimpse of what she was or might be.

I felt her soft hand slip into mine, and it was small but cold. I looked down to where she held me as she leaned into me. She was trying to keep me strong when I should've been the one giving her my strength. Alaric stomped back toward us, and without thinking, I pulled Lexi into my room and slammed the door shut. I pressed my body against it to stop them from coming in.

The door handle rattled, and there were a few bangs before Galen told them all to calm down and that Lexi would come to the living room soon. Galen told them to give her a little time with me, that it would be for her best interest. I felt like Galen was on her side, but as a vampire, he was the weakest member in the pack. Usually in shifter packs, vampires had no say or pull. I suspected he was just as low-ranked as Grayson and Jack, but he was respected by Alaric, which went a long way.

"I won't let them send you back." Her words were barely above a whisper.

I looked down at her, her eyes filled with tears and I didn't know what to say. No one had ever done something like that for me. I vowed then that I would always protect her, no matter the cost.

I'll keep you safe, Lexi.

CHAPTER TWENTY-NINE

LEXI

The room I'd been put in was huge, but it was white and sterile like the rest of the house. It made me feel like a caged animal. It didn't help that the way they treated Raff and me was worse than an animal. God, I hated Nash and Alaric. They played me, they played me well. I wasn't sure if they were serious about sending Raff back to his uncle, but I didn't want to take the chance. I knew either way, I was going to be dragged here. I wouldn't let Raff be taken down too, just because we were friends... well, more than friends. At least, I hoped we still were after what I did. I didn't get a chance to explain to him why I ran.

I could hear talking outside my room again, and I didn't like it. The room was on the second floor. The window opened and I could get fresh air, but I wasn't too sure how the drop would go for me to escape. It was a pretty fair drop, but the pool was down there... I couldn't swim though, so dropping into it wasn't just a bad idea, it was terrible.

I went back to pace the room, the white carpet soft under my toes. There was a huge empty closet with a few bare hangers on one end and shelves to store someone's belongings. I had nothing worth putting in there. Someone—I suspected Jack—had packed up all my things, and they were now here, but I didn't want to open the suitcase. I wasn't going to unpack, since this wasn't my home.

As Ada had said, every room had a full bathroom, and it was the only room in here with color—green mosaic tiles mixed in with the white. There was a full-sized bath, huge walk in shower, and toilet in there. It had been stocked with soaps and some towels, which were white…of course.

This whole house was fucking white.

I heard talking again outside the door—there had been a lot of talking and pacing outside there over the last few hours since school was out, so I guessed Ranger was back home. I heard a knock and froze. I had nowhere to hide here, no protection. This was Alaric's house, and he had five sons. I didn't know that until I got here and met the other two—I'd already met Nash. Fucking asshole.

"It's okay, Lexi, you don't need to be scared." I rolled my eyes. Ranger. He'd finally knocked after lingering out there for so long, I'd thought something was wrong with him. The door didn't have a lock, so I expected him to just open it and barge in.

"It's dinner soon, and my father has requested you come eat with us." I moved into the walk-in closet and sat down in the corner where I'd left my bag earlier. I pulled out my book, since some Mr. Darcy would be perfect about now. I needed to get lost in another world.

It didn't take long before there was another knock, but this time, they didn't waste any time in waiting for me to answer—not that I would have. They just strode right into the room.

Nash.

His face turned to me, and I glared at him, gritting my teeth and clenching my fists at the sight of him. This whole smelling me thing wasn't helping. I needed to show him I wasn't scared of him. I was so fucking mad at him. He was one of the assholes who fucked up Raff on the weekend, and now he'd played me and I was here. *Like a prisoner.*

"So, we can do this the easy way or the hard way. Galen is here for dinner, because Father felt you might prefer to have him here on your first night. I don't care. But if you want Raff to still be living here in Kiba, you'll be at dinner in the next five minutes. And preferably dressed in something," he waved his hand at me, "more suited to company." Then he gave me a wicked smile and turned on his heel. I could hear Ranger tell him that he was out of line as he walked away.

He wants me in something more suited? I'll give him something...

I walked down the stairs to the dining room where I could hear everyone. I'd been asked two more times by Nash to hurry up, but I told them I was a girl and we take more than five minutes to get ready. Not this girl, of course, but I wanted to fuck with them a bit longer. I didn't want to be here, so they got what they asked for.

I rounded the corner, and everyone came into view. One of the brothers, I think his name was Jett, saw me first. Well, I assume from the way he choked on his water that he had seen me. I gave my fake dazzling smile as I saw an empty seat beside Ranger and Galen. I held my head high and didn't look at them as I walked over barefoot. I pulled the chair out, and the whole table was quiet as they watched me sit.

"What...ah, did you need...?" Alaric scratched his head as he tried to avoid looking at me. Nash just stared directly at me, his eyes wide and mouth agape.

Ranger cleared his throat. "You...look nice." That made me want to laugh. I didn't want to see what Galen's reaction was. I didn't want to see his disappointment in me. I knew I was being a bitchy teenager right in this moment, but it was worth it for the looks on their faces.

"I'll give you an allowance for clothing, Alexis, and you'll be able to find something more suitable in some of the local stores. I'll get one of the boys to take you tomorrow."

I placed my hands gently on the table and cupped them together, pretending that I was the Queen of England with good manners. I gently tilted my head and gave my fake innocent smile as I batted my lashes.

"Is this not suitable? I was wearing what I would normally eat dinner in earlier, but Nash told me it wasn't suitable. So, I took it off..." I heard a snort and some chuckles coming from one of them, but when Alaric growled, they stopped.

That wasn't a lie—I did take it all off. I took off my skinny jeans, socks, and hoodie, and just left my tight white tank, red bra, and my black boyleg underwear. I was kinda going for the Harley Quinn look —I was just missing a belt and boots. But my makeup looked pretty wicked. Nothing better than black eyeliner to pop these amber eyes.

No one said anything, so I took that as my clue to leave. I stood, making sure to turn around and show my ass to all of them. I was playing with fire, and I knew it, but I didn't care. From all the times I danced at The Landing Strip, I knew how to work a room full of males. I could hear them all as I started to walk away, and I made sure to put a little extra swing in my hips. Alaric muttered something, and I could hear a chair move, but I didn't turn around to see who it was.

As I reached my room I paused just outside. I could feel him so close, his breath tickled the back of my neck and all the hairs on my arms stood up.

"Lexi..." I let out a shuddering breath. I hoped it would be him, I wanted it to be him so bad. I leaned back a little and felt his hard body against mine. I took a deep breath as I straightened up and walked into the bedroom, my body humming with need. I *wanted him.*

I turned to see him close the door behind us. He hesitated a moment, his hand still on the door handle, and I took a few steps backward, I needed space between us. He didn't say anything, just stood there like he was frozen. All the air in the room felt like it had left, and there was nothing left but a buzz—a pull to him that I'd felt since I first met him. *Vampire.* I had to remember what he was. He'd told me, and I didn't doubt for a moment he was lying.

"Why did you do this?" He sounded hurt. I shrugged like I didn't know, but I did know. Now, with him like this, I felt ashamed of what I'd done. I swallowed the lump in the throat.

When he finally turned to me, his hazel eyes were hooded and he wouldn't meet my eyes. Instead, I could feel them on my body.

"Why do you suddenly care? You said everything would be fine. You told me to come back, to not run, and look what happened. I came back, and they kidnapped me. You can't tell me this is legal. You're just as bad as they are, because you let them do this. You handed me right over to Alaric and Nash. You told them I ran, and now they've put me here... I'll never forgive you for this, Galen."

My heart was pounding, and I was starting to lose it. I wanted to hit him. I wanted to scream. I wanted to wrap my arms around him and have him stroke my hair and tell me everything would be fine.

I didn't want to be here alone. I felt so alone here, like I was being punished. I was doing fine on my own, I didn't need to be here in Kiba, but I was. I'd finally had foster parents who gave a shit, who taught me how to cook muffins and made my bedroom look like mine...and now I was in this house that looked more like a hospital than a home. And the one person I wanted with me in this moment was only allowed to live in Kiba if I was living here. And I needed him...more than I'd ever needed someone.

"I'm sorry, Lexi. If I had a choice—"

I cut him off when I shoved him. His eyes flared to mine, as he wasn't expecting that. Then he left, the door clicked shut behind him, and I sank to the floor and buried my face in my hands.

What the fuck was I going to do? I shouldn't have run...

I fucked up.

CHAPTER THIRTY

RANGER

I *fucked up.*
She was here because of me, and she hated me even more than before. When my father had spoken to me in private yesterday, it was about how I felt this pull to her. Like I knew she was my mate, my wolf could feel it and wanted to be around her always. He didn't understand how that was possible, but said he would help me. I just didn't think this was what he'd meant by that.

"She isn't happy." I looked up to see Lyell shake his head at me. He was the second eldest of my brothers and usually didn't say much, especially to me. So for him to speak up like that surprised me.

If I had to say which of my brothers I was closest to, it wouldn't be him, or even my twin, Maverick. I was closer to Jett. He was only a year older than me, fun, loved doing pranks, and was the closest one of us to almost having a mate of his own. But then she up and left him to go to college, and no one was expecting that.

His best friend and packmate, Mekhi, really felt like this was the one for them. It was normal to have more than one shifter per female, but they'd yet to tell her about our world...and she just left. He'd been different ever since. He wouldn't talk to me about it, and Mekhi wouldn't either, so we'd all been left wondering what had happened. Maybe that was why my father took my claims about Lexi so seriously, because out of his five sons, I was the only one interested in finding a mate and being mated.

Nash grumbled, "No shit." If anything, I wanted to kill him. I stood up and slammed my hand on the table.

"You told her she wasn't dressed for company, and you made her feel like she didn't belong here. You're blackmailing her, I heard you. And now... If I thought I could even have a chance with her...that she would even look at me the same way she looks at—" I just couldn't take it. I wasn't going to sit down with my brothers and father, and share a meal with them. I stormed off and up the stairs.

In the hallway, I saw Galen leaving her room. He ran his hands through his dark curls, and they bounced free like loose springs as he walked toward me.

"Just leave her for now. She needs space." *Like I didn't already know that, old man.*

I heard her call out that night, and I rushed to her door. Lyell and Mav were there also. I knocked lightly, and when she didn't answer, I cracked it open and glanced around the room. It was dark, but I could see she wasn't in the bed. The covers were missing, though.

"Lexi? Lex?" I whispered into the room, trying to find where she was. Mav pulled me back when I smelled her fear. I made her feel that way, and it made me feel like shit. My stomach plummeted. *I really fucked up.*

I closed the door, and Mav led me back to my room, which was only a few doors down from hers. Lyell's room was between hers and mine. Lyell nodded at me before Mav shoved me into my room and closed the door behind us. He didn't say anything at first, and my wolf bristled for a fight, but there were rules about shifting in the house. Not like I was one for rules, but I didn't want to start shit with

Mav. His wolf was much stronger—even though I would never admit it.

"If you're not going to say anything, then fuck off. I know I fucked up. I know you don't understand. Look, I don't know what you have against her, but don't say it. I already know I've lost her before I even had a chance."

Yes, Lexi got his head turning those first few days, but now...he hasn't so much as looked at her without a scowl on his face. He hated her, and I could clearly see that. So when he looked at me then, his eyes full of unshed tears, I froze. I swallowed the lump forming in my throat. "Maverick..." He just shook his head and left my room, leaving me standing there, confused and sad. I'd never seen him that way, and I didn't know if I should go after him or not.

Two days. She'd not left the room in two days. Galen had been over and tried to speak with her, but she wouldn't have it. She shut down even more. She was hiding in the closet in a cocoon of pillows and blankets down at the far end. Each night, I heard her call out, screaming in the dark. The only person she'd let into the room was Lyell. He sat outside the closet, but in her eyeline, quietly reading for most of the day. And when he did, she didn't smell like fear anymore—she was relaxed.

But night was coming again, and I just didn't know how to help her. She was having these horrible nightmares, and I wanted to help her. Mav was even more quiet than usual, and I feared that her being here was the reason she was having these bad dreams. That we...that I did this to her.

"Father, I need to speak with you." I could see he was in a meeting with some of his betas, but I couldn't do this to her anymore. As much as I wanted her here, I knew she had to go back. I knew it was breaking her. I missed the feisty spirit she had. I missed our banter.

"Yes, Ranger. Be quick."

He never had time. He was always too busy, but that was the life of an alpha.

"We need to send her back, she needs Rafferty... She hasn't eaten dinner again. I just don't know how to help her. I know he can, I know he'll make this better for her. She trusts him."

It was hard to admit it, but it was the truth. I could see he was thinking about this. He wanted her here, and not just because I had asked, but because he wanted to protect her.

"He'll move here. I'll arrange it tonight."

CHAPTER THIRTY-ONE

LEXI

Lyell was sweet—if that was even possible in this family. He'd come and checked up on me a few times, and today, he brought me a book. He didn't say anything, he just placed it near me with a bottle of water and sat out in the bedroom against the bed, then opened his book and started reading like this was a normal, everyday thing.

I looked at the book he'd left me and saw he'd brought me *Emma*. I didn't know what to say, he must've seen what I was reading and bought it for me. Or he'd actually read it.

I hadn't been to school, but Galen had been around to see me, a lot. I couldn't face him, because I was so conflicted. On one hand, he gave me over to Alaric, but on the other, he was a fucking vampire, my teacher, and I wanted to...kiss him. My crush had gotten out of hand. I had daydreams where he'd be touching me, sucking my neck while Rafferty was kissing me and rubbing himself against me. It was crazy, fantasizing about them both, but I couldn't stop. I wanted to be mad at him, but I couldn't. So I was ignoring him.

I was hardly sleeping. I felt like shit, and when Nash brought me food, I refused to eat it. I didn't trust him, and I worried he would put something in my food.

Maverick brought me some breakfast, and considering how much he hated me, I actually felt safe eating it. He'd warned me away so many times, and now I knew why.

I heard talking outside my room, and Lyell stood. His nostrils flared—he did that when Galen came around. I was waiting for a lecture from Galen. He'd been sweet the last two days, but the last time he was here, he was growing frustrated. But when I saw the black boots, I looked up. Those amazing blue eyes looked down at me, the silver hair out of place. I sucked in a breath and held it. I didn't move. I feared I was now seeing things.

"Raff?" I whispered. Was I dreaming, or was he really here? "Why? How?" I suddenly realized I hadn't showered since I got here and probably smelled awful. I scrambled out of my blanket fort and got to my feet, then wavered a little from standing up so quickly. His eyes drifted to my bare thighs. I hadn't put on anything since my stupid stunt at dinner the other night.

"They asked me to move in." I saw Lyell behind Raff, who gave me a warm smile before he left the room, closing the door behind him and leaving Raff and me alone in my new white room. My heart pounded in my chest at the sight of him. He didn't look the same—his hair was all messy, he had dark circles under his eyes, and looked thinner. Was that possible?

"Have you been eating?" I went to him, placing my hand on his chest. I felt his arms hesitate at first, then they wrapped around me. I felt his head on mine as he inhaled my hair. I didn't care how bad I smelled in that moment, I just felt like a piece of my heart had returned and clicked into place. We stood like that for a while, breathing, feeling each other, until I pulled away to look up at him and wiped some tears from my eyes. He was really here.

"I should take a shower, I stink." He chuckled, it was deep and rumbling. I smiled, and everything felt right again in that moment.

"I like the way you smell." My mouth popped open. I forgot for a moment that he was a werewolf. Or shifter, as I'd heard so many times, not a werewolf.

"Tell me what I smell like to you. Like, what is it that you can smell being a...wolf?"

He hugged me to his chest again. It was a warm hug that felt like home, and I breathed in deeply, smelling him. He smelled like rain on a hot day. Knowing that I was something different, that I smelled different to shifters and regular people made me wonder...

"Shifters can smell many things—fear, sadness, when you're... happy." That last one made my heart speed up. Could he smell that I was attracted to him?

"Can you smell when someone is like, happy, happy?" I could feel my face heat up, and when he didn't say anything, I put my hands to my burning cheeks. "Holy shit. You can smell when a person is turned on?"

His mouth popped open, but he didn't say anything, he just nodded instead. I put my hand on his cheek, feeling the stubble there. He was beautiful.

"Can you smell me when I'm turned on?" He nodded and smiled slightly, never breaking eye contact.

"Can all the wolves smell it?" He glanced to the closed door, then back to me before he nodded again. *Holy crap.*

Raff was so different than most guys. He knew I was attracted to him—could smell it even—but had never tried anything more with me. I wondered if he was waiting for me to make the first move. I wanted to kiss him so bad, to touch him. My pulse picked up, and I licked my lips. I started to pull his face closer to mine—

"I have to tell you something," he whispered. He looked...*guilty.*

I told him to wait for me, that I would take a shower and then we would talk. I wasn't ready just yet for what he was going to say. He'd just gotten here, and I didn't need any more bad news. That look on his face worried me. *A lot.*

When I returned, I could see the bed was made and that Raff was just standing to the side like it was lava and he couldn't touch it.

"Did you make the bed?" I was a little confused about why he would do that. I was dressed in my pajamas, the same ones I got from Shelly—the large white T-shirt and green-checkered sleep pants. I was naked underneath...which made me feel a little naughty coming out to see him, knowing my top could lift and expose my breasts at any moment. I'd brushed my teeth, trying to smell my best. My stomach did a few flip-flops, but I wasn't hungry. If anything, I was nervous, and I worried that he would smell that too. God, how was I ever going to keep my feelings from these guys?

"No, um...Maverick did. He got fresh sheets and everything. I can't sleep in here, but I can stay until midnight. That was one of the rules for me to come live here."

I nodded, that sounded like a normal rule, but I was still confused about why Maverick had made the bed. That was odd. I crawled up, and the sheets were crisp and smelled nice as I got under them. I patted the bed, signaling for Raff to get in beside me. He shucked off his boots but sat on top of the sheets. That worried me even more.

"God, Raff, what is it? I just can't..." I was freaking out. What was he going to say? Oh my god, maybe he had a girlfriend back home. Maybe he didn't like me that—*No.*

"Jack and Grayson told me—and well, so did the alpha and Galen —that I had to tell you...what I...what I had done to you, been doing to you." I sat up straighter. What the hell had he done? I could see he was struggling to find the words. He wasn't someone who spoke a lot, so this was big. I was a little worried about what he would say.

I reached over and took his hand in mine. "You can tell me. Is it something I should be mad about?" He shrugged at first, then nodded, his head hanging low. What could he have done? They couldn't make you fall in love with them, right? They didn't have those kinds of powers.

"I claimed you. Well, I scent-claimed you without your permission." He pulled his hand away from mine and turned his back on me, his fingers raking through his hair. I could see he was shaking, and this was obviously big news, but I didn't get it. I had heard of the claim thing, and Jack said my smell called to the wolves. The wolves wanted to claim me, but they wouldn't let that happen. How did he claim me without me even knowing?

"What does that mean, Raff?" I pulled on his shoulder, and he finally let go of his hair.

"I have been marking you with my scent. Telling the other shifters that you were mine. Off limits, to stay away. That my wolf had claimed you, but I didn't ask you. I couldn't. You didn't know what I was, what our world was like. I...I didn't want to lose you to Ranger or one of the others. I knew I wouldn't stand a chance if you liked them. Grayson and Jack told me to stop, but I didn't. I should have. I was wrong to do it, and I'm sorry. So, sorry Lexi."

I was confused at first. So he marked me to tell the others that I was his? The first day fights about claims had been about this? I remembered Ranger yelling at Raff about making a claim, and I'd had no idea what they were talking about. He put his scent on me? He didn't want to lose me...

"Why didn't you just talk to me? I know I didn't know your world, but I liked you from the start, Raff. You didn't need to mark me to keep others away." I was conflicted. He did something without my permission, yet it didn't even seem to work anyway. There was a heap of guys who still smelled me and watched me.

Wait, unless the scent was what the problem was. *Oh god.*

"What is the scent?" Oh please, don't let it be something gross. I was thinking the worst thoughts about this claiming scent.

"It is just my pheromones. The other shifters would smell it and know you were claimed. It's like telling them you were dating someone, but through scent." He reached up to his throat. "I would rub myself on your clothes...mark them. They knew I didn't have a real claim, because I didn't smell like you. Well, only when we... The morning we woke up together and I didn't shower, I knew it would set Ranger off, but I didn't care. I wanted him to know what you meant to me, what I meant to you. I'm sorry, Lexi. It was my fault that you saw us shift."

I had so many questions but— "It's not your cum, right?" was the one I blurted out. His eyes flashed to mine. Yeah, I just asked that. Like of all the things I was thinking... The surprised look he gave me made me giggle.

"No, it's not...it's, um...not cum."

I wasn't upset with him, which surprised me. He'd done something that I didn't know about and tricked those other wolves into thinking that we were together, even when we weren't. If anything, I realized now just how much he liked me. I just couldn't smell his scent to know he'd done that.

"That's good. It would've been a different story if it was. I don't want you to be sorry, for any of it. Even if I didn't know you were marking me..." I let out a deep breath and moved a little closer to him. Those beautiful eyes warily followed me. "It tells others that I'm yours, right?"

He swallowed and nodded. That guilty look washed over his face again, but it didn't belong there.

"Do I smell like you now?" He shook his head as I crawled up and over the top of the sheets toward him. He watched my every move until I was right in front of his face, and I knew right then and there that I wanted Raff. I needed him like I needed air.

"Mark me," I whispered in his ear. He let out a low growl that I felt between my thighs as his hand reached out and grabbed my hip.

God, I wanted him to claim my body now.

CHAPTER THIRTY-TWO

LEXI

I woke up from a nightmare with a pounding heart and the bed drenched in my sweat.. The door to my room opened suddenly, and Raff was there. I almost cried at the sight of him, my hands calling him over without words. *I needed him.*

I could see Maverick and Ranger behind him as Raff came straight over, laid down beside me, and wrapped his arms around me tightly as I lay my hands on his bare chest. My eyes burned at the bright light coming through the doorway, so I closed them. The feel of Raff here relaxed me instantly.

"Did you want some water?" I heard Ranger ask, and the concern in his voice had me glancing over at him, still in the doorway. Maverick shifted on the heel of his foot, and when he looked up, our eyes met and my heart sped up a little. He didn't look so upset and angry with me. He looked...relieved? No, I was definitely seeing things. I felt Raff run his fingers down my back in a soothing gesture, and I let out a deep breath and settled into his warmth.

When I didn't answer, I heard Ranger tell Raff that if I need anything to call out. Then the door clicked shut behind them, leaving us alone. It didn't take long for Raff to get under the sheets and spoon me. My body relaxed, and I fell into a deep sleep.

I groaned from the warmth of too many blankets. I felt so hot, and my head was fuzzy, but my body was so relaxed. I'd slept so well. I realized that Raff was still with me, and he was breathing deeply, but I could tell he was awake.

"Raff?" I whispered. I heard him let out a deep breath as his body rolled toward mine. His breath was now on the back of my neck, and his arm snaked slowly over the top of the sheets and rested against me. I liked the feeling of his heavy arm over me. I felt so safe, so protected by him. I looked at the windows, and I almost forgot where I was. This big room at the Lovell's house was so out of my element, so not me.

"Lexi." I closed my eyes at the sound of my name rolling off his tongue. God, his voice was so deep, I could feel it inside me.

"Run away with me." I knew when the words came out of my mouth, I didn't really mean them. There was no way I was going to be able to get away from here, and neither was Raff. I had to finish school, go to college...I had a friend. *Oh god.* Ada. I hadn't spoken to her in days. I made a friend who was really amazing, and then I turned into the worst friend ever. *Shit.* I needed to turn my cell on.

"I would go anywhere with you, Lexi, but I can't keep you safe." He didn't tell me why, but I knew it had something to do with my smelling like something to shifters. That was different to what I thought was normal, but apparently, I wasn't exactly human.

I rolled over in his arms to face him, his hair all messed up and those eyes looking right into my soul. The feelings this guy gave me... I remembered what he'd said last night and what I'd asked him to do...he'd marked me. Then he'd come and saved me from my nightmares, and I'd fallen asleep with him. *Again.*

My body hummed with the sexual tension that always buzzed

between us. My breathing sped up slightly as his gaze wandered over my face to my lips, before he moved his arm from my waist and pushed my hair behind my ear, his hand lingering on my neck. My heart was going to pound out of my chest if he didn't kiss me.

Oh shit, he can smell me.

"Hi," I squeaked out. Why was I suddenly so nervous? Shit, just last night, Raff had spoken more words in the span of five minutes than he'd ever before. I could feel my cheeks heat. He could smell that I was turned on by him, and I had no idea if he felt the same. I wasn't sure I liked that he could smell me like that and that I couldn't smell him.

I reached my hand up from under the sheets and touched his bare chest. His body shivered at the touch, and he closed his eyes as I traced the outlines of his tattoos. I could feel his heart hammer against his chest, and his breathing sped up. When he opened his eyes, I knew he was turned on. I didn't need to smell anything to be able to tell that.

My lips parted as I looked at his mouth. I reached up to his cheek as I pulled him closer, willing him to close the distance between us so I could kiss him. Our eyes never left each other, until our noses touched. When he closed his eyes, I did the same, and then tilted my head, my lips softly grazing his. I could feel him suck in a breath before his lips pressed harder against mine.

I pulled him closer. I wanted our bodies together. I wanted to feel him, show him how much I wanted him, but the sheets were getting in my way. I felt his hand on my hip, and I gasped, wanting to take the kiss deeper, but he pulled back suddenly, and my eyes flared open.

"I'm sorry," he whispered as he pulled his hand away like I just burned him.

"Don't be sorry. I was just getting lost in the moment. I..." I didn't have words. What could I say? I was confused, but I didn't know his past. I might have overstepped or brought back some bad memories. *Fuck.*

He rolled away from me and muttered something under his breath. I felt cold and rejected. What the hell just happened?

"What did you say?" I demanded more than asked. I wished he would tell me, and be like he was last night—more straightforward. He rolled back over, his eyes barely meeting mine.

"I...I did it wrong." *Did what wrong?*

"Hey, I am so lost right now."

I watched his chest rise and fall before he looked at me. He looked a little lost.

"I've never kissed anyone before." I sat up straight and looked down at him. Now I was really confused.

"That was your first kiss?" He made a nervous sound and rolled his face way from mine.

"Yes..." he whispered.

Holy shit. I was his first kiss. Oh my god. If I was his first kiss, then... "You're a virgin." I slapped my hand over my mouth. Fuck, I... He tried to get farther away from me, but I grabbed his shoulders. He didn't pull away when I touched him. If anything, he relaxed into my touch like he needed it. He wasn't scared of me, he was just inexperienced. That was okay—actually, that was more than okay.

"Raff, I didn't mean it like that." When he finally rolled toward me, his eyes danced back to the bedroom door. Did he want to leave? I was having none of that. I pulled the sheets out and saw he was practically naked in my bed. He scooted up so his back rested against the headboard. I could feel my body heat up just from the sight of his body. He had some black boxer briefs on, and there was a tent—a big tent. When he saw where my eyes had landed, he tried to pull the sheets back over himself to cover it.

"Don't hide your body from me." I pulled the sheet down and straddled him. The feeling of his warm, hard body between my legs sparked that feeling deep inside me. I bent down to his face and kissed him, but I didn't back down. I parted my lips, and he followed. Slipping my tongue in, he met mine, and he didn't disappoint. For someone who'd never kissed before, he was a fast learner.

His hands hovered around, not knowing what to do, so I grabbed one and placed it on my hip. When he squeezed, I rubbed myself against his hard cock. He let out a deep moan, so I did it again. Rubbing my clit against him felt so good, I could get off just from that alone. But I wanted more. I wanted him inside me.

"Condoms?" I asked, just so caught up in the moment, my body responding to his in ways it never had before. That was when he froze and stopped me. I was panting, so close to climax, but his eyes darted to the door, then back to me. I looked over to the door, then placed my hand on his chest.

"Sorry, I was just caught up in the moment." At first, I thought I'd pushed him too fast too soon. He didn't move for a few moments, then smiled lazily at me. God, that was so sexy. Pushing my hair behind my ear, he took my mouth again. I moaned loudly when his cock nudged that sweet spot. I was so close, and I could feel my sleep pants slick with need. I started to take over, rubbing more and more until he held me still again. His breathing came out ragged as he looked between us. I could now see the wet patch on his boxers right where the head of his cock was. I traced my finger over the top, and his body shuddered before he grabbed my wrist to stop me. I playfully tilted my head and smiled.

"Did you..." His eyes widened as he looked down again. I could see his muscles tighten with every deep breath he took.

"Yes." He looked up at me, looking slightly embarrassed that he'd done that—come in his boxers. That was what I was hoping for too.

"I'm so close," I whispered as I rubbed my core against him again. He let out a shaky breath as I started to chase my climax again. So close...I could taste it—

"Did you know shifters have good hearing, as well as smell?" he asked, and I stilled. His eyes searched my face before he looked to the bedroom door again. I didn't know why he was telling me that at first, but then it dawned on me. Everyone in the house would have heard...

"They can hear everything?" I gasped. He nodded, and now I looked toward the door. Were they outside the room? I didn't say anything, but I gestured with my eyes, and he looked again. He closed his eyes and shifted his head slightly on the pillow.

He shook his head and pointed down. Oh, they were downstairs. Fuck, I didn't know that they could hear...everything. That was something they left out of the shifter lesson.

"Do you think they..." I mouthed, 'heard us?'

He nodded. I could see he was focused on what they were saying. He rolled his eyes and groaned. Oh my god, could he hear them talking about us?

"They're talking now about...?" I whispered, pointing down between us. When he didn't say anything, I knew that they were. Oh, what assholes. They should try to block it out. They'd get a show if they wanted to listen to something private, and this was between Raff and me. Not them. I smiled as I placed a hand over Raff's mouth. His eyes widened, and I winked at him.

"I want to suck your—" There was a huge banging sound, and my bedroom door flew open, slamming against the wall. My hand flew off Raff's mouth and to my throat in shock at how fast that happened.

Ranger was in my room, his chest heaving, and he emitted a rumbling growl which scared me. I didn't expect that. Maverick appeared just behind him, looking unaffected by the scene in front of him, but his eyes glared daggers into his brother. Then I saw Galen, and my mouth popped open. He was here? They'd all listened to me and Raff as I dry fucked him. My breath hitched. Galen heard me and Raff.

I looked back at Ranger and saw he was visibly shaking. I was playing with fire, but it was his fault. Fucking asshole, he listened to me and Raff. This was none of his business. God, I hated him.

When Galen's eyes met mine, he didn't look happy with me, but when was he lately? I always seemed to mess things up with him, and here I was again, messing shit up. I wanted Raff, I wanted what was happening between us, but there was a part of me that wanted Galen too. It was crazy to want them both. That was not how this worked. I got one, and that was all. But there was still a small part of me that wished he was here beside me.

Though he would never see me as anything more than this—a poor orphan girl who runs away and enjoys pissing off temperamental shifters at an alarming rate. I gave a sly smirk to Galen...the vampire. His brow rose in question.

"Neck. I want to suck your neck, Raff." I leaned over, not breaking eye contact with Galen, and licked just below Raff's ear before sucking his lobe.

CHAPTER THIRTY-THREE

RAFFERTY

Fuck, Lexi took control after I told her she was my first kiss. Like, way more than I thought she would do with me. After she asked me to mark her last night, I just couldn't believe this was happening, that I had a beautiful, amber eyed girl to mark. How did I hold out on kissing someone for all this time? It was the best feeling in the world.

Well, my uncles were the reason why. But now I was here and she was too, so there was no holding back now. I wanted this girl. She was mine.

My wolf wasn't happy about Ranger downstairs, snickering and laughing about my virgin status. I blocked him out as best I could, but I could hear him laugh and Galen telling him to stop it. I knew he was doing it to piss me off, throw me off, but I didn't let it get to me. I kept kissing Lexi.

The one thing I didn't expect to happen was Lexi rubbing her tiny little self on my cock. Our clothes were on, but I was so aroused. I didn't know if it was her scent that had tipped me over, but when she asked if I had condoms, I knew that really pissed off Ranger, and even Maverick was not impressed.

Then I *came*. I fucking came in my boxers. I was so caught up with her, rubbing against me, kissing me, and I tried to stop, but I couldn't. I was so embarrassed that I'd done that. I'd never come that fast before, but then again, I'd never had a girl rubbing herself against me before.

When she said that last line, I knew she was just doing it to get a rise out of them after I told her they could hear us, but I didn't care. She was on top of me, she was in my arms...she was marked with my scent.

The first one up the stairs was Ranger—I could hear him. Maverick was on his tail, muttering about saving his brother's ass. I didn't expect Galen to come up, but now he was there, I could sense he wasn't happy to see where Lexi was sitting. But even more than that, I knew the room smelled of both our arousal and my cum.

I didn't know much about vampires, but the way he watched me, I could tell he wished he was here, under her. I'd gotten that feeling from the way he was always watching her. She was teasing him now. He knew it, and I actually felt bad for the guy. When the tip of her tongue touched my neck and she traced a line up to my ear and sucked my earlobe, I shuddered. How did something so small feel so *good*?

I felt the moment Ranger shifted. The air in the room grew tight, and my wolf begged to come to the surface to protect what was mine.

I growled lowly as I grabbed Lexi's hips and spun her away from him.

"Ranger, for fuck's sake. This isn't winning any brownie points for you," Galen yelled at him. I could see Ranger had shredded his clothes shifting. *Dumbass.* He was so weak, always giving into the anger. He had no discipline.

Lexi squeaked, and I could smell the fear rolling off her in waves. She reached out and held onto my arm, shielding her body from Ranger.

You see that, Ranger? She wants me to protect her from you. She's mine. I growled lowly again, warning him that I would shift if I had to, but only to protect her. I wouldn't fight him unless he charged at me, I would protect her at any cost. Maverick wasn't fucking around and letting this play out this time. He was actually concerned, which set my wolf off even more. I was on the edge and so close to shifting.

"Ranger, shift back. Father will know, and he's going to be pissed. For fuck's sake, she isn't yours. Get it through your head. You. Are. Scaring. Her."

Ranger's jaw snapped at his brother before he turned to me and let out a loud growl that pushed my wolf to the surface. I pushed Lexi away as I let my wolf come forward.

"Raff," she called out as heat and pain hit me for a brief moment, then I was on all fours. I leaped off the bed and stood defensively, protecting what was mine. She was mine, she wore my scent. Why couldn't he see this? When I heard a loud call through the house, my wolf whined. I tried to hold it, but I couldn't. The alpha was here, and he was calling for submission. I looked up and saw Maverick was on his knees.

The thundering footsteps up the stairs told me it wasn't just Alaric. He'd told me the rules last night, one of which was no shifting inside the house.

"I leave and come back to this! Maverick, Ranger, leave now. Go to your rooms, I'll deal with you later."

There was a growl from Alaric when Ranger didn't move. Ranger's eyes locked onto me, letting me know this wasn't over, but I already knew that. He wanted Lexi as much as I did. If I was him, I wouldn't back down either, but I also wouldn't do what he was doing. It was exactly what Galen had said—not winning brownie points. I didn't have a packmate, but I grew up a shifter, just like him. If he was smarter, he wouldn't keep challenging me like this.

"Rafferty was only protecting Lexi," Galen said. He didn't look at me, and I couldn't get up—I was waiting for Alaric to release me.

"This ends now, this is your first and last warning. I told you the rules, and you didn't last twenty-four hours before breaking two of them. If you're going to live under the same roof, you'll need to tolerate each other. The same rules apply to all my sons."

The rules were simple—keep out of trouble, attend school, and get good grades. Don't shift in the house. And the biggest rule was no sleeping with Alexis, and her door was to stay open with any of the boys in there. So yeah, I guess I actually broke more than two rules.

I could hear Lexi's bare feet touch the floor beside me, her fear settling down like she knew she was projecting it and could stop herself.

"Well, Ranger needs to learn how to knock. He just flew in here and growled at me. Then he turned into a wolf and growled more. I would appreciate him not doing that. I could've been naked."

Alaric grumbled under his breath, and I could sense he was conflicted. I guess having a headstrong teenage girl that your son was determined to have as a mate living under your roof was frustrating. Plus, add in the foster kid that she wants and needs, and who has marked her... Well, I could see that this could be stressful. He wasn't a bad alpha, far from it, truthfully.

"I'll speak to him. In the meantime, it would be great to get you to school one day this week. So please, get ready. Galen can drive you both." Alaric waved his hand at Galen, and I felt the pressure release me, then the door clicked as Alaric and Galen left. I stood up on all fours, my wolf loving being so close to Lexi in this form. I felt her shift beside me, and I slowed my movements as I turned to look up at her.

"Can I...pet you?" I laughed, but it came out as a *wruff* sound. I stepped forward to where her arm was stretched out toward me and butted my snout against her hand. When she ran her hands up and over my ears, I couldn't stop. My wolf wanted to twist around her and rub my scent on her legs. She giggled at the movements.

"You're tickling me." She giggled again and sat down on the floor. We were almost the same height like this, and I could see her search my eyes.

"They like, glow. You're so cute, Raff. You're smaller than

Ranger, but I like that because you still jumped in to protect me. You know what?" She was stroking my fur and it felt amazing. "I never had a pet before." I looked up and saw the playful glint in her eyes.

Oh really? Teasing again? I did what all 'man's best friends' did. I licked her face.

CHAPTER THIRTY-FOUR

LEXI

I was late down to breakfast after I took an extra long shower, and I only caught a glimpse of Raff before he was told to get in the car. Alaric told me that I had to keep this to myself. That if I went around telling people about shifters that Galen would have to wipe their memory. That was enough to scare the shit out of me, and then I wondered how the hell he wiped people's memories. I decided I didn't want to know. *Shit.* He was a vampire. He could have killed lots of people, but he didn't look scary. No, he drew you in with those kissable lips, those eyes... He could kill me, and I wouldn't even be sad about it.

The ride to school was awkward. Galen had told Raff to sit up front with him, so by the time I got to the car, I had to sit in the back seat, *like a child*. I was just happy to be riding in this car, rather than with Ranger and Maverick.

Ranger had offered to drive me many times while his father was trying to scare the shit out of me about the 'big secret.' I rolled my eyes at Ranger for the fifth time. *Yeah, sure, ignore what you did earlier. I haven't forgotten, and I won't.* The guy who couldn't control himself, listening in on private conversations... *Sure, I'll ride with you. What a dumbass.*

Galen parked in the teacher's parking lot, and I didn't wait for Raff to get out before rushing into the school. I didn't want any of the girls to know Galen drove me here, because I wasn't in the mood for bitch fights and drama. And when it came to Galen, I could tell there would be a lot of both.

I walked into the school and was instantly stared down by a lot of males, *large males*. All, I assumed, were shifters.

Shit, shit, shit.

"Hey, Alexis. I'm Noah." Ah, fuck. I guess the 'don't talk to Lexi' thing had been lifted. That, or this guy had more balls than anyone.

I spun on my heel and faced Noah. I when I looked up, he was smiling at me. Why were so many of them tall, ripped, and attractive? Were any of these shifters unattractive?

"Uh...do you like living with the Lovells? My mom said you can come chat with her, if you want. You know, about things and, ah... Come over for dinner?" I just stared at him. He knew about me moving in with them? Fuck. Of course he knew, he was a shifter. I bet the whole fucking school knew about me living with Ranger. *Ugh.* Could today get any worse?

Another guy, who looked like an older version of Noah, swung his arm around his neck, put him into a headlock, and winked at me.

"Hey, get off, Callum!" Noah tried to spin around and push away from him, so I took that as my cue to leave. But as I turned, I found more of them surrounding me.

"Hey, I'm Harley." I looked over to a tall guy who I'd seen before in English. My heart started racing. They were intimidating for anyone, and the fact that I knew they turned into wolves...yeah, that made this worse

I looked toward the door I'd come in. Where was Raff? I shouldn't have run off from him. Then again, I also didn't want him to get into more fights, and these guys were the ones who'd been attacking him. I needed Galen. I didn't want to need him, but I knew he'd be able to help me. There was a group of shifters all staring at me, and they had me caged me in like a mouse.

"Get away from me," I shouted as I pushed against the smallest one, who was still taller than me. His chest was warm and hard, and his dark eyes and nostrils flared at my touch, but he didn't budge. It was like he was made of stone. He quirked his brow at me and looked down to where I touched his chest, then his mouth parted just as he was shoved away.

"Move, Luca." Maverick appeared in front of me. "All of you, fuck off. You know the rules."

I could feel the guys behind me shuffle, and I worried what they were doing behind my back, so I turned suddenly and saw they didn't look happy.

"But, but—" one started, but Maverick cut him off with a low growl that scared me. I didn't think I would ever get used to that—the growling like an animal thing. It was so foreign coming from a human.

"Hey, Mav...Ranger and I are packmates, you know that, right?" When Maverick growled again, I was ready for it. He sounded different than Ranger. Holy shit, the others were scared of him, too. I still didn't really like him, but he was growing on me. Better the devil you know and all that. I found myself taking a step backward, away from the others and closer to Maverick.

"There's a claim," he ground out. The guys just shook their heads and started to protest. When Noah took a step toward me, I freaked out that he was going to touch me, so I stepped back and hit a wall...of Maverick. I froze, and all the air sucked out of my lungs. I went to sidestep him, but his hand reached out and grabbed my waist to stop me. My back was flush against him, and I could feel the hardness of his body. The smell of pine made me relax slightly in his hold. He smelled like summer, and I didn't know why it affected me so much.

"Bullshit," Callum muttered under his breath. I looked down to where Maverick's hand was on my hip, and his fingers tightened slightly. Finally, the bell rang and they all disbursed, grumbling and muttering under their breath, but I stood still. Maverick didn't let go of me, and to be honest, I didn't want him to. It was wrong, he hated me...but then he fed me breakfast and, *ugh*. Why were guys so complicated? Why was all of this so messed up?

I could feel his thumb brush over the exposed skin just above my jeans, and I sucked in a breath. What the hell was happening? I could hear him breathe deeply, his breath tickling the hairs on the back of my neck. He dropped his hand from my hip, and I almost stumbled backward to feel him. His head moved over my shoulder beside my ear, and I tilted my neck to his mouth. It was such a natural movement, so I didn't know I was even doing it.

"Go find Rafferty. He needs to mark you before the other packs find you, smelling like theirs...*mine*." The last word was barely a whisper, as if I wasn't supposed to hear it. It sent a shiver down my spine as he inhaled my hair and left me there. I was a little disoriented. Did that just happen?

I couldn't find Raff, and I was freaking out. The bell had rung, and I didn't know what class he had now. I was hoping to see Ada in English lit. Lucky, I had history straight after English today, so Galen would be able to help me. Maybe, hopefully.

"Hey," Ada said as she beamed at me. "I was wondering when you were coming to school." I looked over and saw Callum staring at me. Shit. I just had to get through this class.

"Yeah, I'm sorry. I wasn't feeling well. Had to take a few days off." We couldn't talk more as class had already started, and I tried my best to avoid Callum's gaze. I felt a tapping on my arm as Ada slipped me a note.

I opened it. *'I think Callum Jones has a crush on you.'* Ah...shit. I had a feeling he wanted to have more than just a little crush. I nodded, and she beamed at me. No...no this was bad, not good. But how did I tell her that? I quickly scribbled back that I was interested in Raff. When she read it, she giggled and winked at me. I felt a little giddy too. It was nice to be with her and share this little bit with someone that wasn't a guy.

A few guys followed me to history. Thank god I was late, so I could just get in and take a seat.

"Nice of you to join us, Miss Turner." I looked up to see Galen with that smile, the sexy godlike one. How was anyone not affected by that? I glanced around the room to the mostly female class, and yep, they were all affected just like me. The blonde girl at the front of the class even glared at me. Yeah, and this was why I ran from his car. I didn't want to be seen with him...or Ranger. Because if there were two guys here at school that every girl wanted, it was them. They could have Ranger all they wanted. I didn't want him. *I didn't.*

"Hey, Lex. Saved you a seat." Now it was my turn to glare, since the only free seat was next to Ranger. And for the love of... He called me Lex. I moved between the desks, pissed off and angrily took a seat beside him. He stiffened up a little, then leaned over toward me, and I leaned away. What was he doing?

"Ranger, do you wish to move seats?" We both turned our heads up to where Galen was watching us.

"No, thank you, Galen. I'm perfectly fine here next to my special friend." I groaned when everyone's heads turned to look at us. Today was going to be a day from hell. I gave Ranger a look that was supposed to make him shut his mouth, but he just smirked and winked at me. Then he moved in and sniffed me.

"Freak," I muttered under my breath. 'Cause yeah, that was what he was—one of those sniffing freaks.

"Shit, you don't smell like him. That makes you fair game, Lex. This isn't good." I realized he was telling me the same thing Maverick did, and I started to get worried. This was bad then, if he was being all serious.

"I didn't know, okay?" Like yeah, I couldn't smell the scents or whatever it was, so how was I supposed to know when I smelled like

Raff or not? I guessed I'd washed him all off when I had that shower this morning.

"Shit, did you have trouble on the way to class? Is that why you were late?" I looked into his green eyes. God, he was gorgeous—and he knew it. I didn't answer him as I turned away. He figured it out for himself.

"Look, Galen can hear us. He'll help, okay? Fuck, was it bad? Do I need to call my father?"

I spun to him and watched as he ran his fingers through his hair and swept it over to the side. Where it always was, so perfect and...

"I'm a big girl, Ranger. I can take care of myself."

CHAPTER THIRTY-FIVE

LEXI

Raff wasn't hard to find when you had a teacher who could hear you all the way from the back of the class. As class ended, Ranger told me to stay, and then Raff walked through the door not a minute later. I sagged in relief. I'd never been so happy to see him as I did in that moment.

I stood as he came for me, and we wrapped our arms around each other like we hadn't seen each other in years, when in reality, it was only hours ago.

"I'm so sorry. I didn't smell you when you got in the car. Galen's scent is strong, and I didn't know. I'm so sorry. Are you okay?" I nodded into his chest. I loved that Raff wasn't as big as the other guys —he was smaller in both wolf and human form. I didn't say anything as he started to rub his cheek over mine, my neck—he rubbed any bare skin he could.

"Yeah, I think she's good and well stunk up now," Ranger mumbled.

I wanted to laugh, but instead, I pulled Raff down and kissed him. When he opened his mouth, I melted into his arms. His tongue swept over mine, and I wanted to taste him. Then a throat cleared, and we pulled away, our eyes meeting each other. Raff's eyes were hooded and almost sparkled. I smirked and giggled at getting lost in each other so quickly. I started to remember this morning...

"Alright, you're scented—I can smell that from here—but we don't really want the others to smell what's coming off you now." Galen moved into view, and my eyes met his. My hand flew to my mouth as I looked around the classroom. Ranger looked away, pretending to look out of the window. He didn't even have a comeback for that.

"Oh god." This was... Fuck.

"It's okay, don't worry about it," Raff said as he ran his hands down my back in a soothing way.

I took Raff's hand in mine. "Do you think that this is enough to keep them away? Like, are they going to keep attacking him?" When no one answered, I got pissed. "Why not? What did Raff do? This doesn't make sense to me. I want him, and he marked me. Can't you smell it?" I moved toward Ranger, who'd turned to see my crazy outburst, and stretched my arms out. He gave me a small smile and nodded.

"Then what's the problem?"

It was Galen who spoke up this time.

"Lexi, I thought Jack and Grayson told you everything...but I guess not." He cleared his throat.

"Take a seat, Lex." Ranger took a seat beside me. I looked to Raff, and he nodded but didn't let go of me as he pulled me to sit back down at the desk and then sat across from me.

My heart was racing. They'd left out the super hearing thing. What else could there be?

I turned to Raff when Galen didn't say anything. His eyes went a little wild, and he opened his mouth, then closed it. He didn't want to tell me? Or he couldn't put it into words?

"I'll start, since I come from a pack where this is...well... That this is...um, shit. Galen?" Ranger looked to Galen. His head was forward and his big, dark curls covered his eyes.

"In the wolf shifter societies—and in bears and a few others—they've been cursed. Have you heard of this?" I nodded. The curse was that they couldn't have females, so they turned normal females into wolf-shifters. I pressed my back hard against the chair. What the hell? I wasn't going to be one. *No way.*

"Nothing is happening to you, calm down, Lexi. I was just trying to figure out where to start. So, I guess you know about the venom and how to turn a female. Works the same for my kind. But with shifters, there isn't always success with the transformation. Because of that, what most packs do is pair or group males together. They usually pick their packmates when they're young, typically around their first shift. You still with me?"

Loud and clear, but this time, I wasn't so freaked out like when Jack told me. This was easier. I didn't know if it was because of Galen or because Raff was holding my hand. He squeezed it, like he knew I needed to feel him still with me.

"So, a packmate is like Jack and Grayson?" Ranger let out a strange sound, then coughed. I watched him cover his mouth. He raised his hand up in apology to me.

"Sorry, that is a little different. They're gay and bonded mates. Not bi."

Okay, I already knew that. Oh...*oh*. Callum. He said he was Ranger's packmate.

"Callum is your packmate. You're bi." I didn't realize Ranger was bi with the way he was all over the girls at school and forever tormenting me with his shitty pick-up lines. Plus the way he acted so rudely about thinking his brother was gay...he was deflecting from the real him.

My words had Ranger's eyes flare, and his mouth dropped open, then closed. I'd never seen him speechless. I quickly reached over to his fist, which was holding on to the edge of the desk, his knuckles white, and placed my hand over it.

"I'm sorry. Callum said that to Maverick earlier. I didn't realize you weren't open like that. Raff and I won't say anything." I looked over, and Raff's brows were drawn in a puzzled look toward Ranger. When Raff caught my eye, he nodded and smiled. God, he was such a beautiful guy. I turned back to Galen, who was watching us all, his head bouncing back and forth between us.

"Ranger, I didn't know. I thought that just Mav was bi, but if—"

Ranger suddenly moved and stood. "Mav is bi? What the fuck? He never said anything... He didn't tell me." Ranger looked upset. I guessed since Galen was his teacher, or the wolf vampire guy, and he knew more about his twin brother than he did.

Ranger turned to me. "I'm not bi, Callum is my packmate. He's my best friend. We made that pack together when we were thirteen. It means that when I find a mate, he and I will both mate with her. She'll have both of us, bond with both of us." He looked to Galen for help as I let the words sink in.

"So, are you telling me that you and Callum will share a female?" They all nodded.

"But...wait up. What happens if the girl doesn't want you both?"

I could see Ranger was still distracted by the news about Maverick, so Galen spoke up. "So, there are families in Kiba where there's a female and two or three males. Then there's the Jones family. Callum and his brothers have four fathers and one mother. The only family in Kiba that doesn't have this is the Lovells. Since Alaric is alpha, it would be impossible for him to share, and all their offspring are alpha-born."

Wow, talk about an info dump. Callum had four dads? *Holy shit.*

"Do...vampires share, too?" That caught Galen off guard. He shifted on the desk he was sitting on.

"Not usually, no. And not with wolves...*usually.*" He muttered the last word. *Usually.* Was he saying that he would share if it was the right person? God, when he looked at me like that, it was hard to forget he was like mega old and drank blood. Like, I assumed he did, since he hadn't spoken about himself at all. But yeah... Wait.

"Raff, do you have a packmate?" Shit, how did I not think to ask that? He just chuckled, squeezed my hand, and shook his head.

CHAPTER THIRTY-SIX

MAVERICK

Ranger had been avoiding me today and the ride home was tense. When Rafferty marked Lexi, things calmed down a small bit, but the shifters were still pissed that she was with a rogue wolf. They didn't understand why she wouldn't choose a more 'worthy' mate.

Honestly, Rafferty was worthy. I'd seen what he'd done for her—how he made her smile and helped her sleep through those nightmares she had. If any shifter deserved her, he did. Even though he did mark her without her knowing, which was dodgy as fuck. But he told her, and then she asked him to mark her. I heard them last night. I'd tried not to listen, but after days of her sadness, I wanted to see what made her happy so I could maybe try. But it was Rafferty that made her happy, just by being there.

In the last few days, I'd realized I was fucked. Her scent was around my house, lingering through the doorways...and god, when she wore barely anything to dinner. Yeah, I couldn't keep those thoughts out of my head and spent too much time in my shower afterwards. So did my brothers, which I wished I hadn't heard, especially since they were probably thinking about Lexi too.

"What happened?" I thought that maybe Lexi had said something to upset him, but then again, she was always rejecting him, and he was usually even more determined to be her mate. He just wasn't the usual Ranger—and everyone had noticed today at lunch.

"Is there anything you want to tell me? You know, 'cause you're my brother. My twin?" he snapped at me. I shifted to look at him as he drove us home. I tried to think of what he might be mad about. I didn't think he would've cared this much about how I had to move in and protect Lexi from some Kiba shifters and his packmate. That was over and done with. Fixed.

"You're mad that I didn't tell you about Lexi being unmarked this morning?" I honestly had no clue. When his eyes flashed to mine, I could see he was getting close to shifting. Fuck.

"Just tell me, and don't fucking shift in the car. I don't know what you're talking about."

The air in the car was getting thick, and I could smell his anger, but then there was something else. Sadness?

"Ranger, please. I'll tell you anything, just calm down."

After a few minutes, I could finally feel him start to relax. He took a few deep breaths. "Are you bi?"

I was a little taken aback by that, as I wasn't expecting it. Shit. I'd only told one person that. Years ago, I'd told Galen that I liked boys, but that I also liked girls the same way. He told me that was natural, especially with shifters, but I never spoke about it again. *Fuck.* I hung my head. I could understand why he was upset. I didn't tell him, and my own twin found out from Galen.

"So, it's true. You told Galen, but not me. I didn't know we kept secrets. Shit, is that why you haven't been into any of the girls at school? I feel like such a shit brother. I should have figured this out sooner. Until Lex came along, you never did anything...did you? With girls, I mean. I've never seen you hook up, but I should have known."

I ran my hands down my face and groaned. Yes, I'd been with

girls, but I hadn't been with any guys. That was something I hadn't worked out yet.

"I've been with girls. I'm not a virgin." The car suddenly stopped short, and the belt pulled against my chest before my head hit the headrest.

"Hey, what the hell?" I could see our place just up ahead, but that didn't stop Ranger. He turned to me.

"Look, I know we haven't been the best twin brothers. Well, I probably haven't been the best since Mom died. But I just found out that you're bi, and you're also not a virgin. These are things you could've shared with me. I know, I know...you're the quiet brother, the steady one, and I'm the loose cannon with a big mouth." He looked out the window, and I could see what he was staring at—Lexi was getting out of the car and Rafferty swung his arm over her shoulder and walked her into the house. They looked so happy, and I wished I was there, part of that.

Wow. Okay, hold up. Where did that thought come from? No, I didn't. I didn't want that. *I'll just keep telling myself that.*

"Who was it?" Ranger asked. Who was who? I looked at him confused. "Your virginity?"

Fuck. I didn't want to tell him that, but I'd rather just get it out since he was kinda into her for a while. "Olivia."

Ranger's mouth dropped open, and his brows creased. "Really? Olivia the one I was fucking?" I nodded. The very same one, except before Ranger came along, she had taken my virginity. When I realized the shitty mistake I'd made, I told her that I wouldn't tell Ranger or any of the Kiba boys if she wanted to move on with them. I knew that some of them might not have liked that I'd been with her, especially since I was the son of the alpha. She would've been off limits to the others. I didn't want to do that to her because I'd made the mistake.

"Huh, anyone else? Like...Saint?" I didn't look at Ranger, but I knew why he would assume Saint. He was my closest friend, practically my packmate, but we'd never really spoken about that—it wasn't official or anything. I wasn't sure about his feelings toward me in that way. I was pretty sure Saint was straight, but I liked him, a lot. He was attractive, but I didn't see myself with him—we had too much history. There'd only been one guy I'd ever wanted to kiss, and I wasn't about to tell my brother that.

"No, no. I haven't even told him. Just fucked Olivia, and that was one time and I regretted it right after. It might seem old-fashioned, but I wish I'd saved myself. You know, for the *one*. My mate. Instead, I was horny and had a few beers in me. Olivia asked if I wanted to fuck, and my cock said yes...and my head was too drunk to tell me no. But my heart reminded me straight after, and I felt like shit. I promised not to tell anyone, because I didn't want her that way. It was stupid mistake I made last year. I'm sorry I didn't tell you, but then you two were really together for a time there. I wanted to tell you for so long, but as more time passed, I realized I was too late. I took too long, so I didn't say anything."

Ranger moved over and surprised me when he wrapped me in a hug. My arms wound around his body, and I released a deep breath, relaxing into his forgiving hug.

"Mav, fuck. Dude, you've gotta talk to me more. You have to let me in. I hate this. We used to be so close. We need that again." There was a long silence. I debated whether to tell him about my feeling toward Lexi or not. I held him tighter, worried he would pull away.

"Lexi, she smells like mine. She's mine."

Lyell was waiting for me in my room when I got inside the house. I felt emotionally exhausted, and I wasn't in the mood for anyone, even him.

"Lexi came and spoke to me." Her name had my ears pricked. Lyell was not one to talk, so this must be important. I flopped onto my bed and turned to show him I was listening.

"She finished *Emma*, so I gave her the copy of *Sense and Sensibility*."

I nodded. That was good. I was glad she was seeking out Lyell and he could help her like that.

"Well, you only gave me those two. I thought you might want to stock up on more. Or maybe get her a Kindle? Then she can load up on all the books she wants."

Why didn't I think of that?

"That's a great idea, and I'll look into it. I'm just tired. I'm gonna have a nap." He left, closing the door behind him, and I sunk deep into my bed. I tried not to think of all the day's events, but my mind wouldn't be still.

Ranger didn't speak to me after I told him that Lexi was mine. I wasn't sure if he was upset with me or upset that she smelled like that to so many shifters. But it had to be said, because I couldn't keep lying to him.

Lying to myself.

CHAPTER THIRTY-SEVEN

LEXI

I was in the kitchen making a sandwich when Jett appeared. He surprised me at first, since he just kind of snuck up on me.

"That looks good."

I didn't know what to say to that. Did he want me to make him one? He just smiled and moved around me, pulling out a large bag of Doritos. He opened it and proceeded to watch me clean up the mess I made.

"Did you want to watch a movie with me?" I looked back at him. Um... I looked for someone else, but it was just the two of us here. Why did he want to watch a movie with me?

"I saw you like reading Jane Austen. We have like, every movie you could want, so I'm sure we have all the Austen adaptions. I've seen *Pride and Prejudice*, the one with Kiera Knightly. That one's pretty good. Or we could watch *Clueless*...that's based off of *Emma*." I took a bite of my sandwich and just watched him as he spoke to me, like this was normal. It was normal for him to have me in his kitchen fixing myself a sandwich while he ate his Doritos and talked about watching a movie with me.

Raff had gone upstairs to his room when we got home. I followed him up and found Lyell on my way. I returned *Emma* to him, and he gave me a new one. I'd never read *Sense and Sensibility*. I thought I would make myself some food—I couldn't believe how much food was in this house.

Raff had told me to come in his room whenever I wanted, as he was just catching up on some homework. He was giving me space, which was nice. I'd never been in a relationship before, and well...I guess this was what we were now. He was my boyfriend, right? Was he? Honestly, I was still trying to process the whole 'multiple mates' thing from earlier.

"We have a popcorn machine." They did? I cocked my brow, and he knew he had me at popcorn. He chuckled.

"Come on, bring your plate. You haven't had a tour yet, have you?" I shook my head. I didn't know what half this house held. It was huge, and I'd only been in a few rooms. As Jett led me down a hallway, I started to worry that this was a bad idea. Was he leading me somewhere to get me alone?

"It's okay, you don't have to fear me, Lexi." He smiled again, and it was warm and he seemed genuine. I nodded and followed him. Raff said shifters had really good hearing, so he would hear me if I called out. *Right?*

"Here's the movie room. It's got a stocked fridge, and here's the popcorn machine. I'll start it up." I slowly edged into the room. *Holy shit.* He wasn't joking, it was a full movie theater with the red velvet walls and seating. There was a row of seats across the top and the bottom row was like a giant bed, with pillows and a few throws. This was the most colorful room in the whole house, and I felt like I could spend all day here.

"Take a seat." He gestured to the seating, so I moved down to the front and sat down. I positioned a pillow behind me and took a bite from my sandwich. "Water?" Jett held up a bottle of water, and I nodded. He threw it at me, so I held onto my plate and flinched away, but it landed just away from me then rolled gently toward me. "Sorry, I wasn't throwing it at you."

It didn't take long for me to relax and the screen started up.

"The one with Keira Knightly?" he asked, referring to the movie that I'd never seen. I didn't watch very many movies. I'd only really seen *Twilight*, and that was because I read the books. So I was a little excited.

"Yes, please." Most of the lights went off, just a small strip of light where the stairs were leading down to the bottom glowed softly. Then the sound switched on and the movie started, and it was all around me like I was inside the movie. I placed my empty plate beside me and pulled a throw up over me. This was perfect...too perfect.

When I felt the spot beside me dip slightly, I saw Jett had a huge bowl of popcorn between us. He reached in, grabbed a handful, and brought it to his mouth. He shoved so much in at once, he started to cough, and I laughed. His eyes flashed to mine, and they crinkled at the edges.

"Glad you thought that was funny...I was dying here." And with that, I turned back to the movie, smiling as we ate and watched in a comfortable silence. It was the first time since being here that I felt comfortable in the presence of a Lovell brother. Other than Lyell, but this was different. This wasn't sitting with me out of pity. This was wanting to hang out with me.

While the credits were rolling, Jett leaned over and wagged his eyebrows at me. "Pretty good?"

I giggled. "That was so much better than I expected. Oh man...all the feels," I said as I held my hands to my chest. It was so romantic, and the scene in the rain... *So hot.*

"Now, let's watch a real movie," someone shouted from behind. I turned and saw Ranger standing in the doorway just as he started to bound down to us. I rolled my eyes. Really?

"You're spoiling a good moment here," I told him, wishing he would just go away.

"Not that it wasn't a real movie, that was great. But I mean, let's watch something with more...action," Ranger said, a smile on his face. I looked over to Jett, who was watching Ranger as he bounced over and started up the popcorn machine again. I looked down to our bowl and saw it was empty except for a few un-popped corn kernels. Ranger reminded me that it was time to leave, as Raff was waiting for me in his room. Shit, which one was his room again? I got up, and some popcorn fell off my lap. I reached down and started to pick it up to put it on my used plate. Jett stood and did the same.

"Don't leave because the dumbass arrived. We can order some pizza, sit back, and watch something else. Maybe make a night of it?" Now I felt weird. Was there something going on? Was he trying to keep me in here on purpose?

"No." I pushed past Jett and heard Ranger call my name, but my heart started to race. Was the door locked? Did they lock me in? When it opened, I felt like I could breathe again. I quickly made my way down to the kitchen, still holding the dirty plate. Then I saw Raff, and he was laughing. Wow, I'd never seen him laugh like that. I was trying to look at who he was laughing with when Raff turned, those beautiful blues twinkling at me.

I guess I couldn't sneak up on him, even if I wanted to.

"Was the movie good?" he asked as I slowly padded toward him.

"Huh?" Oh yeah, he could hear the movie. I wasn't sure I would get used to this amazing hearing thing. I nodded and smiled to myself. The movie was just as good as the book, maybe better because Mr. Darcy was so hot. At first, I wasn't sure, but as the movie progressed along, he was every bit the Darcy I dreamed of.

"Jett mentioned pizza and watching movies? I think that's a great idea." I turned to see Galen. He had on a dark sweater and tight blue jeans. Oh man. His lazy smile made my heart skip a beat. No, no...he wasn't for me. He was old—okay, he looked young but was old—and a vampire, who may or may not drink blood. I was still curious about that, but the number one reason I had to stop thinking like that was because he was my *teacher*. I had Raff, the sweet and amazing Rafferty King. I quickly made my way to him and, as if to prove to Galen that he didn't affect me, I hooked myself under Raff's arm. He laughed again, this time at me, and the sound was like music to my ears.

"Hey," he whispered to me. I looked up and smiled

"Hey, back." Then I heard a clearing of a voice. I turned to see Nash was here. *Great*. Followed by Maverick. Guess the whole family was home.

"I'll order the pizza. What does everyone want?" Nash asked a little louder then needed. I didn't say anything, since I still didn't want to speak to him after what he did to Raff. But then I saw him nod a couple of times. Holy shit, Nash was taking their order and I couldn't even hear them. This was crazy. When he looked to me, I shrugged.

"I will eat whatever there is. I like pizza," Raff said. Nash raised his brow at me, then shrugged as he looked to Galen. I placed the plate down in the sink.

"Pepperoni."

I looked over to Galen, who smiled at me, knowing I was watching him. He never ate... Why was he getting pizza?

"Let's go pick a movie, before Ranger picks what he wants," Maverick said as he walked out of the kitchen to the movie room.

CHAPTER THIRTY-EIGHT

LEXI

Twenty minutes later, I was seated where I was earlier. Jett had moved places, I guessed he didn't want to sit next to Raff. I didn't care, I was snuggled up with him while the boys all argued over a movie choice.

"Pizza is here." I could smell it as Nash brought a stack of pizza boxes down and placed them on a table in the corner. Everyone got up, and there were some plates handed around. I turned and passed a plate to Raff, then reached back and gave one to Galen. He smiled at me as I turned back to the pizza. Oh my gosh, so many types. I waited for the guys to all pick some. Raff put a few on his plate and gestured for me to do the same. I nodded, but I wanted to wait to make sure they all had enough. They all started to take their seats again, and apparently, Ranger had picked the perfect movie and was going to surprise us all when we sat down. Maverick groaned at that. It made me laugh.

"Here, I got this for you." Galen held open the box of pepperoni. He passed me a slice, then a second, then when he put a third on there, I looked up and caught him smiling at me.

"Um…didn't you want any? You ordered it?" I was so interested to see if he could eat it.

He winked. "I got it for you." My heart sped up a little at that statement. Oh my gosh, he got pizza for me?

"What…why?" He placed a slice on his plate, and my eyes followed it. He picked up a napkin and wiped his fingers.

"Because I knew you wouldn't ask Nash. You're stubborn like that." He winked and walked away, then took a seat just off to the side. I guessed he was staying for the movie. Nash wasn't here anymore, and Lyell hadn't come down at all. It was just all the other Lovell brothers, Galen, Raff, and me. It was strange how everyone was acting so…normal. Like this was a regular night, hanging out in a room with four werewolves—shifters. And a vampire. And me, the girl who smells good to them, or something weird. Maybe I was a unicorn?

My eyes found Galen's. He was holding his untouched pizza, but his eyes were on me. Oh hell. Was I something he wanted to eat? I quickly turned back to the screen. Shit, would I want that? Was it bad that I wouldn't mind if he did…?

"Okay, everyone. Tonight's movie is one we'll all enjoy. Including Galen here… That's right shifters, vampires, and a mystery girl. Tonight's movie of choice—my choice—is none other than—" Ranger started tapping on his thighs like a drum roll, and I heard Jett groan in embarrassment. *"Twilight."*

Everyone groaned, well…except for me. I looked back at Galen. Did he tell them? Did he tell Ranger what I'd said at the diner? It was as if he could read my thoughts as he shook his head slightly. I let out a deep breath as everyone settled down and the movie started. Considering how many of them complained, nobody moved to change the movie or leave the room.

We were about halfway through when Ranger paused the movie. I was nice and full, Raff was stroking the back of my hand, and I was almost falling asleep.

"Popcorn time." Ranger bounced down over to the machine and started loading it up. While we were waiting, I stole a sneaky kiss from Raff. I pulled him closer to kiss him deeper when Ranger popped up in our faces. It scared me a bit, and I pulled away.

"Pop quiz time." I looked over to Raff, who looked just as puzzled as me.

"Since Galen has so lovingly decided to have dinner with us... again, even though we know we haven't served anything he would normally *eat*."

Maverick stood. He'd been sitting nearest to me, but just below Galen.

"That's out of line. Galen is welcome here for dinner. It doesn't matter what he eats." Ranger took a step back, placing his hand over his chest.

"Oh dear, brother, tis all in good fun. I was only joking." But when I looked to Maverick, he didn't look like he thought it was funny. In fact, no one laughed. That was not very nice. He was still a person with feelings.

"Ahh...well, my question here is for our young Lexi. A.K.A Bella. I'm curious, with your own Jacob here... Were you Team Jacob or Team Edward before...you know, all of this." Ranger waved his arms around at everyone. Jett stood and pushed Ranger away from me.

"You don't have to answer. He's just being his usual dumbass self, so just ignore him. Most of us do anyway," Jett said as he smiled down at me. Ranger pretended to be hurt and dropped to the floor like his brother had injured him. I rolled my eyes, but I couldn't help the smile on my face. Ugh...I hated this guy.

"She doesn't have to answer...but it would be fun to know. Team Jacobs, maybe?"

I pressed myself closer to Raff, and Ranger chuckled.

"Oh, so Team Raff only?" I wasn't going to take the bait. I'd only just found out about the whole multiple guy thing, and now he was pushing me, obviously wondering if he had a chance. I knew he wouldn't stop, no matter what I said, so I sat up and looked at all of them. Everyone was watching me, but Galen looked away. I felt a little sad. Did he wish I was Team Edward? I wanted to be Team Galen.

Ranger was bouncing around in front of me, and I could feel Raff tense up a bit. *Fuck it.*

"I think Bella should've had them both. It wasn't fair she had to choose. I say have your cake and eat it, too." Ranger bounced super high, and he made a large happy wooing sound.

"Hell yeah... And maybe a few from the wolf pack too, right?" I rolled my eyes and everyone laughed.

Raff wrapped his arms around me and whispered into my ear, "I think that sounds like the perfect ending to the movie."

I didn't want to look over at Galen, but I could feel the heat of his gaze on me. When the movie restarted and everyone had popcorn, I shifted so my head was in Raff's lap. I could see Maverick watching me, and he gave me a small smile before he looked over his shoulder to Galen. When I did the same, our eyes met. It was dark, but I could see them. He didn't smile, he didn't move. He was frozen, and so was I. Maverick touched his knee, and Galen's eyes flicked to where his hand was. It lingered there for a while before Maverick looked over to me. I gave him a small smile, even though getting caught staring at him again was a little embarrassing. When he realized his hand was still on Galen's knee, he jerked it off fast, and I quickly looked away.

Holy shit. Galen knew that he was bi because... I looked back over and Maverick was glaring at me.

Oh fuck. Were they together?

CHAPTER THIRTY-NINE

LEXI

There was a dull ache in the pit of my belly. I squeezed my eyes tighter and pressed the heel of my hand to my stomach to stop the cramp. *Ugh...great.* It was that time of the month. I rolled over and felt movement in my bed. I opened my eyes, and Raff was looking at me.

"Are you okay?" Oh man, shit. These were white sheets, and I'd probably just left a nice stain on them.

"No, I think I just got my period... Nope, I'm one hundred percent sure I have it."

His eyes widened at my statement. He looked around the room, then back to me. I guessed he wasn't used to females and their cycles.

"How did I get to bed last night?" The last thing I remembered was the movie and feeling sleepy as I lay on Raff's lap.

"I carried you here, then got kicked out by Galen and Alaric. I came back when you needed me." I rolled to be closer to Raff, but then realized that wasn't so good and I needed to get to the bathroom quick.

"I don't want to be rude...but well, I'm leaking everywhere. I need to get up to clean myself off." I almost laughed at the look on his face.

He nodded, then was out of bed and over to my door fast. I pulled back the sheet, and as I suspected, I'd ruined the sheets. Why were they white? It was just asking for trouble.

"Do you need anything? Like, you know...for...it." He couldn't even look me in the eyes. I'd scared the poor guy with female problems.

"Fuck, I don't have any tampons. I left them at Jack and Grayson's house. Can you maybe ask Alaric to get me some?" I didn't think Alaric was exactly the right person for this, but he wanted me to live here. Raff nodded and gave me a cute little smile as he ducked out. I moved slowly and awkwardly so that I wouldn't get any mess on the white carpet, because that would be hard to get out. As soon as I was in the bathroom over the tiles, I relaxed. A nice hot shower would help with the cramps.

I was in the shower a good twenty minutes before there was a knock on the bathroom door.

"Did you get some?" I called out around the glass shower door. I couldn't hear anything, so I shut the shower off and grabbed a towel, wrapping it around myself. My hair was still wet and dripping everywhere. I opened the door to the bathroom, but it wasn't Raff on the other side.

"Galen." I tightened the grip on the top of the towel. He was wearing some dark jeans and an army-green knitted sweater. He held up a bag and handed it to me, and I took it, my wet hands slipping slightly.

"I heard Rafferty...he was a little concerned. So, I dashed out to get you what you needed. If there are any brands you prefer, just let me know for next time." My mouth dropped open. He got me tampons? My sexy as sin history teacher got me tampons?

"Thanks," was all I could muster up as I closed the door on him. I rested my back against the door and looked up to the ceiling. I wasn't sure if that was embarrassing or sweet. Sweet, I'd go with sweet.

I opened the bag. "Oh my god," I sighed. There were three

different boxes of tampons, some chocolate bars, and Advil in the bag. I was being all girly and sappy now, but Galen was the sweetest.

I quickly took some Advil, dried up, and took care of my lady business. I packed away the boxes and left the bathroom with the bag of chocolates in my hand. When I stepped out into my bedroom, I noticed the bed was freshly made. I froze. Who did that? I was going to take the sheets down. *Oh man.* They would've seen the mess. Like, I knew it was normal and natural and shit, but these guys didn't live with women.

I hadn't asked them yet about their mother. I'd seen photos of her around the house and assumed she had passed away. I was waiting for someone to tell me or bring it up, but they never spoke of her. It was like she didn't exist. I didn't want to pry in case it brought up painful memories and that was why they didn't speak about her.

I grabbed a pair of jeans, a fresh T-shirt, and a hoodie from the closet and got dressed. They were clean and smelled so nice. I reminded myself to find Raff so I could get marked before I left for school.

"Good morning." I smiled at the table full of huge, sexy men when all their eyes flashed to me. Galen moved from behind me and made me jump slightly.

"Here." He handed me a glass of orange juice and a bagel as he proceeded to pull out a chair for me to sit. Shit, I could get used to this treatment.

"How are you feeling?" Jett asked.

I felt my cheeks heat up a bit. "Can you smell me? Like smell that I have my period?" All their eyes darted around at each other. Jett looked right at me and nodded. *Fuck this.* I wasn't going to school with that many shifters smelling me and then smelling this.

"I'm not going to school, fuck that. Can you bring me my work?" I placed a hand over Raff's as I looked at him. He smiled, and everything felt right in the world.

Alaric happened to enter the room right then. "No, you can't take off school. Other females at the school get their...*you know*. You need to go." To hell with that statement.

"No. Fucking. Way." I crossed my arms over my chest. I already had to deal with the weirdness on a normal day, and I had no idea what menstruating would do to them.

"What do I smell like? Because it's already grossing me out that you can smell it." No one said anything, they just looked at me like I was crazy for asking.

"I think this is a good opportunity for Alaric to find more information about what Lexi might be. What do you think?" I turned to see Galen look at Alaric. I spun more and could see Alaric clench his fists, and his eyes were not like they usually were. I swallowed the lump in my throat. Shit, did I piss him off? I tried to give him a smile, but that just made him growl low.

"She doesn't understand, she isn't from here. She's right, the other shifters will have a field day with this. You know it, we all know it. I'll make sure that Lexi gets all her work. She'll graduate, because she's doing very well. Plus, this gives you a chance to find out some things so we can work out what she is. Isn't that the reason she's here? To find out and keep her safe?"

Galen was good with words, because yeah, I wasn't doing very well at school. I knew for a fact I wasn't where I wanted to be academically, but I was coming to terms with never going to college. I'd moved schools too many times, and it'd set me back over and over. And once again, I was just a mediocre student.

"Yes, that is part of why she's here. That's actually a good idea. Maybe we can do that DNA test we thought might help. If that's okay with you, Alexis?"

DNA test? To see if I was some supernatural thing? Fuck, yeah. Might as well work out why I smell good to all of them. I nodded to Alaric. This was the best idea. I hoped I turned into something cool like a unicorn or a dragon. I turned back to the table to find all the guys were watching Alaric, except for Maverick, who was watching Galen. I smiled at that.

"Are there like dragon-shifters?" All eyes were now on me. The look on Jett's face was comical.

"No... Why?" Ranger asked in a funny tone.

I glared at him. "So I could burn you." There were a few chuckles at that.

"I'll do the DNA test. Maybe I turn into a unicorn?" I wiggled my brows, and a few of them snorted. When Ranger opened his mouth, I beat him too it.

"So I can stab you with my horn," I directed at him. Raff started laughing, and it warmed me up. I reached over for him and pulled him in close. "Don't forget to mark me before you leave." I didn't know where this DNA place was, but I wanted everyone who came near me know that he was mine and I was his.

He looked down to where the brothers were all sitting, then back to me. Then he did something that surprised me. He kissed me in front of all of them, and as he pulled away, he winked.

"I won't forget," he practically growled under his breath. Fuck, that sent shivers down my spine—the good kind.

Everyone started talking and doing their own thing as I ate my bagel, but I couldn't keep my mind off the chocolate bar tucked in my hoodie pocket. It was probably melting, but I didn't care. It would still taste so good.

CHAPTER FORTY

GALEN

I gave Rafferty a lift to school, and he was quiet, more so than usual. I tried to make conversation, but he gave me nothing to work with, so I stopped and tried to give him some space. Obviously, he had something on his mind, and he wasn't in the mood to share.

I knew I should've gone back home and fed as soon as I walked into school. I had something in my office to hold me over until the end of the day, but first, I needed to speak to Karen about Lexi's grades. I headed straight for the office.

"Oh, Mr. Donovani!" She clutched the gold cross around her neck. "You frightened me. I wasn't expecting you."

I nodded and smiled as I casually walked over to her. I was hungry, and I could hear her blood rushing through her veins. My fangs were itching, but I held myself. I'd never fed on someone at school, and I wasn't about to start today with her.

"I wanted to speak to you about changing grades for a student." Her eyes went wide behind the hideous pink frames she wore. "You will change the grades for Alexis Turner. You will give her passing marks in all of her classes. She will graduate with a B average."

She was a little stunned at my compulsion before she blinked and came to. "Well, yes, of course. Is there anything else?"

Your blood.

"Give her perfect attendance."

I pushed through the glass doors and rushed straight to my office. I unlocked the door, and as soon as I was inside, I ran to my desk and pulled out the bottle of Jack Daniels hidden in the bottom drawer of my desk. I was shaking from the need to feed, so I didn't have time. I drank straight from the bottle. I could feel the alcohol warm me, helping me with the hunger. Then my office door swung open, and Ranger stood right in its place.

I almost had to pry the bottle from my lips as his eyes flashed to me. I could see that stupid smirk on his face at catching me at a bad time, and I wiped my lips on the back of my hand. "Close the door, young man."

He kicked his leg out behind him, and the door slammed shut. I rolled my eyes, at his dramatics.

"And how can I help you today, Ranger?"

He walked over and dropped his bag before sliding into the chair at my desk. He put one knee up and laid back like he didn't have a care in the world. "Why the fuck do you keep turning up at our house? Like ever since Lex got there, you keep showing up. Like at breakfast today..." He raised his brows and smirked. "You don't eat breakfast. At least, not the kind we serve, *bloodsucker*."

I returned his smirk and took my seat, still clutching my bottle of Jack. Though with Ranger here, stinking up my office, I wasn't so hungry anymore.

"Are you worried about the competition? Worried that maybe— just maybe—she wants her cake...and to eat it, too?" His hands went to the armrests, his knuckles almost white from gripping so hard.

"No, fuck you. It isn't fair if you're in the game. This is bullshit. How can someone compete against... you?" He blew the hair out of his eyes and sank back into the chair. When his head bent down to his lap, I watched him take a few deep breaths. That made me feel like shit for teasing him. I didn't realize that he really thought it would be unfair. I never thought I'd have even a small chance of Lexi considering me as a mate.

Well, that was until last night, and of course, I could barely sleep. I kept running that over in my mind. That and the way Mav put his hand on my knee—it felt electric when he touched me. I could see in Lexi's eyes, she was wondering if we were more than friends, especially after the conversation from yesterday.

But the thing was, Mav and I... Well, I never thought we were even friends to begin with. He'd always avoided me. He never spoke to me, until last night. Did Lexi say something to him? When I saw Ranger put his head up, I could see the unshed tears in his eyes. *Oh, fuck.*

"Fuck, Ranger. I was just messing. I know you like her, but shit. You really like, like her. Are you in love with her?"

He quickly looked away and ran his sleeve over his face. "Yes," he mumbled. "And you're...well, you're you. And you just have to be you, and you get the girl and—"

I put the bottle on the desk and pulled out some books and pens I needed for class. The bell would ring very soon.

"Ranger, apart from the fact that you said 'you' one too many times in that sentence, yes, I am me. Why would a girl like Lexi want to date me? I'm three-hundred and twelve. She's seventeen. I've lived eighteen times longer than she has."

He just shrugged, but didn't make any effort to leave.

"Are you upset that she's with Rafferty?" His eyes flashed to mine. At first, I thought he was going to say yes, but he surprised me.

"No. If anything, I understand they have a connection that she and I won't have. It's different. He understands her in ways no one else can. And it pisses me off, but that's because I feel so much for her that I want that. But instead, I'm breaking inside. I put on the happy face every day, but I don't feel like that. Not on the inside.

"And then last night, when she said that Bella should have had them both—a vampire and a shifter. That... *Fuck*, I couldn't sleep. I waited to speak to her this morning. I wanted to know why she said that. Was she trying to tell me that I didn't have a chance, not even a small one? I've been showing her I can get along with Rafferty. He isn't so bad."

I couldn't help but chuckle at the last bit. I shook my head and waved my hand for him to continue.

"Well, have you ever heard of shifters, vampires, and human being together?"

I tried to think back to all the packs I'd met along my travels, and not once could I place three of them together.

"Shelly is a vampire. She's the case worker who brought Lexi here to us, and she's dating a wolf-shifter, who's a cop. My friend Benedict, he...he dated a human once, but that was before I met him." Ben didn't date at all, so he was a bad example. I tried to think of others I could draw from, but I was struggling. Vampires dated humans all the time, so did shifters.

"Are you saying that you want Lexi to stay as she is? That you won't want to turn her? You are an alpha's son," I reminded him. Alpha's sons produced more alphas. But without a shifter female, he wouldn't. "But Lexi isn't human, so don't overthink this."

He opened his mouth to say something when the bell rang. I waited to see what he was going to say, but he just picked up his bag and left. I followed and was hit by a powerful hunger. I would have to get someone to take my classes for today. I needed to go before I did something I couldn't fix.

CHAPTER FORTY-ONE

LEXI

I felt like the worst friend again. Ada texted me, asking if I was coming to class. I felt bad that I wasn't there again. It wasn't like me to ever take time off school. I shot her back a quick text, telling her we could hang out this weekend. But of course, now I had two huge secrets I couldn't tell her. Oh wait, make that three—*me*, the strange smelling girl who turns shifters' heads. And to that my vampire teacher who bought me stuff for my period.

Oh god. Could he smell blood? If so, he would've been able to smell me. I hadn't thought about that.

But I was glad for the tampons and chocolate, of which I was onto my fifth bar. I didn't know if that was a bad thing or a good thing. I didn't care either way, it was yummy brown goodness and it made my PMS happy. The cramps were just a dull ache now, and I was just finishing off my makeup for the day.

"How long does it take, Lexi?" Jett called out. He'd asked me to hurry twice. I was hurrying, he just had no patience for me to look my best.

"Rome wasn't built in a day," I hollered back. I could hear his footsteps as he entered my room, and then his beautiful face peered around the open bathroom door.

"Oh man, was hoping you were naked." I threw a towel at him, and he caught it, laughing.

"You don't need all this, Lexi. You're a natural beauty." Well, of course no one needed makeup, but everyone needed a mask, something to hide behind at times. Mine was eyeliner and mascara.

"You seriously have the most amazing eyes. I bet they have something to do with what you are. I really hope we get answers today. But that's only going to happen if you get your butt moving. Come on." He threw the towel back at me, and I didn't get a chance to catch it as it hit the side of my head. I just laughed and threw it at him again, but he'd run off laughing.

"Well, for that I might take another twenty minutes," I yelled back, but then realized that he would've heard me even if I'd whispered it.

I brushed my hair again, then put it up into a messy bun. I grabbed the leather jacket that I loved so much—I definitely need to call Ada for girl talk later— and walked out of the bathroom with a swing in my step. Today was the first day I'd felt so...I didn't know the words for it...happy and like nothing bad was going to happen.

I had the most amazing silver-haired boyfriend. I smiled to myself as I skipped down the stairs. Yeah, I was going to say that to him tonight. I was going call him my boyfriend. God, how much had changed in just a short time? When I got to the bottom of the stairs, I was shocked to see someone different in the house.

"Hey, Lexi. You might remember me?" Oh, I remembered him—from the party where Raff got fucked up by a bunch of wolves. I looked down to his outstretched hand, then glared back at him. His hair was all neat and gelled, and he was wearing dark jeans and a navy sweater. He moved his hand and rubbed it over the front of his sweater.

"Uh...maybe not? I'm Saint." He looked over to Jett.

"Yeah, you tried to give me poisoned water, then you fucked up my boyfriend. I remember you. You're a fucking asshole." I lunged at him. I didn't know I had this kind of strength, but when I shoved him hard in the chest, he stumbled back a few steps. He looked surprised. You'd be surprised how strong someone can be when they have adrenaline running through them. The images of Raff's back that night, the blood...so much pain came rushing back. I lunged at him again, but this time, my fist was clenched and aimed for that stunned look on his face. But before it collided, warm arms wrapped around me and pulled me back against a hard chest. I pulled to get away, but Jett held me tight.

"What's going on in here? I can smell that from out there. Alexis?"

I was shaking. I couldn't stop the memories. It was only a few nights ago that he did that.

"Ah, yeah. I'm really sorry about that, Lexi. I truly am. I'll even apologize to Rafferty for what I did. Luckily, we heal fast, and I knew he would. So no damage. He's fine."

No damage? What about emotional damage, asshole? I used my elbow to get free from Jett. He snatched my wrist, but not before I slapped Saint across the face. He looked over to Alaric. I was breathing hard, and my heart was racing. This day, this one day that seemed to start off half decent, just got ruined.

"Alexis, please control your anger. Saint is here as our driver today."

Saint held his hands up at me. I could see he regretted what he did to Raff, but it didn't change a thing. He still did it.

"I deserved that and more. I'm sorry, Lexi. I really am."

"You don't get to call me that. Don't speak to me, and I'm not going in any car with you."

There was a loud growl, but I didn't care what Alaric thought.

"I'll drive us. Saint can drive you, Father, and I'll follow in my Jeep."

A few extras came along. Apparently, they were some council guys, who rode with Alaric. I was worried a little about being alone with Jett. He hadn't done anything for me to be worried about...yet.

He was sweet and playful, but I wasn't too sure what his intentions were. Was he like the other shifters? Was he affected by my scent, or was he okay with everything? He was only a year older than me, and he'd just turned nineteen.

"You're really quiet. Did you want to talk about what happened back there?" I shook my head and watched the trees as we drove. After a few moments, I saw deep blue water.

"Did he really try to give you poisoned water?" I snorted at that, and Jett laughed. It helped the mood a little.

"No. Well...for all I know, he could've. I think he was maybe trying to chat me up at the party. He gave me water, but I never trust anyone with an open cup. So, I tipped it out."

It became quiet again as we followed the black SUV in front of us. The one that Saint was driving.

"Thanks for driving me. I can't forgive him for what he did, not yet anyway. I know that Raff healed fast, but still. He didn't see the pain he was in. It broke me how bad it was. I washed his wounds and dressed them. I was scared he was going to die." I tried to stop the feelings, but they flooded me. Stupid period. I did get a little emotional when it came. I wasn't immune to it...I was a regular girl.

Well, I was a regular girl until I came to Kiba.

"Well, do you know what you need?" I looked over to him, and he gave me a small smile, then winked. I let out a small chuckle.

"You need to be fed. You need a juicy burger, *yum yum*. Some fries, *ooohh*...maybe a milkshake? Something sweet like apple pie? Yeah, you need apple pie. Ice cream...cake. Oh, you need some of that...and to eat it, too."

I laughed as he made sounds like he was eating between the words. He was cheering me up, and it was working.

"You know, you seem to know all the right things to say. How come you're single?" I'd kind of figured out they all were single.

Either that, or their girlfriends were invisible and they forgot to mention them.

"Well, I did have a girlfriend. We dated for a while... She wanted to go to college to be a vet. So, we broke up."

Oh, man. *Shit.*

"But you could still chase after her? How far away did she go? Or you could've maybe followed her to college?"

He watched the road ahead and didn't say anything for a while. I guessed I hit a sore spot. I'd just met Raff and we'd only just gotten together, but even now, if we were to break up, I knew I'd be heart broken. But I didn't fully know him, either. Or what his plans were for after high school.

"It's a hard one, because it wasn't just me. She was dating my packmate, Mekhi, too. She was—no, is beautiful. The sweetest girl I'd ever met. And she accepted Mekhi straight up. I told her we came as a pair, and she was happy. We all were. We were open about our claim to her, and everyone knew the three of us were together. Father thought that we'd...claim her. But she'd told us of her dreams to become a vet. All her life, she'd wanted to heal animals. We thought that was perfect. We wanted her to do what made her happy. When she was accepted into Colorado State, I asked my father if we could move down there. We'd get a place, and she could live with us while she studied.

"I knew the answer before he told me. We don't leave our pack lands. We can go to college, but it's online. We don't leave Kiba, unless on business. She wanted to do the long-distance thing, said we could visit her. But the thing was, if we did visit, we'd end up like what happened to Raff. Or worse..." He took a deep breath. His words were thick in his throat. I could tell this really hurt him still. He must really love her.

"What's her name?" I asked after he didn't continue. I could see the glassiness of his eyes, the tears threatening to spill over.

"Clare, Clare Briggs." He made a funny chuckling sound. "Well,

I called her Clare bear, and Mekhi called her Pooh bear." He wiped his eyes, but there was smile on his face.

"She sounds amazing, and so does Mekhi. How come I haven't met him yet?"

"Well, Father has instructed the other shifters to stay away until you settle in. We can't have any of our packmates or friends over, human or shifter." My mouth dropped open. Oh man, that made me feel like shit. Like was he and Mekhi...together also? Fuck, I didn't know what he looked like, but with shifters, they were all hot. And the thought of Jett and this Mekhi guy together, touching each other's bodies, sucking...

Jett laughed. "I don't know what you're thinking about, but I can smell it. You have dirty thoughts, Lexi Turner." I could feel my cheeks heat up. Holy shit, how did I forget that? I couldn't even have dirty thoughts without giving away what I was thinking. *Fuck it.*

"I was just wondering if you and your packmate, you know...fuck too?" I turned and wiggled my brows at him.

He cracked up laughing. "I don't kiss and tell, Lexi."

CHAPTER FORTY-TWO

LEXI

The place they took me to was very similar to Kiba. Just bigger.

"Bardoul are our allies, they are a very large wolf pack. If anyone knows what you are, they will, and they're the largest pack in the state."

It was like having a history lesson with Jett. I enjoyed learning more about the wolf-shifters. He'd never met a panther-shifter, but he said they were out there. He honestly didn't know much about them, but only because he'd never been interested in learning about them more.

But bear-shifters lived in Port Angeles, and he'd met a few before, but not in bear form. Which would have been so cool. I told him I would love to pet a bear, just to see what they felt like. He told me not to pet shifters unless I wanted them as a mate. That it was very intimate. So there would be no bear petting for me in my future. *Only wolf petting.*

When we rolled up to a large building that looked like a school, I turned to Jett.

"They have a school here where they teach all their shifter pups without humans. The council offices are all connected with the school. So you might pass some students." I gave him the dirtiest look I could give him. *Really?* I was not going to school today because of the whole smelling thing, and now he drops this on me?

"I didn't think about it, okay?" He chuckled. "I'll try my best to block you from anyone." I could see Alaric and Saint had hopped out, along with the other two men that were with them.

"Fine, but I swear if one of them sniffs me, I'll hit them. That shit is fucked up." Jett just laughed as if I was joking. I wasn't. I think he was hoping I was.

I got out of the warm car and into the cooler day. It was overcast here compared to Kiba, but it smelled so fresh and nice. Jett gestured, and I followed them all into the building.

"When you spoke to us, Alaric, I was excited to hear you were bringing the mystery girl." A tall, dark-haired man greeted us. He was just as big as Alaric, so I guessed he was the alpha around here.

"Hello, Alexis. I'm Ralph. It's a pleasure to meet you." He held his hand out for me to shake, and he didn't seem weird, so I took it. He had a firm but gentle grip.

"Nice to meet you, too." He shook Alaric's hand next and told us to follow him to the testing center.

We passed a few classrooms along the way. It was like looking into an all-boys school. There were a lot of heads turning as we passed. Jett moved to my side to block me from the onlookers and smiled at me, then sniffed a few times. I chuckled and smacked him in the chest.

"Stop it, you dork." He laughed, and I heard Saint laugh behind us. I turned and pointed at him, which shut him up quickly.

When we got to the testing center, it was like a hospital, but with no patients.

"Alexis, this is where we test blood samples of many different shifters. We've been trying to find a cure for our reproduction complications and other ailments shifters may have. This here is our staff of twelve scientists. They'll take your blood sample, and hopefully, we'll be able to find out what you are very soon.

"I don't want to upset you—in case you were hoping for this outcome—but you're not a shifter. I've never smelled a scent like yours in my sixty years. But don't worry, we'll soon find out what is in your blood. Are there any abilities you have?"

He led me over to a female scientist, and I took a seat. She smiled gently as she rolled up my sleeve. "Have you given blood before?" I shook my head no. "It just feels like a little prick. It'll be over fairly shortly."

She prepared my skin as I started to think of an ability I could have.

"Like super hearing? Or super strength? Flying?"

Jett snorted, and Alaric glared at him, warning him to shut up. But when I caught Jett's eyes, a smile dazzled his face. Hey, this was awkward. I had too many people staring at me, and it made me nervous and—

"Ouch. Prick, my ass," I blurted out. I watched as my blood filled a tube.

"Sorry, won't take long," the lady said, trying to reassure me.

"Yes, any of those. An ability that is not human."

I shrugged. I didn't know what made me different to humans until I suddenly wasn't one. When the nurse finished, she took a band-aid out. I looked down and saw that the hole she'd made was already healing.

"No need, it'll be fine in a moment."

"So you heal faster than humans? How fast do you heal?" I was stunned, and all eyes were on me again. A man in a white coat held a clipboard. Oh...well, I never really thought about it.

"I guess so? I don't get sick either?" I'd never had a cold in my life. I watched as the man furiously write down what I said.

"This is very interesting. Well, this will take us a day or two, but if you can think of anything else we should know, please let Alaric know. It might help us in finding what you are. You're all welcome to stay and have lunch. I hear today's menu is roast beef," Ralph said.

I shook my head and looked over to Jett.

"No, thank you. I was promised burgers." Alaric shot me a look which told me that wasn't the right thing to say. But I wasn't his puppet, and I wasn't having roast beef.

But Ralph just chuckled. "Well, if you were promised burgers, then that means more roast beef for me. Thank you so much for stopping by. It was lovely meeting you, Alexis. I'll be in touch soon." Then Ralph shook my hand again.

CHAPTER FORTY-THREE

LEXI

Three cheeseburgers, large fries, a super large chocolate milkshake, and a warm apple pie to top it all off. I had a belly ache, but it was worth it when we got back to the house.

"Well, Miss Piggy, I had a great day with you. I hope you did, too. I'm off to see Mekhi now...and no dirty thoughts." Jett pointed at me with a huge grin as I started to walk toward the house.

I just laughed. This was such a fun day. When I got inside, I heard my name...and it didn't sound great.

"Um, yes?" I turned to see Alaric. He wasn't upset like I thought. I felt like it was just the way he spoke. His voice came out like a growl and a little dominating. But if you looked at the guy, he radiated top-dog vibes...*wolf vibes*. I smiled at the thought, and he smiled back.

"Could you please meet me in my office in ten minutes? I have something I need to speak to you about." I nodded. That sounded fair enough, right?

I ran upstairs to get into some comfy clothes. I was cramping bad again, and my belly needed room to stretch. The only pants I could find were my sleep pants, but I didn't want to wear them in front of Alaric. Maybe I could borrow some of Raff's sweats.

I snuck out of my room and looked down the long hallway. The stairs were to my right, and to the left was another room and then the end of the hall. There was a door there, but I was pretty sure was a linen closet.

"Fuck." Which one was his again? All the doors were white, and the walls were white. Yesterday, he went to his room without me while I looked for Lyell, so I didn't see which was his. There were pictures on the walls, and I knew mine was the one with the boats. I was four doors down from the stairs that led to the kitchen area. This house lacked so much color it was so...blah. Now, I knew they didn't put Raff in the room beside me. I think Lyell was next to me. Or wait, was he across from me, and Raff was next to him on my left?

I cracked open the door, and the room looked the same as mine. It was kind of weird. I hadn't been into any of the other rooms until now. This one was bare, like someone had just moved in. I looked in the closet and bathroom and there was nothing in there. *Shit.*

I closed the door and made my way down to my room. It was the only door that was open and the only way I could find it without counting.

Fuck it, maybe he was three doors down from me and across the hall? I opened a door and this room was lived in—this was one of the Lovell brothers.

"Hello?" I called out into the room. When no one answered, I looked around the hallway to make sure no one was coming. I was running out of time to get to Alaric. Maybe this was Jett's room. He was nice to me, and I was sure he wouldn't mind if I borrowed some sweats. I walked into the huge closet, which was full of clothes.

Huh, maybe this wasn't Jett's. As I turned to walk out, I saw a stack of books on the floor next to an Amazon box. I crouched down to look and found that it was filled with Jane Austen books. *Holy hell.* This was Lyell's room? I was really bad with the room set up. He didn't just have these, he'd been buying me books? I'd have to tell him not to do that, that was... Oh my gosh, was that a hardcopy of *Pride and Prejudice*? I ran my finger along the top. It looked so old with the gold and black detail. Shit, I hope this was for him and not me.

I didn't have time. I just looked over and saw a gray pair of sweats lying in the corner. I grabbed them, saw that they looked clean enough, and I ran out, closing the door behind me, then I raced back to my room. I took care of lady business, took some Advil, and ran to meet Alaric.

"Alaric?" I called out when I got to the hallway. I knew the movie room was to my left, but there were lots of doors on my right, and I thought that was where he went.

"Second door on your right," his voice boomed out. I opened the door, and saw that his office was huge with a beautiful window overlooking the green grass.

"Come in, Alexis, take a seat. I'd like to talk to you about a few things that I've been thinking about for the past week."

This didn't sound good at all.

I tried to give him my confident face, but I was sure he could smell that I was anything but. I took a seat and noticed that his desk was tidy—nothing like Galen's desk at school.

"Today was a good start to finding out what you are, but I've been thinking about your future here. My son, or possibly sons, have taken a keen interest in being your mate, Alexis."

Holy shit. This wasn't the way I thought this was going. Before I could say anything, he continued.

"I understand your birthday is coming up soon, yes? May? Spring break is just a week away. So not long now until you age out of the system. But the same goes here as it did with Jack and Grayson. You'll be able to stay here as long as you wish, and I hope you choose to stay. Ranger has really taken to you. And from today, I can tell you like Jett—"

"Hold on a second." I put my hand up. "I like Jett as a friend. He's been good to me and hasn't tried to *claim* me. Or attack Raff. Unlike some others..." I didn't name anyone, since he already would've known.

"Yes, you're right. But Ranger...he wears his heart on his sleeve. He's been acting like a young wolf in love. I don't think he's expressing himself correctly in front of you. As you've already taken Rafferty as yours, I believe he's trying hard to show you he would make a good mate as well and doesn't want to miss his chance." I glared at him. Where was this going? Did he want me to break up with Raff? No way.

"I like young Rafferty, he's strong. He thought to protect you, though he did things wrong in the beginning. But anyone can see he did everything for you, and he asked for your forgiveness. He will make a great pack member for Kiba when he turns eighteen.

"What I have brought you in here to discuss is that I've looked over your files, though not all. I didn't pry into places I didn't need to. But even from what my sons and Galen have told me, of how strong and resilient you are, I would be proud to call you Kiba on your eighteenth birthday. If you wish, I'd like you to join the pack."

I didn't know what to say. Ralph said I wasn't a shifter, but Alaric wanted me to join his pack anyway?

"I see that you've been studying hard to make it to college. I'll pay for your online college, and you may live here. I'll continue to provide for you."

There was a but, wasn't there? There was always a but.

"But? Like, what's the catch?"

He shook his head, and a slow smirk appeared. "Ah, see, you're a smart girl. There's no catch. Rafferty will be here, and I know you wouldn't want to be apart. I just wish for you to be a little more... understanding of Ranger's actions. The boy is doing everything he can to show you how much you mean to him. He requested Rafferty be moved in here for you. And he's tried hard forge a friendship with him. Because that is something a mate would want from her men—unity and support.

"I know this is a lot to take in, and that you still might not wish to take Ranger as a mate. That doesn't change my offer. It still stands. Does that sound like an offer you would consider?"

I was still running the words Alaric said to me over in my head. Ranger had asked for Rafferty to move in. Why? And Alaric would pay for my college? Rafferty would be part of their pack? Free housing, food...and a college education. If I play nice with Ranger.

I stood as Alaric rose from his chair. I put my hand up, since I wasn't too sure. I didn't like this—trusting the Lovell family. This was a huge step. One I had to think about. "Can I think about this?"

Alaric nodded, and I left his office, closing the door behind me. I ran straight to the movie room. I needed popcorn and a sad love story.

CHAPTER FORTY-FOUR

RANGER

Jett had texted our group chat a few times today, telling us what he and Lex had been up to. He even sent a photo of her smiling as she ate a huge burger. I'd be lying if I said I wasn't jealous of my brother because, fuck, he was making her laugh and doing all the things I wanted to do with her.

And well, I know he found her attractive. What if she picked him? What if she never wanted those things with me? My wolf was struggling. Jett was my brother, and I loved him. He would be good to Lex. I knew he would, I'd seen him with Clare.

But now it was my time, and she was mine. I'd told them over and over. And if he—

"Seriously, I can't deal with this today. You're up and down. I know why, and don't. I saw the photo, too. They're just friends. Okay?" Mav grumbled next to me.

I'd taken a detour on the way home to get her some things for her period. I'd found Lex's only friend, Ada at the end of the day and asked what girls like when they were having their periods. Her eyes widened in shock at first, and I wasn't sure if I'd said the wrong thing.

Like, girls talk about it, right? She stuttered at first, then asked me why I was getting her things like that.

"Because she's living with us now, and she got it this morning. I wanted to make her feel better." That seemed like a surprise to her, and I could tell in her voice she didn't know.

"Chocolate, um...ice cream is good too. Sugar for the win." She giggled. "Hot water bottle, a back massage. Um...flowers?" Apparently, she wasn't sure on the flowers. I wasn't either, but fuck it, I was going the whole hog.

"We'll see, Mav. After I give her this, maybe she'll want to be more than friends with me." He growled at me as he slipped out of the car and into the house. I had my hands full. I went with the biggest bunch of flowers I could find. I held onto the bags and walked into the house. I could hear Father working in his office, and Mav was already upstairs.

I was happy to have beaten Raff home, or he would've been with her like he always seemed to be. She was never alone. But he was catching a lift with Galen again.

I could hear a movie playing and smelled popcorn drift up the hallway. As I made my way down, I could smell her. She was sad? My wolf was unsettled by this feeling coming from her. He wanted to crawl up and wrap himself around her.

I opened the door and saw that she was sprawled out in the same spot from last night. Her head whipped around, and her mouth formed an "O" as I walked down with the huge bouquet. Now I kind of felt stupid with these flowers.

As I got closer, I could see she'd been crying. *Shit.*

"Lex, oh my god, are you okay? What's the matter?" When I reached her, I put everything down and looked her over. Was it the testing? Did they do something to her? My wolf was getting agitated, which wasn't good. I really needed to control him better, I'd just never cared before. But I didn't want to scare her by shifting here.

She gave me a watery smile and pointed to the screen. Was that...*Paul Rudd?*

"Is it the movie? Is that why you're sad?" She laughed and wiped her tears away. I didn't know what to say. The movie made her cry? Was that what girls did?

"She was blind...clueless. She was in love with him, her stepbrother. And..." She sniffed. "They kissed on the stairs, and now they're all together and the teachers are getting married."

She was talking to me, like really talking to me, and now I didn't know what to say. She wasn't pushing me away or snapping at me or trying to punch me in the face. I needed to speak up before I lost this chance.

"I got you some things. I hope you don't mind... I got flowers and chocolate." I put the flowers next to her and gave her the bag filled with fifty dollar's worth of chocolate. Her eyes went wide at the flowers, and then she peered into the bag. I heard her sniff again, and she wiped her eyes as she pulled one out.

"Holy shit, Ranger. That's a lot of chocolate. Thank you."

I shrugged like it was nothing, but the way she said my name and the grin on her face made me smile and my wolf happy again. I did good. I thought I did the right thing. Mav helped me pick out most of the chocolate, but I told him I wasn't giving him credit for my idea.

"I also got chocolate ice cream, a hot water bottle. And um...the lady behind the counter asked if this was for a woman *with monthly pains*. I told her yes, and she gave me chamomile tea, which she said can help with cramps. I can make you tea, or I can warm up the water bottle..."

She crinkled her nose at me. Those big amber eyes were surrounded by a lot of black. I think her crying had made her makeup smudge a little.

"Or some tissues?" She laughed at that and nodded.

"Ah..." She looked to the door, but didn't say anything. I knew in that moment she was looking for Raff. "Yes, please, to all of it...and maybe a spoon for the ice cream."

I jumped up and saluted her. "Your wish is my command." I ran out of the room. Mav was waiting in the hallway, and I stopped.

"She likes it all. She's happy." I jumped up in the air.

When I returned, I was upset to see Mav was sitting in the room, talking to Lex. I shot him a glare and jerked my head for him to leave. What the fuck was he doing in here? I was trying to spend some time alone with her, and he knew it. But Mav just raised his brows. Yeah, I fucking heard them too, and I could smell him coming. It wasn't long before Raff and Galen walked in.

"Hey." Lex waved to them and patted to a spot besides her. Raff went straight to her, and she wrapped her arms around his neck, kissing him on the cheek. He didn't bring her anything, and she did that. I could feel the jealousy rise up, but I tried to calm my wolf down. I was getting better at holding him back today.

Galen placed his hand on my shoulder. He must have sensed me getting worked up. They were together, and I knew this, I just... I wished that was me, too. I had the tea in one hand, and the hot water bottle and spoons in the other.

Galen looked down. "Is that chamomile tea? I forgot about that one. Anti-inflammatory," he stated. I moved down and gave her the tea and the hot water bottle, and she instantly moaned when she pulled the blanket away and placed it against her belly.

I looked over to Raff and found his nostrils flaring just as mine did. I looked down to what she was wearing. He looked at me, and then we both turned to Mav. Did he give her those after he marked them? What the fuck? Did Maverick want her still? He hadn't shown that much interest since he told me in the car the other day, and now this?

"Maverick," I growled out. Lex jumped slightly at my words and sucked in a gasp. I didn't mean to scare her.

"Sorry, it's just..." I pointed to the sweats. It was his scent, and it was strong. Her eyes went wide as her hand covered her mouth. Her gaze darted to Raff, and she shook her head.

"I'm so sorry. I didn't think about the scent thing when I put them on. I forgot."

Raff just shook his head and pushed her hair behind her ear. "It's okay, I don't mind." She nodded like that was it. He wasn't mad, he was okay?

"Did Mav give them to you?" Had she been wearing them all day? If she had, Jett would have said something. Wouldn't he?

"No, what? Oh...I feel terrible. I was bloated, and I didn't really have anything to change into. I tried to find which room was yours, Raff, and then I ended up in Lyell's room, so I just snatched them. Honestly, I didn't even think he wore sweats. My jeans were just so tight."

No one said anything, we just nodded, but I watched Mav from the corner of my eye. He'd moved closer, and I could see that he'd smelled himself on them, too. I wouldn't have noticed if she hadn't pulled the blanket back, since all our scents were mixed in this room. I looked at Raff, and he didn't look like he was going to say anything to her. But I would.

"They aren't Lyell's sweats, and you're right, he doesn't wear them. They're Mav's."

Her mouth popped open as her head swung back to Mav. He gave her a small smile and shrugged.

"Oh god, I'm so sorry, Maverick. I didn't mean to go in your room. I had to grab them quickly before talking to your dad and stuff. I didn't even think about it. I'll wash them and give them back."

She blew the top of her tea and took a small sip. The room was quiet, except for the music and credits rolling on the movie.

Galen moved around and stood in front of us. "Don't worry about the sweats. There's like a hundred pairs here. Isn't that right, Maverick?"

"Yeah, you can keep them. I have more if you need some." She wouldn't stop looking at Mav over her teacup. Why? I wanted her to myself for just a little while, and everyone in here had messed that up for me.

"Let's watch a movie and eat ice cream." I held a spoon out to her and kept the other. I was going to eat with her. I reached into my back pocket and produced some tissues.

She giggled. "Oh, thank you. I didn't realize how good that movie was."

I didn't think it was good…it'd made her cry.

CHAPTER FORTY-FIVE

LEXI

*S**hit, shit, shit.*

Maverick's sweats... which meant it wasn't Lyell's room. That was Maverick's room, and he had all the Jane Austen books. Why would he have them in his room? Was he going to read them? I looked at him for the longest time, but he didn't say anything. He just smiled at me. And holy hotness, that guy had dimples... Like, how had I never seen them? I guess because he was always so angry at me before. But now, he wasn't...and he hadn't been. He was giving me whiplash.

Ranger had sat down beside me, while Raff had sat up to give us more room for the ice cream. I guessed Ranger didn't expect everyone in here when he gave me a spoon and kept one for himself.

I'd been thinking about what Alaric had said, and I really had judged Ranger unfairly. Well, he was a bit full of himself, and that got my back up fast. I decided I would stop being such a bitch to him and get to know him better. Not because of what was put on the table —with college and everything—but it was fact that this wasn't how Ranger normally acted apparently, and he got Raff to move here. That in itself was a huge plus in the 'be nice to Ranger' column and a reason to give him a second chance. And now with the flowers...he was growing on me.

"*Romeo and Juliet?*" Galen asked from over near the popcorn machine. Ranger and Raff both nodded. I wanted to giggle at the way they were so in sync with each other.

I nodded. "Yes, sounds great." I wasn't going to cry in front of any of them. No more sad, sappy me. I looked over at Maverick sitting alone and waved for him to come over. He couldn't just sit alone when we had a picnic going on here. When he didn't move, I knew I would have to make him.

"Come on over here, Maverick. We have everything. Did you want some ice cream?"

Galen sat on the floor in front of me and laid his head back on the blanket close to my feet. He picked up a chocolate and then put it down again. His head tilted back, and his eyes met mine, but I wasn't sure what he was thinking. I felt bad for him since he couldn't eat it. I would die if I couldn't eat chocolate.

"Do you only drink blood?" I whispered. I felt everyone's eyes on me. I looked around at them all. Maverick had come over and was now sitting next to his brother, yet still farther out than I was hoping.

"Yes, and alcohol," Galen responded. Ranger let out a snort and a small chuckle, and Galen pinned him with his eyes. I could tell he didn't want him to say something. Oh...what did Mr. Donovani do?

"What's so funny?" I asked, really curious now. I scooped some ice cream, and the flavor burst in my mouth. I moaned. So cold, chocolatey, and creamy. God, that was good. I scooped again and turned to Raff, aiming for his mouth. He opened, and I put the spoon on his tongue. I watched his lips wrap around it as I pulled out slowly.

He smirked, and I couldn't help it. I kissed him and licked away a little ice cream that was left behind on his lip. I licked my lips as I turned back to see what Ranger was going to say, but instead, the three of them were staring at me.

"What?" I asked again. Ranger shook his head with a smirk and cleared his throat. Galen jumped up and, in a flash, he held his hand over Ranger's mouth. I think my eyes bugged out of my head like Ranger's did. I forgot how fast Galen could be.

"Nothing was funny. I do drink blood. I also drink alcohol to keep my body warm to the touch and to stave of hunger. That's all. I don't get to taste chocolate and popcorn." When he took his hand from Ranger's mouth, Ranger wiped his mouth as he cocked his head, and that grin on his face turned wicked.

"Galen was *so* hungry this morning that he drank straight from the bottle." Galen's face paled as he looked at me.

I didn't know what that meant. Was it because...? My face felt hot, and I put my hands on my cheeks to hide it.

"No, no. I can tell what you're thinking. I skipped breakfast, and I'd never done that before school. It was...a little harder for me than usual."

The movie had started, but no one was watching, since we were all still watching each other. It wasn't awkward or anything. It felt... right? We were all just hanging out, like what normal people did. It was nice. Plus, well, they were all nice to look at. I kept that part to myself because I didn't want to make that mistake again. No dirty thoughts with shifters around. I took a scoop of ice cream and caught Maverick's eyes following it as I brought it toward my mouth.

"Oh, sorry, did you want some?" I leaned forward and held the spoon out close to his mouth. He looked to me, to Raff, then to Ranger.

"Shit, you probably don't want my germs—" He took my hand in his, guided the spoon to his mouth, and sucked the ice cream off. *Holy shit.* That was so hot—*no dirty thoughts.* Oh god, I just figured out what I did there. When he let go and I took the spoon back, I moved a little closer to Raff. His arm went around my waist, and he smelled my hair. I was worried Raff would be mad, since I'd fed him from the same spoon too, but he didn't say anything. He just held me close. and my heart calmed a little.

No one said anything about what I'd just done. We just all turned and watched the movie. I wanted to ask Galen more about being a vampire and how he drinks. Did he drink from humans or did he go to a blood bank? Did he have a blood slave at his place? I couldn't concentrate on the movie, as I kept looking at the back of his head. His curls were extra curly today, and I wanted to mess them up a little and run my fingers through them.

At the end of the movie, everyone packed up quickly because dinner was ready, and then Galen went home. I didn't realize that Nash was a cook, but it turned out that all the boys took turns cooking dinner. Jett wasn't back for dinner, and I wondered if he was with Mekhi still.

"What are you thinking?" Ranger asked me with a huge grin. I realized I did it again. Holy shit, *no dirty thoughts... Fuck, fuck, fuck.*

"Stop smelling me. It's rude." Alaric agreed with me, then gave me a look that reminded me about the conversation we had earlier. I gave a small nod. I wouldn't call Ranger out, but I would slap him later because no one else said anything about my scent. There were times he could've just pretended like everyone else.

There was discussion about the boys going to a shifter party over at a neighbor's place later, with a bonfire, marshmallows, and a little bit of drinking. I was surprised that Alaric was okay with this, but I guessed this was just how shifters lived. I'd never seen the boys or Alaric drink since I'd been here, so maybe they only did it at parties?

"You want to come, Rafferty? Meet the boys?" Maverick asked. I felt my insides want to burst and cry with happiness. I could feel Raff tense beside me, so I nudged him with my elbow.

"You should go, it sounds like a great idea." He looked conflicted. I reached my hand under the table and squeezed as I gave him a warm smile, willing him to get out there. Then maybe later, we could kiss and cuddle.

"I wish we could take you, Lex. But it's a pack only thing, so *no girls*," Ranger told me. I shrugged.

"I was going to take a bath and read some more of *Sense and Sensibility*." I looked over to Maverick as I said that. I wanted to ask him if he was the one who'd bought the books for me. When his eyes met mine at the words *Sense and Sensibility*, the greens of his eyes lightened and they were almost bright. My heart sped up. *It was him.*

"But you should go, Raff, and then when you come back, give me a goodnight kiss?"

"I think this is a great idea, Rafferty, Ranger, and Maverick. You'll all have a great time together. Some bonding time will be great for you all."

I hoped so, for Raff's sake. Or I was going to go to this party and kick some wolf-shifter ass.

CHAPTER FORTY-SIX

LEXI

"Lexi, Lexi, I'm here," someone called, and I pried my eyes open. The sunlight was bright coming through the curtains, so I buried my head under the covers. I wasn't getting up, why was someone calling my name? I felt the bed dip, then dip again and again. *What the…?*

The bright light was back, and I opened my eyes to see a little face with a huge grin, those big brown eyes, and jet-black hair.

"Joshy?" Was I dreaming? He giggled and nodded.

"Do you want to go in the pool with me? I can't swim good." *Yeah, neither can I, buddy. I was never taught.*

"I can't swim good, either." He just giggled as his little hands went to my cheeks.

"I missed you. We didn't get to watch our shows this week." I nodded and felt a pang of guilt. It wasn't my fault I was here, but still. I should've made more of an effort to see Josh. When I saw Jack and Grayson at the bedroom door, they gave me apologetic looks.

"Josh, you should have knocked and waited."

I pulled Joshy in for a hug. "He's okay. How did you…" 'Find me' was at the tip of my tongue. Maybe 'smell me' would have been better? "Ah...when did you get here?"

Jack looked around at the bedroom as I sat up and glanced beside me. Did Raff come in last night? I didn't remember if he did or not. Shit, I hope he got back okay.

"I just need to check on Raff, then I'll get ready for the pool." I didn't have a bathing suit, but if I just wore my underwear and a tank, that would be okay. I think. Crap, was it even warm enough to swim?

"Raff was downstairs with the big boys," Josh said as he got closer to my ear. "You know, the ones that are like the same, but one is nice and the other—"

I put my hand over his mouth and laughed. "And the other is nice, too?" He shook his head, and I could hear Jack and Grayson laugh as they told Josh to get out so I could get ready.

I made my bed and took a quick shower, then I rummaged through my stuff and found my razor. I quickly shaved my legs, my armpits, and yeah, I shaved my pubes. I didn't have money to get waxed, so shaving was just a normal part of my life. Plus, I liked to look neat down there, and it only took a tiny bit of maintenance. I still had my period, but at least I didn't have cramps today. Maybe chocolate, flowers, and ice cream really was the cure for cramps.

I put my black boylegs on, since they looked like bikini bottoms. I only had a lace black bra that was clean, so that would have to do. I looked through my tank tops. Fuck, I'd done laundry, but I was missing some. I only had a white one, and no, I couldn't wear that in the pool with Josh. It wasn't appropriate. I dashed back to grab the fluffy white towel and wrapped it around myself. I'd ask Raff if I could borrow something.

I felt a little exposed out in the hallway. I headed down to where I'd learned was his room, the one right next to the stairs. Then I remembered Josh said he was downstairs.

"Raff?" I called out. It didn't take long before I heard him bounce up the stairs. I laughed when he froze as he took in my appearance.

"So, I was wanting to borrow a top to use in the pool, preferably dark because I don't exactly own a swimsuit." When he didn't move, I heard more footsteps, and then Ranger's head popped around the corner.

"Oh," Ranger said, which snapped Raff out of his daze.

Raff bent down and kissed me, his hand on my hip. I grabbed his top and pulled him as I walked backward toward his door. I reached behind me and found the door handle without us breaking apart. As I pulled it down, I looked from the corner of my eye and saw Ranger watching us from the stairs. We stumbled into the room, falling onto the floor. Raff held me tight to break my fall, but we ended up all tangled together, not that I was complaining. The towel was now long gone as Raff hovered above me.

I felt his heated gaze as his head dipped to take me all in. I could feel my pulse picking up when he made a sound deep in his chest, telling me he liked what he saw.

"Are you really mine?" he asked, his brow cocked, and that cute smile he had made me feel breathless.

I reached up and pushed his hair out of his eyes. "I could ask you the same." His hand went behind my head and pulled me into a kiss. His tongue swept out to mine, and slowly, his body lowered. The heavy weight of his body was welcome as he pressed his erection into me. He rubbed himself against my core, and I trembled. I loved the more confident Raff. Kissing and licking, I wanted all of him. If only I could just will my period away right now.

A throat cleared, and Raff quickly pulled me to his chest to block me from whoever it was.

"Sorry to interrupt, but Josh is getting a little restless waiting for his Lexi." It was Jack. Oh gosh, how embarrassing... He could probably smell how aroused I was. When Jack left, I quickly got up with the help of Raff. I watched as he reached into his sweats and rearranged himself so he didn't have a tent out the front. He grabbed a black T-shirt, which wasn't exactly what I was looking for, but it would work. I slipped it over my head, and he gave me another kiss before he rubbed his neck on me. I giggled. I didn't think I would ever not like this marking thing. It proved that I was his and he was mine.

I grabbed the towel and swung it over my shoulder. The tee was long enough to cover my butt, but if I put my arms up, it was exposed. It would be fine in the pool. No one would see it then.

"Marco."

"Polo."

Josh was wearing some floaties, which really helped him. There were times I wished I was too, but I just avoided the deep end. It was warm, and the pool was heated and so nice. I was so nervous when I dipped that first toe in, but the air outside wasn't too bad for spring, and with the heated pool it felt so good.

"I got you again, Lexi. You keep losing." Josh laughed as he held onto my arm. I gave him a look of surprise again. I let him catch me over and over. I wasn't going to tell him I let him win. I just loved the laughter and innocence that came from a six-year-old.

Jack, Grayson, Nash, and Alaric were all sitting outside at a table, drinking lemonade and talking. From what I could gather, Jack and Grayson didn't come here often. And by the way Josh was excited about the pool, I think this was his first time here.

"You have to come visit me every week, and I'll visit you, okay?" I told Josh, holding out my pinkie finger. He took it with his little one, and we shook on it.

We played until it was lunch and they had to leave to get the other boys. Apparently, Harry and Jaxon were at their friend's house, and this was just a special visit for me and Josh. It made my day that they brought him here. When it was time to go, I gave him the biggest hug, and he burst into tears. I promised him I would see him after school during the week.

I'd ask Galen to drive me, which helped calm Josh. Then it was just me, alone in the pool. Alaric had walked them out, and Nash was just sitting at the table. He wasn't looking at me, rather he was looking behind me at the forest—the one that held bad memories of last Saturday.

How was it only a week ago? How had my life changed so fast? This was insane. What had happened to me since I moved to Kiba? Maybe Shelly was right—this was where I was meant to be. I wasn't just in the Lovell's pool, I was still here living with them. I hadn't run, I'd stayed.

I inched closer to the edge of the pool, but I didn't want to talk to Nash. I still didn't like how he'd threatened to send Raff away to get me to move here. His eyes flicked to mine, and I froze.

"I'm only waiting for Ranger...he's on his way with Rafferty. I didn't want to leave you alone in the pool in case something happened and you needed help."

I nodded. Huh...that made sense. I'd mentioned many times to Josh that I wasn't confident swimming too far from the shallow end.

I guess that was nice of Nash to be concerned. *I think.*

From out of nowhere, I heard a "whoop" as someone flipped and bombed into the deep end. Water splashed everywhere as Ranger emerged from the water, his hands pressing his hair back, his muscular chest all wet and shiny. My nipples hardened at the sight.

Shit. I was in trouble.

CHAPTER FORTY-SEVEN

RAFFERTY

I hadn't been too sure about going to the party last night. With me living here at the alpha's house, I'd come to some kind of truce with Ranger and Maverick. We seemed to be getting along fine. I knew they felt the same intense pull to Lexi as I did. I couldn't blame them for the way they acted toward me, or to her for that reason. I might've done the same, if I was in their shoes.

Maverick thought I didn't know, but I could tell he liked her, and I knew he was the one giving her those books she loved, not Lyell. He was just the in-between guy. Lyell was really quiet, but you could tell he had a good heart. Lexi felt relaxed when she was around him, so it made sense in the days before I was here that Maverick had him deliver the books to her.

The party was at the Jones brothers' house, which was just a few houses down from the Lovell's. But they all had such big properties that it was a good ten-minute walk before we even got to their front gate. I was nervous, since in my old pack, I'd been the only teen. Hell, I'd been the only one under forty. So, for this place to have so many teens, it was intimidating and my wolf was pacing. I was looking for danger everywhere, trying to calm him when I saw nothing.

"I need to talk to you before we go in. Is that okay?" Ranger asked. It was dark out, but I could see him quite well—a benefit of being a shifter. I shrugged, for someone who talked a lot, he'd been really quiet as we headed toward the party.

Maverick hesitated, but Ranger waved for him to go ahead. I realized he wanted to speak to just me, and I think I already knew what it was about.

"So, I have a packmate, and I'm going to walk in there tonight and tell him that I'm breaking that with him. For now, at least. But before I do, I wanted to speak to you. And well, I know Lex is with you now. And I'm happy for her and you, but you know how I feel about her.

"I want to... Is there any way you can forgive me, for everything I've done? I want to make this work, us work as friends and show Lex that I would make a good mate. Fuck, I'm in love with her. I can't stop myself. I want her, to share her with you, and I swear on my life, I'll protect her. She'll have the backing of the whole pack, even if she doesn't want me like that.

"You're one of us, even though it's not official yet, but you are. And I wanted to tell you that you can trust me. I'll have your back always."

I was taken aback a little. I'd only just been told about Pack Kiba's offer to join them on my birthday. I thought about my uncles—the assholes who tortured me—and it didn't take any thinking to say yes. There was no way I could go back to Pack Russet, they would kill me and take Lexi for their own.

I didn't even want to think about the horrors they would inflict on her, and I didn't want to be a lone wolf my whole life. Lexi needed a pack, and with Kiba, I could give her that. She would be protected by me and the pack. And maybe, if she wanted, by her other mates.

I held my hand out, and Ranger smiled as he took it, then he pulled me into a hug. I was a little surprised by that as he patted my back.

"That feels so much better, thanks so much, man. And...ah, can you like, maybe talk me up? Like, talk to Lex for me?" At that, I shook my head and chuckled. If he wanted her, he had to do all the work himself.

"Oh, man, really? You suck," he said as he playfully pushed me away. "You're making this hard on me, aren't you?"

"Yeah, well...just be yourself. If she likes you, she'll tell you." I didn't know what else to say, but my wolf knew that Ranger could be trusted. That he would make a good packmate to me. I could feel my wolf getting closer to the surface. He wanted to run with Ranger, to show him that I liked this arrangement. I turned to see Ranger's eyes flash—his wolf was thinking the same.

"Let's go say hi, then go for a run?"

Hell yeah. I needed this...we needed this.

We'd been in the kitchen while Josh and Lexi had their little play date in the pool. I loved the connection they had with each other. That was something special, and it wasn't just for Josh, it was for Lexi too. She really cared about him.

Ranger and I were talking when Nash called for us to come watch Lexi. He said he was trying to be discreet, but he could smell the fear coming from her, so we ran up and got changed for the pool. I didn't own any boardshorts, so Ranger loaned me a pair. He was built larger than me, so I had to really pull the drawstrings in.

"Dare you to dive in." I shoved him playfully before I ran off down the stairs, but the guy was still bigger and faster than me. He beat me to the pool, and I watched as he flipped in the air and dove in. I watched the back of Lexi as she tried to block the water from splashing her face. She didn't smell like fear now. No, I could smell her arousal. *For Ranger.*

Nash nodded and walked off as I made my way to the stairs into the pool and walked down, the warm water lapping at my skin. Ranger was right, these boardshorts would've come off if I dove in.

"Hey, where were you?" Her big smile and those gorgeous eyes sparkled at me, and I couldn't get over how lucky I was. How the hell did I get such an amazing girl? I could smell her arousal stronger now as I got closer, and I knew that this was for me, too. My wolf nuzzled her neck, feeling happy at being close to her.

"I was just chatting with Ranger." She climbed my body like a monkey, wrapping her legs around my waist, and then she kissed me. My cock grew hard at her tiny body pressed against mine, wearing my T-shirt. When my hands went under her ass to carry her toward the deeper water, I was met with more skin than her underwear, and I growled softly as I nipped her lips. I might be inexperienced, but I was a quick learner.

She responded as she ground herself against me, and when I moaned against her lips, she giggled. I moved her away from my body to reach down and adjust myself. I seemed to be forever needing to readjust myself around Lexi.

She ran her hands all over my chest, then traced a path lower...

"I love your tattoos. You have so many for someone so young."

I could hear Ranger laugh before he called out, "Yeah, well, that's because someone has good control of his wolf, and he wears the proof of it on his body. If only I had that much control. Raff is one of a kind, Lex." She pulled back and looked over to Ranger. He only had half a sleeve, it was a wolf in a forest scene, and most the Kiba teens had something similar. It was very detailed, and I'd been meaning to ask who his artist was. I still had a little time before my eighteenth to get a couple more, and I wanted to get Lexi's name tattooed to me. I knew she was it for me.

"What does that mean? Does your wolf not like you getting tattoos?"

I realized then that she didn't know. I'd never told her...but I guessed there was a lot she still didn't know that was just so normal to us that we'd forgotten to mention it. She looked back at me. "What's he talking about?" I shook my head and laughed.

"I heal fast, we all do, but if I was to shift into wolf form too fast after getting a tattoo, it would heal too fast and be gone. It takes about two weeks before my body fully accepts the tatt. So it would all be for waste if I didn't have control over my shift."

Her little brows crinkled in the middle, and I kissed her there. She was confused, and I wasn't good at this.

"He's just being modest. Trust me, he's strong. Mav's probably the only other shifter our age that has such control of his wolf." Ranger had moved closer, and she started tracing some of them on my shoulder.

"Is that why you only have that one?" she asked Ranger, her voice teasing.

"Yeah, and to be honest, this was the second go. But then I turned eighteen, so no more for me." She nodded, then gave us another puzzled look. Ranger laughed. "Man, we're shit at this. When we turn eighteen, we become full shifters? Is that what you would say, Raff?" I nodded. "So, I heal fast. Like super-fast without shifting, so the tattoo would be rejected by my body before they've even really started it. But Raff's healing will still take time, until his birthday. Then he won't be able to get anymore tattoos."

I could see Lexi's brain was working overtime, and I hugged her close. I could smell Galen coming...with Maverick. That had my ears perked.

"Yeah, okay. I'm just not going to think about it and just enjoy them instead."

That was when Ranger splashed us and Lexi squealed, clutching her legs tight around my waist. She moved her arms to the side and splashed him back. Then she turned to me, so playful and happy, and she smacked my chest. "Go get him." She dropped away from me, and I pushed her to the side of the pool so she could hold on, then I wrestled Ranger down under the water in a mock fight.

CHAPTER FORTY-EIGHT

LEXI

I was laughing so hard when Raff and Ranger tumbled around. It was a sight that I wouldn't forget...and might even use when I got myself off. God, they were so hot. The tattoo thing was still reeling over in my mind, and I wondered if what Ranger said was true, then Raff was like super tough or something for a shifter.

"Good to see the peacocks are out today." I laughed when Galen walked over, wearing yet another sweater. Wasn't he a little warm? Oh fuck. The alcohol thing made him warm to the touch, he'd said. So, I guessed he was cold right now? Or he didn't feel the sun or the heat? Actually, how did he walk around in the sun? Or was that one of those myths? He was a myth, what was I thinking?

"Hey, who you calling peacock?" Ranger called out as Maverick pulled a chair closer to the edge of the pool. He was wearing a tight white tee, his colorful tatts out on display. I wondered after that conversation if he had more. He smirked at me, dimples out, and I felt it between my thighs. I clamped my legs together, which just intensified the need. Oh god, I gotta stop this. I still had my period, but my body was all hyperaware of sexy bodies and dimples. Galen pulled a chair beside Maverick and took a seat. I looked away, since I didn't want to get caught out, and I knew Galen would send me over the edge.

Ranger appeared from the water in front of me. I giggled as his hair lay limp in his eyes. He shook his head like a dog, little droplets spraying my face. He winked just as Raff popped up, and Ranger jumped on his back and took him down under the water again. I could feel Galen and Maverick watching them and me.

"Lunch is ready," Jett called out as he brought a huge plate of subs.

My stomach growled as I walked over to the edge and grabbed one before Jett moved on to Maverick. Jett shook his head at me. "Don't eat and swim." I laughed, yeah, like I could actually swim.

Ranger and Raff waved Jett on, since apparently, they'd already eaten. I was surprised at how fast they'd formed a friendship, even though Alaric did tell me this was happening between them.

But what surprised me the most was how fast this was becoming so comfortable—the four guys here with me.

I sat on the edge as the boys swam races up and down the pool. I moved back into the pool as I watched them swim underwater again and got into position for Raff to swim into me. I wanted a little bit more now. I was feeling a little horny again, and I missed his lips on mine.

He grabbed my waist as he popped up. "I win," he said, just as Ranger popped up at the edge of the pool.

"Yes, you do." He chuckled as he leaned back against the ledge. I wrapped my legs around Raff and pulled my lips to his. I could feel him walk backward past Ranger, backing himself into the corner. My back was to Maverick and Galen, so I was hidden in a way.

I licked the seam of Raff's lips, and he opened for me, his hands cupping my ass as he pulled me closer. I could feel one of his hands start to travel up my back, under the heavy, wet tee. I wanted to take it off so I could feel his skin against mine.

I trailed my hand down his chest and between us as I toyed with the drawstring that held his shorts up. He groaned into my mouth, bucking his hips up, and I smiled. He pulled away from the kiss, and I could see his hooded gaze trail down my body. The wet tee stuck to me, showing off my body without me being naked.

"You are so sexy, Lexi," he whispered in my ear, and I could feel my body heat up. My clit wanted to be rubbed, and I wanted to rub his cock, watch him come... I turned back to see Ranger had moved closer to us, like really close. I looked over and saw Galen was now leaning forward on his chair, his elbows on his knees. Maverick was in the same position as Galen, but he'd moved over to see me, his knee touching Galen's. I could see them both look to where they were touching, then back to us. But their knees didn't pull apart.

"You're beautiful, Lex. Inside and out." Ranger hadn't moved any closer, but I could feel the air around us full of built-up sexual tension. He gave me a small smile before he checked out my ass. Holy shit. Could everyone see my ass? I reached behind me and tried to pull the material down, but it had ridden up a lot.

They were all looking at my ass? I looked back to Galen, who just cocked his head slightly, but his expression didn't change. Did my history teacher just look at my ass? Holy fuck, I think he did. The thought alone had me growing wetter. Raff started to grind his hips into me, his hard length rubbing against my clit. It sent heat flaring through my body, and I turned back and kissed him. I rubbed myself more, chasing that blissful feeling of climax, and knowing I had an audience made it feel all the more intense. I wanted it. I wanted to fall apart in front of them.

I felt something press against my back, and I froze. My chest was heaving, and I felt Ranger pressing gently against me. My eyes flashed to Raff, and the corner of his mouth turned up slightly.

"You make me so hard, just watching you rub yourself against his hard cock. Are you going to come, Lex?" I sucked in a breath. Ranger, holy shit... My heart pounded as his chest pressed heavily against my back, but Raff didn't tell him to leave, he just nodded at me. He was telling me he was okay with this if I was.

I didn't move, since I wasn't sure. But when I felt the pressure from my back leave as Ranger moved away, my hand flew out and grabbed his arm to stop him. I didn't know what I wanted, but I didn't want him to leave.

I pulled him back, and this time, I could feel his hard cock against my ass as his hands grabbed my ass cheeks. I let go of his arm and held on to Raff's neck.

"Tell me to leave, and I will," he whispered into my ear. When I didn't reply, he took that as a silent answer and squeezed my ass. I started to move against Raff, but this time, there were three of us, breathing deeply, getting closer, chasing that climax. I took Raff's lips again, and I was rough as I bit his bottom lip, then licked it better. He growled, and I could feel it in my chest.

My nipples were rubbing against him, and I wanted this wet tee off. I needed to feel his chest against my nipples, I needed him to touch me. I reached down and pulled it up as high as I could get it. It was stuck to my body, but with four other hands helping, we got it pulled up over my head. I heard Ranger gasp from behind me, and he ran his finger down my spine. I arched back toward him. I hadn't even kissed him, and he was touching me in ways I didn't think would turn me on. *Was this what it was like for a female shifter?*

Double the pleasure. Raff pulled down the cup of my bra, exposing me. His thumb brushed over my hard nipple before he took it in his mouth. I let out sound that was almost cat like.

"Fuck, I'm close," I said. God, I wished I wasn't on my period. I wanted to fuck him so bad, but this was good enough for now. Ranger wrapped his fist around my hair and pulled it gently, my back bowing and giving Raff better access to both my nipples. With my head on Ranger's chest, I watched as his eyes asked for permission to kiss me. I gasped, then turned my head to the side, exposing my neck to him. He bent down, kissing and sucking my neck, giving me small bites, then kissing them better. I was pressed so hard against him, and I wanted to kiss him, I just...I wasn't ready.

I pulled free of Ranger and grabbed Raff's shoulder just as pleasure crashed through my body in waves. I moaned loudly, closing my eyes, and a hand went to my mouth as I rode out wave after wave from that intense orgasm.

As I started to come down, the hand was removed, and I realized it was Ranger who'd stopped me from screaming out and alerting everyone to what we were doing in the pool. He didn't pull away from me though. He held me with Raff, all three of us panting hard.

"Shit, you didn't come in the pool, did you?" I didn't think about that as I looked down to Raff's crotch. I didn't think many people would want to swim in here after something like that. Raff shook his head with a lazy smile, and I could feel Ranger chuckle from behind.

"No, but you're so fucking sexy when you come, Lex." My body shivered at his words. Ranger certainly knew how to talk.

Now that I was down from that high, I didn't know what had come over me. Did I want more with Ranger? I... Fuck, Galen and Maverick. I tore my eyes away from Raff and glanced behind me, finding Ranger smiling at me. I cocked my head to see Maverick and Galen were now standing, watching us.

I couldn't tell by Galen's expression what he was thinking—it was unreadable—but as I looked down, I could see Maverick had the heel of his hand pressed against his crotch as he rubbed himself through his jeans. His eyes widened like a deer in headlights, and he stopped as he looked right at me, his mouth dropping open. I quickly looked away, breaking apart from Raff's body. He pulled gently on my wrist, and I pulled him down for a kiss.

Ranger had stepped back a little, but his hand was still on my ass, until I spun around and looked up into those pretty green eyes of his. His breathing was still heavy as he looked down to the space between us. His hand went out and found mine. He didn't say anything, he just held it, waiting for me to make the next move.

I just didn't know what that move was. I dropped his hand and quickly made my way out of the pool, forgetting I was now only wearing my wet underwear and my bra was exposing my nipples to everyone. I flicked them back up as I looked over to where I'd left my towel earlier, but then I felt it brush over my shoulders. I grabbed hold of it, looking over my shoulder and catching the hazel eyes of Galen.

"Thank you," I whispered as I wrapped it around me tightly. He rubbed my arms through the towel to dry me off, touching me.

This was too much. I was in way too deep, and I needed to talk to someone. *Right now.*

CHAPTER FORTY-NINE

LEXI

I needed someone, so I texted Ada to come over. This was what friends did, right? They helped you, and they talked about boys. Plus, I had to tell her I was living at the Lovell mansion. I was nervous about that, because I guessed that was something you told your friends when moved. She called me back and screamed about how I didn't tell her, and that she learned about it from Ranger yesterday, and that she'd been waiting for me to tell her. Then, once she calmed down, she said she'd be over shortly, and we'd have a full girls' night sleepover.

I agreed, because the more distance I could put between me and the guys until I could clearly think about this, the better. Plus, Ada was a good reason for them to not talk to me about what had just happened, because even I didn't know what had just happened.

I'd just got out of the shower when I heard a knock at my bedroom door.

"Lexi, it's me." I could hear her giggle as I opened the door in just my towel. She rushed through the doorway, suitcase and backpack in tow.

"Lexi...dang. Do you always open your door in nothing but a

towel?" Jett waved his hand, fanning himself in a dramatic way, before he gave a low wolf whistle. If I didn't know how fun he was, I would've been worried at that. I clutched it tighter and shoved him from the doorway.

He laughed as he put his hands up in surrender. "I was just showing your friend to your room, being a good host. And to let you know that everyone has left for a run..." He winked. "So, you girls have fun with girl talk, and I'll be outside chilling if you need me, listening to the sounds of rock." He pulled some earbuds from his pocket and popped them in before walking off, waving to me over his shoulder. I laughed as I closed the door and watched as Ada flopped onto the white king-sized bed.

"Holy hell, this bedroom is amazing. And what the hell happened? Is this where you've you been hiding? You didn't tell me you were living here. I heard that from Ranger. And oh my god, Ranger talked to me. At school, in front of like, a heap of people." She was talking so fast, then she jumped up and squealed loudly at the flowers that Ranger had brought me.

"This is what he got? Holy crap. I told him I wasn't sure about flowers, but I wasn't expecting it to be this big when I told him." I laughed. The bouquet was a huge bunch of wildflowers mixed together, which was kind of funny because that was how he smelled to me that first time we met.

"You told him to buy me flowers? What did he ask you?" Shit, did he ask her how to impress me and she told him to buy me flowers?

"Oh yeah, he said you had your monthly and wanted to know what to get you. I guess he wanted to cheer you up or something. Did you get chocolate and a massage?" Her eyebrows wiggled, and she laughed. I was so glad she was here right now. I needed this.

"Yes to the chocolate..." How did I tell her the massage was maybe a little different than how they're normally given, and in a pool? "They have a movie room. I say we raid the kitchen and watch movies, and maybe we can sleep in there? It's amazing. Just let me get dressed real quick."

When we were all comfy with our goodies all laid out, I tried to think of how to ask her if she thought the whole Raff and Ranger thing was crazy and weird.

"What is it? You have a look," she said. I knew I needed to be quick. Jett told me they were going for a run, and his wearing headphones and listening to rock were code for 'we're not listening.'

"So, Raff and I are like... He's mine—"

Her hands flew to her mouth. "Oh my god, you're with Raff? I... Wow, he's so fucking hot and mysterious."

I laughed, because she didn't even let me finish. I nodded. "Oh, hell yeah. I know right? So many tattoos." Her eyes were wide, and she nodded, waiting for me to proceed.

"So, like earlier, in the pool..." She gasped. I didn't know if I could finish with her doing this. I was nervous to tell her for some reason, but I guessed that was because I'd never told someone my boy problems before.

"Just let me finish. So earlier, I was in the pool, making out with Raff...and you know, dry humping him in the pool." She held her hands tight to her mouth and nodded. Fuck, why was this hard?

"And um, Ranger..." I waited for that to settle with her. "He, um...joined in." Her hands fell from her mouth, but she didn't say anything. I'd made Ada Stephens speechless.

"I didn't kiss him, but he... Well, he wants to go out with me, too... I think. Well, no, he said that he does, even with Raff being my boyfriend. Like, is that normal? Do girls really have more than one boyfriend? I've never had one before, so two at once seems like...like a lot?"

She held her hand up and nodded. Shit, she probably thought I was some greedy whore.

"Girl, that's normal, and no, that's not a lot. You're crazy for even thinking that. Holy hotness, you come to school and score the most-wanted guy in our class. And the new guy, who is a total mystery, and god, those eyes." I laughed and agreed, because Raff really had amazing eyes.

"You know, my sister's best friend, Kiara, has two boyfriends. We all thought people might say something rude about them, but they walked around school all holding hands and kissing. The guys didn't, you know, kiss each other, but they both kissed her, and I always thought, that's what I want. And you, lucky thing, can have that with Raff and Ranger."

I sat up straighter. There was a girl Ada knew who'd already done this?

"Oh wait, Jett and Mekhi were dating Clare Briggs last year, and that was all in the open. But they broke up... It was sad because I was friends with her, not close, but still. She was upset at first, but then she was all happy and moved off to college. I wouldn't go to college and leave them yummy guys behind. I would've stayed. We thought they would get married and everything."

Wow, that just made me feel even worse for Jett. She was all happy to move away and leave him. I couldn't bear to think about moving away from Raff... Ranger... God, Galen and Maverick. I wouldn't want to leave here. I felt the same as Ada.

"Where's this friend now? Your sister's friend, Kiara?" Because if she was with these guys, I had to assume she knew about them being shifters and everything. And maybe I could talk to her.

"She lives in Rawlins with them. They all got a house after graduation and moved in over there. I saw her last week, she stopped by to say hi to my parents. She's getting married...well, not to both of them. More like having a commitment ceremony thingy. She invited us, and my sister is coming home, and I can't wait for you to meet my sister. I told Destiny how the jacket fit you like it was destiny. She didn't find it as funny, but she's excited to meet you when she gets back over spring break."

Wow, this was amazing. I felt a lot better hearing that someone else did this two boyfriends thing and was still living like that, having commitment ceremonies, and people were accepting it. Well, for the shifters, it was normal. It was the regular folk that I thought might have some problems.

"Did you like...you know...with Raff? Is he big?"

I slapped her arm and told her to shut it. We hadn't gone that far, but I'd seen it, and I couldn't help it... I showed her the size with my hands. She whistled and I nodded, and then we both laughed.

"Let's watch a movie with hot guys and pig out."

CHAPTER FIFTY

LEXI

When Monday morning rolled around, I felt amazing, like everything was going to work out. Talking with Ada had really helped. I'd avoided Ranger most of yesterday after Ada went home, but he'd spent a lot of time talking with her during breakfast, which was nice. She'd been a little overwhelmed by the Lovell brothers. Lyell didn't know what to make of her, and I was starting to suspect Ada was a bit of a nervous talker.

"You can ride with us, if you want?" Ranger had been acting very sweet toward me, like not so in-your-face as he had been. I had a feeling he was worried I was upset with him, or that was my guess after what had happened in the pool. *No dirty thoughts.*

I was starting to come to terms with the whole two boyfriends thing and how, like maybe, I might be okay with it. *Ugh.* I didn't know. I hadn't even wanted a boyfriend or to fall in love when I moved here. I had plans, but all that had changed for the better, and I wouldn't take it back. I could never give up Raff. What was an extra boyfriend...or two or three?

"Um, okay, Thanks." Ranger's face lit up, and he stumbled out of his chair as he stood. Everyone laughed, but he didn't care. He had the biggest grin on his face, like he'd just won the lottery.

The school day didn't start off bad. If anything, it seemed a little too easy. An essay I wrote in English came back with amazing marks. I didn't think I'd done that well, to be honest, since I was a little distracted about the whole move to the Lovells and I didn't get a chance to study much for it. Statistics was boring, but Raff being in class with me was the best part.

When lunch rolled around, Raff came and took my hand in his. I didn't think I would ever get used to it, this feeling of floating whenever he was around and the little pulse of electricity that seemed to thrum between us whenever we touched.

"Hey." I pulled him down for kiss him in the middle of the cafeteria. Some students watched us, but I didn't care.

"Did you want to sit with the boys?" he asked, pointing toward the table that Ranger and Maverick sat at each day. Ada stopped next to me and wiggled her brows.

"Hey, Raff, how are you?" she asked. He looked a little stunned that she was talking to him. I knew he didn't talk much, well to other people at least. He talked plenty to me now.

"I'm good," was all he gave her. She gestured with her head to the table behind her, knowing she was talking about Ranger, and I rolled my eyes and laughed.

"What, haven't decided yet? 'Cause, wow, if I was you, I would have, and it would be a 'hell yes.'"

Raff didn't say anything. I guess he knew I'd spoken to her about it—but left out the whole wolf part. If Raff was going to sit over there, that meant that the Kiba boys had accepted him. Then I should as well, if I was going to be Pack Kiba, too. And because he was mine and I wanted them to know, I would kill them if they touched him ever again.

"Okay, I'll eat with them." I kissed him again as he made his way over to the table. I watched as Ranger's eyes found mine as he moved over for Raff to sit beside him. All the guys smiled and nodded at him, accepting him. It made me feel such relief. He had a pack now. He would be protected forever.

"You gonna invite me to come sit?" I spun back to Ada. She was wearing a little more makeup than I'd seen on her before.

"You better sit with me, because that's way too much testosterone for me."

She looped her arm in mine as we took our trays over to the table. Instantly, Raff and Ranger moved for me to sit between them, and it was almost as if it'd been planned. I watched as two other guys on the opposite side moved, and one waved for Ada to come over. I think that was Noah. Yeah, Noah. I smiled. I felt great, and they even accepted Ada.

I placed my tray on the table and stood over the bench seat and sat down. The extra space that was beside me was swallowed up with two warm bodies. Oh boy, my heart sped up a little.

"How's your day going so far?" Ranger asked, his voice a little strange sounding. I cleared my throat as Ada looked between us, and her eyes lit up as she smirked.

"Good." I didn't know what to say. All the guys at this table were shifters, and well...maybe this was a bad idea. I should've gone to Galen's office. I'd been wanting to talk to him, but also, I wasn't too sure what to say to him after the pool incident. He'd been around for dinner last night, but it had been awkward to say the least. Even Maverick was...well, he wasn't the same. I was worried I'd messed something up there, and I wanted to make it right again.

After a few minutes of sitting there, it wasn't too bad, and they started talking about football and other stuff. Obviously, being careful not to mention anything about the fact they could turn into huge gray wolves. I eased into the conversation, nodding like I had a clue about football and eating my pizza. Even Ada was smiling as Noah talked to her.

"Hey, Ranger." I turned to see Olivia standing behind Ranger. Her hand rested on his shoulder.

He turned around and gently brushed her hand off. "Hey, Olivia." He seemed a little unsure what to do as he looked at me. I didn't know what to do, either. We hadn't said anything about what was going on between us, and we hadn't even kissed. When he looked at me again, I stole a glance at her, and she gave me the good old death stare. Like I would shake in my boots. I just shrugged my shoulder, turned back to the table, and pretended she wasn't there. Funnily enough, so did Ranger. She threw a little hissy fit before she stomped off.

I rested against Raff, and he slid his hand around my waist. I wanted to laugh about her dramatic exit, but instead, I just nestled into him and secretly sniffed him. He smelled so good. Then I reached under the table and held my knee. When Ranger was talking about some story, I slowly crept my fingers across to his knee. He stopped speaking for a moment as I felt his warm hand move over mine, so I flipped mine over, intertwining our fingers tightly. He kept on talking, but now there was a lightness in his voice that wasn't there before.

I felt someone watching me, so I looked over and saw it was Maverick. He quirked his brow at me, and I winked at him, and was rewarded with a smile. It was worth it for the dimples.

When the bell rang to tell us lunch was over, I couldn't believe it. The time had gone by so fast. Ada was chatting a lot to Noah, and yes, we were getting looks from other girls, but I didn't care. Fuck them. I didn't think they could tell I was holding hands with Ranger under the table, but even if they did, they couldn't say anything to me that would make me change my mind about it.

As I lined up for history, I could feel Ranger close behind me. My pulse sped up, my mind going back to holding his hand, and the feelings I got from that gave me butterflies. It was the same feeling I got when I held Raff's. It felt...right.

"Hey," he whispered into my ear. My skin prickled. *Holy fuck...* How was my body responding so strongly to him just being this close? I looked over my shoulder and saw his goofy smile.

"Hey, back at you." He straightened up and looked around before he leaned in again. I could feel his hot breath on my neck as he sniffed me, and I giggled.

"You smell like Lexi and Raff. So fucking hot. I wanna lick your pretty throat." I trembled slightly, then I heard a throat clearing, and my head whipped around. It was Galen, and my cheeks went red. Fuck, he'd heard Ranger. This... Oh man. I looked around, and there were two guys looking at me. Dirty thoughts...they could smell my dirty thoughts. This was...ugh. I turned around and smacked Ranger across the chest. He laughed and put his hands up.

"I only tell the truth. You should know that by now." The Ranger I thought was lost had now returned.

"Yeah, well, you don't play fair," I grumbled back, but I didn't really mean it. I was smiling as I went into class and sat in the front, while Ranger followed and took the desk next to me.

This was going to be the longest class of the day.

CHAPTER FIFTY-ONE

GALEN

It was so hard to teach a bunch of teens, and it was even harder to teach with a hard on. God, why did Ranger have to say that, the prick. He would've known I was close, and he knew it would affect me, especially with the whole vampire, shifter, and Lexi conversation.

He knew I liked her more than I should, and I knew I shouldn't. I'd been wrestling with this for some time now, but I couldn't stop. The feelings for her grew every day, and I had to keep reminding myself that this was wrong. I was too old for her. She needed better than someone like me.

I'd wanted to speak to Lexi all day, and I'd been waiting for her at lunch. Her DNA results had come back, and Alaric wasn't too sure how to break it to her. He'd asked if I would do it, since I helped with the shifter speech last week. I half agreed, only because I wanted to get her alone. The shifter speech had gone terribly, so I was hoping to do much better today.

How was that only a week ago? It felt like a lifetime.

When class ended for the day, I called Lexi over as the other students left the room. Ranger could hear this, too, I didn't care. He lingered around, not wanting to leave. Maybe he was worried that I'd steal her away. And to be honest, the thought had crossed my mind for a moment.

"Lexi, I was wondering if it would be okay for me to drive you home so we could go back to my place, where we can talk?" I could see her cheeks pinken up. Was she blushing?

Oh man, this girl. I was done for. Her smell drew me in, and I wanted to taste her, her blood, her... But I knew if I did, I wouldn't be able to stop. I wanted her in a way a teacher shouldn't.

"Yeah, that sounds like a plan. Did you want me to come now?" I didn't know why, but that had all the blood rushing down to my cock. Fuck...that pool scene. I couldn't get it out of my head, and it played over and over in my mind, torturing me in the best possible way. She was so beautiful, sensitive, and the way she just let go like that... *Fuck.*

"Yes, let's go." *Before I come in my pants like a teenage boy.*

The drive back was full of tension. I wasn't sure if it was coming from me or her—probably the both of us—but it wasn't helping.

"Did you want me to stop and get you something to eat first?" I remembered that it was only last week when we were at a diner eating breakfast, and she told me she was Team Jacob, letting me know I didn't stand a chance. But then, days later, she was Team Have Them Both. I just couldn't stop thinking about it. I knew I should leave it, that I shouldn't interfere, but I'd never felt like this for anyone before.

"Yes, please. I'm a little hungry. Maybe we could get some burgers to go?"

I also shouldn't be going over as often as I was to the Lovell's. I shouldn't be watching movies and doing all these things that teenagers do, as I was well past that. I may have been frozen at the ripe age of twenty-one, but I had more experience than Rafferty,

Ranger, Maverick, and Lexi, times four. I was hundreds of years old, and I should tell her that today.

"Did you want to ask me anything? Now is a good time if you have any burning questions." That got her attention. She had her hair down again today, and she ran her hands through it, pushing it out of her face as she turned to me, her foot cocked up on the seat, relaxed.

"Yes, you mean vampire ones?" I chuckled at the way she asked, like she wasn't sure that was what I'd meant.

"Yes, vampire ones. I'll tell you anything, but...please, don't judge me." I turned and saw that she was still focused on me. Her gaze wandered over my sweater.

"Do you have tattoos?" I let the question linger for a few moments. That was not what I thought she would ask.

"No, back in my day—" She started laughing, and it was a deep laugh. She clutched her belly and bent forward, and I started laughing, too. God, I was an old man. I just didn't feel it when I was around Lexi, and that was bad. I needed to remind myself who I was. "As I was saying, back in my day, tattoos weren't something people did. Not the same as nowadays. You'll see the older wolf-shifters don't often have any. Alaric doesn't have any. And so, the answer to your question is no, I don't, and no, I can't get any. I heal too fast."

She nodded as I pulled up to the Wendy's drive-thru. I could see she was reading the menu, so I waited for her to decide. When I got up to the little box, I heard the scratchy voice of a woman ask for our order.

"Get whatever you want," I told Lexi as she hesitated, but she surprised me when she ordered three burgers, fries, and a Frosty. Wow, she must've really been hungry.

She turned to me. "Did you want to get something?" I was confused by her question. Did she forget that I didn't eat human food?

She giggled. "I mean...like get something you would want to eat, and then I can tell you how it tastes. I saw you eyeing the chocolate the other night, and it made me feel sad that you don't get to experience foods like I do."

If I was on the fence about whether to leave Lexi alone...I just jumped off and ran straight toward her. I didn't know what to say, I was so stunned. The lady in the box asked if that was all.

I looked back at the menu. I'd never been here before, I'd never needed to. I didn't know where to start.

"Yes, can I have also a crispy chicken sandwich?"

She ate two burgers and the fries before I even got to my place on the Lovell estate. She described every bite, and I think I enjoyed it more experiencing it through her words than I would've ever eating them.

"You can ask me all the questions you want when we get inside. I have a device that keeps out unwanted ears. There are a few around the house. Alaric has one in his office and his bedroom. Most shifters have them in their bedrooms." Her eyes perked up at that.

Yes, well, vampire hearing was much better than shifters, and I didn't want any outsiders to hear what was said in here. Not that we'd done anything to draw the attention of other shifter packs or vampires, but it was always nice to talk to someone in private.

It was a strange feeling when she walked inside my place with her bag of food and backpack.

"Wow, it's a lot bigger in here than it looks from the outside." I nodded, there was a basement too, but I used it mostly for storage. She walked around the sitting room, looking at some of the trinkets I had collected over my lifetime. I just kept the ones that meant the most to me here. She eyed the wooden horse my father carved for me when I was only four or five.

Most of my belongings were in my many houses and apartments around the world. With time on my side, I'd amassed considerable wealth, and I owned many properties. But with money doesn't come happiness, and it doesn't give you a purpose. That was why I was here, in Kiba.

"So, I guess the burning question to follow up the 'in my day' spiel is, how old are you? Like you look young...maybe twenty?" I shook my head and pointed up, she smiled as she took a seat and curled her legs under herself, making herself comfortable. She was so relaxed in my presence, and I realized I was the tense one. Why did she make me feel nervous? I took a seat across from her as I watched her unwrap another burger and take a bite. "Twenty-three?" Her voice was muffled as she spoke. I shook my head and pointed down. "Two, one?"

I smiled as she took another bite, not caring that she was speaking with her mouth full.

"Hey, you said you'd answer my questions." She ate some of her Frosty, and I laughed. It made me relax more.

"Yes, I did. I'm stuck at the age of twenty-one, but I've just celebrated my three hundred and twelfth birthday. So I am old, but not the oldest... There are vampires that are older than me. But to be honest, when you're around...I don't feel old or like a vampire."

She stopped eating and put her burger back inside the wrapping. I could see her brain ticking over. She was always thinking, and I liked that. She was switched on at all times.

"Is it something to do with what I am? Or...me?" She didn't meet my eye, maybe worried about my answer.

"Not what you are, but who you are." I waited for her to be disgusted, to leave my place. Grossed out that her teacher—an old man—was saying this to her.

"I like that," she whispered. Her smile was so genuine, her eyes so beautiful, they almost glowed from within. I almost forgot myself for a moment.

I let that sit and watched her lips as she licked them. I wanted to lick them too.

I wanted nothing more than to kiss her.

CHAPTER FIFTY-TWO

LEXI

Galen said that when he was around me, he didn't feel old, or like a vampire. I liked that it was me and not just the what I was that made him feel like that. There was a quiet in the room after I spoke, but it was nice. He was waiting for me to ask more.

"Do you drink human blood?" I decided to just dive right in. I wasn't afraid of Galen. He made me feel safe when I was around him, the same way I felt when I was around Raff and now Ranger.

"Yes." When he didn't go further, I waved my hand for him to continue and that sexy chuckle he had came out to play. "I drink from humans, and I also go to blood banks." Oh wow, that I guessed, but blood banks... That made me feel a bit better.

"What are you thinking?" he asked, his eyes searching my face.

"The truth?" I asked. Being bold, I wanted to tell him I didn't want him drinking other people's blood, and not because it was wrong, but that I was jealous. I wanted to be the one he fed from, and that should scare me, but it didn't. It just felt right. He nodded and crossed his legs as he sat back and got a little more comfortable.

Though I could tell from the way he was holding himself that he was anything but comfortable.

"I don't like the thought of you sucking blood from someone..." I could see his face harden slightly, but before he could speak, I quickly added, "I want to be the one you take blood from."

I could feel the air in the room thicken with desire as the words lingered between us. When he didn't move or say anything, I felt like maybe I was reading this wrong and he didn't feel something for me like I did for him.

"I can't, I... Your blood is different. It calls to me, but I don't know what it would do to me. If I drank from a shifter, it would make me weak, but it wouldn't kill me...like their venom does."

Before I could say anything, he blurted out, "Your DNA results are back, and that was one of the reasons I brought you here."

That had me sitting up straighter. Oh my god, I was going to find out what I was...

"Before you get too excited, they're still running tests to find out what you are. They haven't seen blood like yours before, and they're comparing it against everything they have. The news I have is different, so it might not be what you wanted to hear. Alaric thought it would be better coming from me."

I was truly freaking out. What the hell could it be if they didn't know what I was?

"Give it to me, I can handle anything."

Galen nodded as he placed his elbows on his knees, leaning closer to me. I mirrored the same movements, not wanting to miss anything he said.

"You don't share any DNA with your father. He was not your biological father, Lexi. We don't know who was, but he's the one who passed the supernatural element onto you, your unique scent, and the fast healing. I am so sorry to tell you this..."

That was it? My mom cheated on my dad with some supernatural guy? I didn't know if I was numb to the fact that he just told me that the man I called 'Dad' for five years wasn't my real dad. He didn't act like I was his daughter, but then again, neither did my mother. They were always drugged out, and I was left hungry more than I could count the times they fed me.

"That's okay...no need to be sorry. They weren't exactly loving parents."

Galen was in front of me in an instant, and I gasped at the sudden movement. His curls bounced on his forehead like they were trying to keep up with the sudden shift. I giggled as I reached out and twirled one in my finger. It was silky and soft.

"You're like super-fast." He was so close, and I was touching his hair. My stomach felt like it had butterflies, and I bit my lower lip as I slowly traced my fingers down his forehead, his cheek, and to his jaw. He was cold to the touch, which reminded me of what he really was. It didn't put me off, it just made me more curious. I wanted to know... no, I needed to know how he would feel on my lips. My breathing had sped up as my lips parted, and I was sure he could hear my hammering heart. My breath hitched as I ran my thumb along his bottom lip, his eyes never straying from my own.

"Show me your fangs," I whispered almost breathlessly. I was so turned on, my body tingling all over. He tried to pull away from me, but I reached out and grabbed his shoulder and held him. He would've been able to get out of my hold, but he stayed.

His big hazel eyes turned dark. "Your eyes are so amazing when they turn dark. You don't have to show me your fangs, but you also don't have to be afraid to be yourself. I won't run screaming. I'm a lot stronger than you think."

When he faced me, I could see the dark swirling with the hazel. It was like there was a fight for dominance happening in his eyes—the vampire side taking over from the human. But it didn't alarm me. I trusted Galen with my life.

I watched in fascination as the dark won and his mouth dropped open slightly. I could see this was hard for him. He didn't want to show me this side of himself, the part he'd kept hidden.

His tongue swept out and licked his lower lip where my thumb had just been moments earlier. I could see two white fangs protruding. I moved closer to him and he didn't move. He watched me with curious eyes as I reached out and ran my thumb along his bottom lip again. This time, I stroked a finger down the exposed fang, and Galen shivered.

"Sorry, I should have asked." He shook his head and nodded for me to continue. He was waiting for me to finish exploring. I touched the other one and tried to imagine it piercing someone's skin.

"Does it hurt? When you bite people?"

He pulled away slight to talk. "No, I compel them. Something I can't do to shifters...or you. I tried once." He looked a little ashamed at that, but I shook my head. I didn't care if he tried, just that he couldn't made me feel relieved. That what I felt for him wasn't put inside my head, that this was really how I felt.

"How do they explain the holes in their neck?"

He let out a deep, rumbled laugh. "Ah, see there is our secret. Vampire blood heals humans as fast as it heals us."

Oh wow. I raised my brows. So, the person wouldn't feel it happening, and then be healed and not even know they'd been fed on by a vampire. I guess that was the way vampires survived for all these years and no one knew that they were real.

I wanted to kiss him so bad, but I'd already created a bit of a mess with Ranger that I needed to fix first. I didn't want to throw Galen in the mix and add a bigger mess. But his face, his lips... I wanted nothing more than to kiss him. He was the sexiest teacher I'd ever had, and I think that was why this was such a bad idea. I shouldn't be touching him like this. I shouldn't want him like this. It was wrong. Until I graduated.

"What are you thinking?" he asked.

"About kissing you." I held my hand over my mouth as my eyes widened. *Holy shit.* I'd said that out loud.

"Hey, don't do that. Don't overthink it. I asked, and you told me... I would be lying if I told you I wasn't thinking the same, Lexi."

I drew in a shuddering breath at his words. His hand went to my knee, and when I didn't say anything, he smiled and moved in closer. My body hummed in response.

"Did you mean what I think you did? When you said, 'have your cake and eat it too'?" His left brow cocked, and I could see a tiny smirk on his face. I pushed his shoulder lightly, but I didn't take my hand away.

"I want to eat cake," I whispered. His hand moved farther up my leg, and I could feel the cold of his skin through my jeans. "I want every slice." His hand stopped, and my skin tingled everywhere he'd touched like he was lighting me up.

"Rafferty?" I nodded. "Ranger." I rolled my eyes, but smiled and nodded. "What about Maverick?" That didn't know, so I shrugged. How many was too many?

"Me?" It was so low, I didn't think I would hear it, but I did. I didn't speak, instead, I looked him in the eyes and slowly nodded. He was so close, just another inch and we would be kissing.

My eyes drifted closed as our noses met, his cold against my warm. I sucked in a small breath just as there was a loud bang on the door. My eyes flew open, and so did his. He was up instantly and over to see who it was. My hand on my chest tried to calm my racing heart.

Alaric...

And now the moment between Galen and me was gone.

CHAPTER FIFTY-THREE

LEXI

I ran back to the house. I needed to get some space to clear my head. I almost kissed Galen, and I'd dry humped Raff and Ranger in the pool in front of Maverick and Galen...and he'd asked me if I wanted Maverick. I wasn't sure what was happening. Did I want them all? Could I have them all? I'd started to really like Maverick, but now everything was crazy.

As soon as I got into the house, I went toward the kitchen to grab a snack. What I didn't expect to see was Maverick...topless. He had a tattoo on his chest, and it was some words.

"Hey, Lexi. Do you like steak? I was going to grill tonight." I looked up at his face, and he smiled. Oh god, those dimples. I needed to think with my head, not my body.

"Ah, yeah." I thought I did. His brows furrowed as he looked at me closer. I tried to be casual and put my hands in my pockets. I desperately tried not to give away that I almost kissed my teacher and was busted by his dad.

"Are you okay? Was it bad news? Did you want to talk about it?" Huh? Oh, oh...the whole parent thing.

I shook my head. "No, I'm fine. It wasn't anything big. My dad isn't my real dad. It's some supernatural guy... Are you making potato salad?" I was just now seeing what he was doing. He looked at me, concern written over his face, but then he smiled again as he nodded.

"Yeah, for dinner tonight. I hope you have room, because I made a pasta salad, too." Wow, just...wow. The Lovell brothers didn't just look like works of art, but they could cook and were smart, too. It wasn't helping me stop thinking about how sexy Maverick looked right now.

"Yep, I have room." I'd make room for that. I quickly dashed past him, grabbed some cookies, and made my way up to my room. By the time I flopped onto the bed, I realized I'd left my backpack at Galen's. Ugh...I didn't think I could face him again tonight, and I had too many things on my mind to sit and do any homework right now.

I was actually lucky that Alaric brought my bag back for me, so I didn't have to go get it. He said that Galen had to excuse himself from tonight's dinner, that he had somewhere he needed to be. I groaned internally, since Alaric would have smelled me at Galen's. He'd know that something else was going on there, that I was turned on by Galen. This was bad. So, so bad.

I was quiet at dinner. Ranger and Raff both sat beside me. Jett was cracking jokes, and I was trying to laugh along. Lyell was discussing something to do with the weather and Nash... Well, he was Nash. After dinner, Raff invited me to come spend some time with him in his room. I agreed, but I wanted to take a shower first and get comfy for the night. I thought some time alone with Raff would be good for me.

If I could, I'd live in pjs, like every day. It was warm inside the house, so I opted for some sleep shorts and the oversized white tee. But I was going bra free tonight. I loved throwing off my bra at the end of the day. I needed to be marked now, and I was hoping Raff would be into marking more than just my neck tonight.

I giggled to myself as I made my way down to his room. I was surprised when I passed by Ranger's room, and his door was open as Raff came out. I stopped and spun around.

"What were you doing in Ranger's room?" I asked as I lifted my arms up to hug him.

Raff smiled and wrapped his arms around me, kissing me softly. "Were just hanging out. Talking about shit." I raised my brow at Raff as I saw Ranger casually lean against the doorframe. He looked like he'd really gotten his confident, cocky self back.

"Do you guys want to hang out in here?" Ranger asked. I looked up to Raff, trying to work out if this was what he wanted. I'd been looking forward to the one on one marking time, but if he wanted to hang out with Ranger, then I was okay with that. Plus, I was sure it wasn't us just hanging. I had a feeling Ranger's words meant more than that.

I just wasn't too sure if Raff was really okay with this, and I needed to be sure. If he wasn't, I'd put all my other feelings aside and walk away right here with Raff. I knew in my heart he was for me—he was my forever.

But there was a pang in my chest that told me I couldn't do that, that I knew Ranger had a piece of me now, Galen too. And I couldn't just let go of this feeling I had for Maverick. Raff's eyes told me all I needed, and I nodded. Raff smiled and took my face in his warm hands and kissed me deeply. When we pulled apart, I sagged against his chest, trying to catch my breath. He was an amazing kisser, and I noticed Ranger was openly watching us.

"Come in." Ranger gestured with his hands to his room. I'd never been in here before. There was a desk with a laptop, some trophies, and there was a photo of him and Maverick when they must've been ten, both smiling and wearing football jerseys.

"Do you want to sit on my bed or..." Ranger trailed off, and I shrugged. The bed was fine. I jumped up on it, and Raff came to sit beside me, holding my hand as I smiled at him. The bed felt the same as mine. Even the white covers were the same. When no one spoke for a few minutes, I didn't know what to say. We just looked at each other, and I waited for someone to speak.

"Did you want to play a game?" Ranger asked, breaking the silence.

I nodded. "Yeah, why not." If no one was going to talk, then this would get boring fast, and I would've been better off in Raff's room, making out.

"How about...truth or dare?"

I laughed, because of course Ranger would pick that game. The door to his room swung open, and Maverick was standing there. He'd put a tee on before dinner, but now he was only wearing tight white boxers. Holy fuck, they were struggling to hold what he was packing there. I felt heat flare up my cheeks. He had that sexy V that I wanted to trace with my fingers. *Shit*. My eyes snapped up to his face.

"Ah, Mav is here. You ready to play, brother?" His face showed his confusion at his brother's words.

"I thought we were all just hanging out?" Maverick asked as he walked in, closing the door behind him.

"Yeah, but I thought it might be more fun to play truth or dare." Maverick hesitated, his eyes darting straight to me before going back to his brother. Oh yeah, I already knew where Ranger was going with this. He moved and took a seat across from me. The four of us were in a circle. I crossed my legs, ready for the many dares that would be aimed at kissing me.

"How about I start?" Ranger asked. I laughed because I knew he would start. "Raff, truth or dare?" I looked over at Raff, and even he was confused by being picked first.

"Truth." He rubbed his warm hand over my bare knee. Ranger leaned back on his elbows, his T-shirt tight against his chest. He gave me a smooth smile as he cocked his brow at me.

"If Lex wanted more than one mate, are you okay with that and... do you care if they aren't all shifters?" My mouth dropped wide open. What the...? *Galen*. Ranger knew, and he was talking about Galen. I looked around at Raff and Maverick. I fidgeted, and Raff just patted my leg, trying to calm me. Ranger somehow knew about us.

"I'm okay with all of that." Raff turned to me. He could obviously smell how anxious I was at the question, but he didn't know it was because of Ranger knowing about Galen, not the sharing me part. "I really am. This is how I was raised, and if you want that, then I want that, too."

I nodded. I believed him, I just couldn't get over the fact that Ranger must've been listening to me and Galen. How? Galen had said he turned the device on so others couldn't hear us.

Ranger just watched me as I panicked. If he knew, how many others did? Would Galen lose his job? Oh god, was he in trouble with Alaric?

"Maverick, truth or dare?" Raff asked, snapping me out of the thoughts I was drowning in.

Maverick's eyes found mine, and he gave me wicked smile "Truth." My heart was racing. There was just something about Maverick, but I didn't know what. He was artistic and a bit of a mystery.

"Would you share a mate with your brother?"

Maverick didn't even blink or have to think before he said, "Yes."

My eyes widened. This was not the way I thought this night was going to go.

"Lexi, truth or dare?" Maverick asked. Well, there was no way I was going with truth, that was too hard right now. I had too much going on in my head.

"Dare." I grinned. I knew it was going to be kissing Ranger, which really was a strange way to trick someone into kissing them. He could've just asked me outright, since he was always so cocky and sure about himself. He didn't need his brother to dare me to do it.

Maverick must have clued in to what I was thinking. He tapped his chin in a dramatic way as he thought for a moment. I gave him my best 'dare me' look.

"I dare you to play spin the bottle, and the person it lands on is the one you *don't* kiss." I think all the air left my lungs. Oh, I so wasn't expecting that. Before I could get a chance to change it to truth, a large textbook was placed in the middle of us and a half-empty water bottle was placed on the top.

"Man, I gotta give it to you, Maverick. That was well thought out," Ranger praised him. Maverick chuckled, and those dimples came out to play again. Well, I guessed I could understand what Galen was asking me earlier about Maverick...he must like me more than he'd let on to come up with this sneaky game.

My heart was racing a little, and I was more than excited. I was trying to calm myself, but I knew I was giving off that turned on scent. None of them said anything though. I took the bottle and spun it before I could overthink this. We all watched as it slowed down, and when it stopped, I laughed so hard.

"Oh, that wasn't fair. Spin it again," Ranger teased and pouted. I turned to Raff, who didn't need to be asked twice. He held my face and kissed me. Our tongues met and danced for a brief moment before he pulled away, smiling. His eyes then traveled to Maverick.

I was a little nervous, only because I was doing this in front of Raff for the first time, and I still wasn't sure how he'd react. He could feel like he was okay with it, but then change his mind when he saw it. Saying and doing were two different things.

I leaned across the book, and the bottle rolled off as I tried to get closer to Maverick. His nose flared. "You don't smell like him," he muttered more to himself than he meant it for us. His bare chest rose and fell as his breathing sped up, and he took my face in with his eyes.

"You are so beautiful, Lexi. You don't have to..."

I smiled and shook my head, my hair falling around my face and framing it. I liked that he was leaving it up to me, but now that I'd really thought about it—about him—I wanted to kiss him, even if it was just a chaste kiss to begin with.

"I want to." I could hear a low growl in his chest as he moved toward me, his fingers lightly touching my cheeks as he pushed my hair behind my ears. His eyes searched mine before they closed and our lips met. I gasped at the contact, his lips so lush, so soft. This feeling washed over me that this was right, like a piece of me was just put back together. When his tongue brushed over my lips, everyone in the room disappeared but him. I moved across the bed until I was straddling him, my hands in his hair, his tongue sweeping inside my mouth, and the feeling of his growl deep in my chest.

My heart was racing wildly, and I could feel his hard cock against my core. I was wet and felt a need deep within me. I smiled, knowing that I did that to him, that his hardness was for me. As I kept kissing him, I wasn't the only one affected by this, then two throats cleared.

"Okay, well... That was hot as hell, but now it's Lexi's turn to ask me." Ranger almost sounded like he was going to sulk like a puppy. I glanced into Maverick's eyes quickly before I pulled away and crawled back to my spot on the bed. I glanced back to see Maverick had pulled a pillow over his lap.

"Eeewww... I don't want your cock touching my pillow," Ranger joked as he tried to pull the pillow away from Maverick, but he held on tight. Raff laughed and held onto me as the twins fought and jostled the bed.

"Ranger, truth or dare?" I asked. That brought his attention back to me.

"Ah, this is a hard one. Dare. No, truth...no...dare. I'll go truth." I chuckled, watching him decide. He sat up straight and brushed his hair out of his face. "Truth, Lex."

I pretended to think about it, but I'd decided to go with the same question Raff had asked, since it made sense. Or I would've dared him to kiss me, but he picked truth.

"Would you share a mate with your brother?" Ranger's eyes went to Maverick as he nodded. When they came back to mine, I could tell he was being very serious.

"Forever, yes."

I didn't move or speak. Then I decided to just go for it. I put my arms down on the mattress in front of me and it dipped lightly as I leaned forward toward Ranger. He gave me a cute smirk as he raised his brows.

"Well? Aren't you gonna kiss me?" Raff and Maverick laughed. "This was what the game was for, right?" Even I laughed.

Ranger moved slowly toward me, the playful glint gone and replaced by need. His hands went to my face as he angled his, and our lips met with an almost uncontrollable hunger. I could feel myself being lifted into his lap. The same feeling of rightness washed over me, and I felt almost complete.

I'd found the missing pieces of my heart... I was just missing one more piece.

CHAPTER FIFTY-FOUR

LEXI

I couldn't believe it was Saturday already. How did the week go by that fast? Oh...because I was busy making out non-stop with Rafferty while sneaking kisses from Ranger and Maverick all week. I'd told them I wasn't ready to go further than that, not just yet at least. I wanted to keep it a secret for now. I wasn't sure how this would go, but I had a feeling that Olivia and her friends wouldn't be too impressed that I took Ranger and Maverick.

Galen had avoided me all week, and he wasn't even at school. I'd seen his car at his place a few times, and I found Alaric on Thursday to ask if everything was okay with Galen. I was really worried he'd lost his job and was being punished for the almost kiss, because that was what it was...an almost kiss. Alaric said Galen was working on finding out what I was for the pack. That they needed a day vampire to help out the pack at Bardoul with their investigations.

Day vampire...I'd asked if there were night ones, too. Alaric looked at me like I was joking, and when I didn't laugh, he realized I didn't actually know. He told me that there were a few vampires who could walk during the day, and they were rare, but there weren't different breeds. Most couldn't or they would burst into flames. Okay,

I just guessed that part. Alaric told me to ask Galen about them, that he didn't know all about them and it would be better coming from him. I would've asked him if I could've found him, but Galen didn't come home last night, and I hadn't seen him all day.

"Oh my god, I can't believe I'm here for another Lovell party. And like, you kissed the brothers. *Twins!*" Ada squealed. "Like, can I have a little bit of what you got? I want me a sexy boyfriend, and just one will do for now, you greedy bitch, taking them all. Leave some for me." Ada giggled as she bounced around my room. The party had started a while ago, but she insisted that we be fashionable late. Plus, she was excited to walk out of the house with me. She wanted to make an entrance and have people to see her.

I had no idea what went through her mind, but she'd been sitting with me and the Kiba boys for lunch the whole week. They saw her in the halls and said hello to her and made the effort to make her feel welcome in the group. No other girls got that kind of treatment...well, apart from me.

I looked out my window and could see some of the girls from school were in tiny bikinis at the pool and calling out to Ranger. I felt a small pang of jealously, but smiled when he waved and moved away from them.

He was looking super sexy tonight in jeans and a white button-down shirt. I couldn't wait till later, when I was going to unbutton it while I kissed him silly. I smiled at the thought. I could have all the dirty thoughts I wanted up here, since the shifters couldn't smell me from here. I looked down again and found Ranger watching me. "*Oh shit*," I hissed under my breath, and I could see him chuckle. Maybe he could smell me...

"Oh my god, is that Mr. Donovani lurking over there?" Ada gasped as she pointed toward the forest edge. I could see him, and he was...lurking. I was confused about what he was doing there and upset that he didn't come see me. I'd left a message under his door to come see me when he got back. Maybe he was looking for me, or waiting for me over there. That made more sense.

"Yeah, he's friends with the family," I said, trying to make up a story of why he was here. I still hadn't told her about him, I didn't know how to even start. She'd been so great and understanding with me, but this was a little too much for now. She nodded at my answer, but still looked a little confused as to why he was here. It would still be weird for a teacher—even as a friend of the family—to be at a high school party. I looked around and could see Raff and Maverick talking with some other guys, one of which was Saint.

I had to stop hating him, Raff certainly had.

"Oh man, do you think Saint is single still? I want *some* of him." I laughed as I saw Raff glance up toward us and smile just as the other two did.

Oh yeah, they heard that.

"You'll have to go ask him yourself." I put my hands on her shoulders. Unlike two weeks ago, tonight, I was really looking forward to going down there and joining the party. I'd decided I was going to kiss all three of them tonight in front of everyone. All the Kiba boys knew anyway, and there were fewer non-shifter people here. So I didn't feel so...judged. Not that I ever cared what others thought of me before. I just wasn't good with being the center of attention, and having three boyfriends would make for huge gossip at school. But it was spring break, and that meant I had some time before I had to see them all again.

"Do you think I look nice?" I could see the vulnerability in Ada's eyes.

I pulled her into a hug. "You look gorgeous, and I'm sure one of the guys out there will think so, too. And then they'll find out that you're a beautiful person on the inside and ask you out on a date." Ada giggled, and so did I, but that was my little subtle warning for the guys out there—they'd better treat her right, or they'd have me to deal with.

"Let's go. You have three sexy boys out there waiting, and you've got to kiss them. Show those girls which guys are yours, and that they need to back the fuck off." I just laughed as I grabbed the leather jacket, and we made our way down the stairs and out into the cool spring air.

You could feel the damp chill outside. Ada said she would meet with me in a moment, since she wanted a small amount of liquid courage. I, however, didn't want any. I grabbed a bottle of water and watched her, scanning the guys, making sure they knew I was watching them. I saw Noah walk toward her as soon as he saw her and smiled. He was sweet to her, even though he was much younger at fifteen.

As soon as I wrapped my arms around Raff, I felt warmer. Mav winked at me and rubbed my back a few times before pulling away. I smiled and told him that it was nice.

"I want more, I'm cold." I was ready for this. The family knew, Alaric seemed really okay with the fact that I didn't just give Ranger a chance, but Maverick, too. There were some extra strict rules about bedrooms, and who could be in them and when. Unfortunately for Jett, he'd become more or less our babysitter. He had to make sure we didn't get up to too much, but this was Jett, so anything pretty much went.

"Wow, you really need to warm up. Your hands are so cold," Raff said as he twisted me around into his warm embrace.

"Well, you can both warm me up." I felt Maverick rub my back. It was only a small move, but I was glad for it. Small steps. I could hear Saint talking away, was he talking about hunting? When I looked at him, he gave me a small wary smile. Then he glanced at Maverick and me. Ah, I forgot Maverick and him were best buddies.

"What do you hunt?" I was curious because Raff was talking more than ever with them and was just so comfortable here, like he really fit in. More than me. And even though I wasn't into hunting or guns, I wanted to be supportive.

"Deer mainly, rabbits for fun. They give the best chase." And then I realized they weren't talking about hunting with weapons—no, they were the weapon.

"When you catch one, then, you know...switch back. Do you have like, fur and blood in your mouth?" They all laughed, *all of them*. I could feel Raff hold me tightly as his body shook, and Maverick's hands were now on my shoulders.

"What? It's a serious question." Saint nodded and gave me a face that told me it tasted just as bad as it sounded.

"Eeeww, remind me not to kiss you after a hunt." I turned back to look at Maverick, then up to Raff. Ada came over with a red cup in her hand, smiling, but I could tell she was nervous—and nervous Ada talked about a lot of random stuff.

"Hi, Ada. How have you been?" Saint asked, and my mouth almost dropped. Okay...he was alright, but not forgiven. Just alright. For now.

Everyone started to feel the effects of the alcohol as the night wore on. Drunk people were everywhere, probably more of them than sober people. I wanted to look for Galen, since I remembered seeing him over the near the forest, and Ranger had disappeared that way a while ago. I wanted to kiss him, but he'd run off before we could. Maybe he was with Galen?

I left Ada chatting with Noah. She kept telling me he was too young for her, but she enjoyed that he was flirty. I just laughed at her. Age was just a number. Galen was old, but I didn't care. And Noah didn't look like a fifteen-year-old, but I was sure he still had the personality of one.

"I'm just going to see if I can find Ranger," I told her, a little white lie. I felt bad, but I really needed to see Galen.

It grew darker and darker as I made my way across the green lawn, reminding me what had happened here only two weeks ago. I saw the fallen log, and again, there were the glowing eyes of a wolf. I froze and saw it was a huge gray one. I looked back to the party. Everyone was unaware that he was here.

"Ranger?" Maybe this was why he'd been gone for so long. He moved forward toward me, then did a little playful jump. I laughed. "Oh, man. Ranger. I didn't expect to see you like this." I reached out my hand, and he bumped his head against me. I pet him and stroked his ears. He was so fluffy. I hadn't seen the guys turn into wolves since that morning I found out, because they weren't allowed to shift in the house. But out here, man... I was missing out. I'd have to make them shift everyday so I could lay down outside and snuggle with wolves.

"Hey," I said as he moved around me so fast, I almost fell, "slow down. I'm not like you." I guess he didn't realize how big and strong he was in this form. Actually, he was big and strong in both forms. When he did it again, I fell on my ass and pain shot up from my leg. I let out a scream as I looked down and saw he had my thigh in his mouth. He was biting me. I tried to shove him away, but he wouldn't let go. I started to panic when I felt an intense burning. What was he doing to me?

"Ranger, stop," I called out. I heard a snap and a loud thump as he let go of my leg and let out a yelp. I reached down to stop the pain, but the burn traveled higher. My chest felt heavy, and it was hard to breathe.

"Lexi, oh my god. I'll get you help." I was scooped up into some arms. I felt the air pass me by at a high speed. *Galen*. I felt safe. I'd be okay, because he was here. When I gasped, trying to catch my breath, I realized I was in trouble as the pain flooded my body. My stomach heaved.

"Fuck, what happened?" I heard Ranger now.

"Why would you bite me?" I ground out, gritting my teeth to stop the pain coursing through my body.

"I didn't do this, Lex. I...fuck. It was Callum. I can smell him on her. Shit, he gave her his venom. She's gonna change. No. Fuck no."

I heard voices all around me, but my ears were ringing, and I felt like I was drowning. My leg hurt so bad, and I didn't know if this was what was supposed to happen when they gave you venom to change, or if I was dying. It felt more like dying. My heart was slowing down, and I couldn't think straight.

I gasped again for air that I couldn't take in.

CHAPTER FIFTY-FIVE

MAVERICK

My stomach was in knots. It was if all my nightmares had come true all at once. I didn't want this for Lexi. I didn't want her to go through this. I could smell her body, the pain and fear that leaked from her was one of the reasons I never wanted this.

She was in so much pain, and everyone was just standing around, yelling and cursing, not knowing what to do. This wasn't good. Her heart rate was slowing.

We were in the living room, and my father had drawn the curtains to stop others from seeing in and watching this happen to her. To my strong Lexi. *Come on, fight this.*

"Fuck, what do we do? This isn't right," Raff called out, holding her hand and trying to offer her soothing words. Her eyes had rolled into the back of her head. Then there was a gasp from beside me.

"Lexi, oh my god. What's wrong with her?" It was her friend Ada. She must've snuck in here when Father wasn't watching. Shit, I didn't have the heart to turn her away. I was paralyzed where I was standing, watching. It almost felt like an out-of-body experience.

"Is she dying?" I managed to ask. Her heart was getting slower by the minute. I could hear it, everyone could. I didn't know what to do, no one did.

Jett rushed into the room, and my eyes met his. They were wild and panicked.

"I'm going to kill him," he growled low, his hands clenched into fists, and I could see his eyes flash—he was going to shift. I'd never seen him lose it so fast.

"No, we deal with this now. This isn't the way it was supposed to go, and she isn't responding in the usual way. Galen, do you think you could give her some of your blood?" I watched as Galen—who was looking unlike his usual well-kept self—dragged his hands through his hair, pacing, touching her, then pacing again. His dark eyes flashed up to my father.

"Yes." He pulled his sleeve up, and I could see scars on his arm. I didn't think much more on it as his fangs descended and he bit open his wrist. I'd never seen him like this, as he never showed his vampire side around anyone. He looked dangerous and hot as sin. Ada gasped from beside me, and I watched her as she took it all in.

She turned to me and said, "I knew he was too good-looking to be human." I shook my head, stunned at her words. She was like Ranger and Jett in the way they masked their pain with witty humor. We both turned to watch as Galen fed Lexi his blood. Her body stopped spasming, but her heartbeat was getting so low, I could barely hear it.

"I don't know what else to do. I..." Galen looked around the room. When his eyes found mine, I felt my heart skip a beat before his face fell. I looked down to Lexi, who was so still, so lifeless. I fell to the floor beside my brother and shook her leg.

"Wake up, don't leave me. You can't—" Tears started to roll down my face. I could see them on my brother. Raff was shaking so hard, I grabbed his shoulder to stop him from shifting. He was losing control of his wolf, and Lexi needed us here. I needed him here.

"This wasn't meant to happen... I don't know how to help her. How do we stop this?" Raff called out.

Her breathing was so shallow. I reached over and placed my hand on her chest to feel for it. "God, Lexi. Breathe, babe." *Just survive this. I can't live without you.*

"I...I think I can save her," Galen spoke up.

My father's voice bounced around the walls in an echo as he screamed for Galen to do it. Galen's eyes met mine, and for a split-second, I felt like he was saying goodbye. Before I could say anything, he brushed her hair from her throat, and he bit her. The room watched in fear as Galen drank from her, but not in a way that it was shocking to see. We knew he was sucking the venom from her—the very stuff shifters used on vampires to kill them.

He pulled back and swayed lightly as he watched her chest. She was breathing steadier, her heartrate increasing.

"Lexi?" Ranger asked. She didn't move, but she wasn't dying anymore. Galen stood and then stumbled. Ada screamed out his name as he crashed to the floor.

I jumped up and ran over to him and tried to get him to sit up. No, this wasn't happening, he wasn't dying.

"No, this isn't fair. Vomit, get it out," I begged him. His mouth was coated in her blood, but he still smiled up at me. I brushed his curls back as I watched his face turn paler, but he was still so beautiful.

"It was worth it...for Lexi." He coughed up some blood, and it coated the white rug.

"Let it out, get it all out, Galen," my father yelled. I tried to push him onto his side, but he wouldn't have it.

He reached out to my face and stroked it so gently. I started crying harder as I clutched him tightly to my chest. I couldn't lose him, too. I needed them both. I had to have them both. This wasn't fair. Hadn't I had enough loss and heartache in my life?

"Lexi? Lexi?" I heard Raff call out beside me. Galen's body spasmed a few times, and everyone watched on in horror. Galen knew this would happen. He knew taking the venom from her blood would kill him, and I didn't get a chance to tell him how I felt about him.

I stroked his hair from his clammy forehead and moved him closer to be next to Lexi, because I knew he was in love with her. He would only do this for her, exchange his life for hers because he loved her so deeply. Ranger's eyes went to Galen, then to me, and his mouth opened slightly before he gave me a sad smile. That was when I realized that Ranger had put two and two together.

"Galen," I whispered into his ear. He started to move more. How long did venom take to kill a vampire? I'd never seen this before. Galen was the second vampire I'd ever known.

"Galen, how do you feel?" Jett asked as he came over and wiped his mouth with a cloth and tried to make him look more like the Galen we all knew. If he was going to die, he would die in my arms beside Lexi, looking like the Galen I fell in love with years ago. Not wanting to know how he got those scars, I pulled his sleeve down over his wrist. It wasn't like I'd be able to ask him about it anyway.

Lexi started to stir. She groaned and grabbed her leg where she'd been bitten, then reached up to her neck.

"Shh, shh... Don't strain yourself, you're here with us. You're going to be fine," Ranger whispered gently. Her eyes fluttered open and blinked a few times, trying to focus.

"Lexi?" Galen croaked out. She slowly turned her head toward him, and her nose crinkled up.

"Galen..." Her voice was dry and rough. "What... Ouch!" Her hand flew to her neck. "You bit me." No one said anything as she turned to Ranger. "You bit me?"

He shook his head. I could see he was still holding back his anger at his packmate. I knew why Callum did this. I'd heard Ranger tell him that they wouldn't be packmates anymore, and he was angry at Ranger, but this was going too far. Lexi did nothing to deserve this.

"It wasn't me, Lex, it was Callum," he explained. Galen reached over to her and placed his hand on her neck. He seemed to be a little stronger as he pulled himself up to go to her.

"Callum bit you. He tried to turn you. I had to bite you to save you."

I could see the words roll over in her head. She tried to sit up, but the boys wouldn't let her. Eventually, Father told them to help her, and they sat her up. She was a little dizzy, but once she settled, she smiled softly.

"I got bitten twice... You drank my blood? And now you're being all cozy and lovey with my Maverick?" I could hear the teasing in her voice, and some chuckles came from Jett and Ranger. I had a feeling Lexi didn't know what he meant by that—that he drank her venom filled blood.

"Do you remember the venom thing, Lex? Vampires die if bitten by a shifter...or if they ingest it. He just sucked the venom out of your body." When Ranger finished, she started to sob. Her hands reached out to touch Galen, to stroke his face, his curls.

"Is that true?" Everyone nodded. "But why? When you knew it would kill you?"

We all knew why, and any one of us would've done the same.

"Because I wanted to eat my piece of cake, too." He chuckled at her, smiled, then made a pained groan. We all froze. Lexi moved in, Ranger and Raff holding her, and she swept back the curls on Galen's face and pressed her lips softly to his.

"I love you, Galen," she whispered. "How did I taste?"

Galen chuckled and took her hand in his. "Lexi, you tasted just like...*heaven*."

The end
   ...of book one

ALSO BY BELLE HARPER

Pre Order Blood Moon Here

You can have your cake and eat it too… can't you?

Galen is a Vampire, Rafferty is a Red Wolf, and the twins, Ranger and Maverick shift into Grey Wolves.

What the shifters don't know is there is a war brewing and Lexi is caught right in the middle.

But Lexi isn't human…

Is she the cure they all have been waiting for?

Or is she the destruction that ends them all.

Can she save the packs and the people she has come to call family and friends?

** Coming late June/Early July**

Buy It Here

LOVE BITES: A paranormal romance anthology full of bite!

Explore your wild side with these sizzling stories.

A paranormal romance anthology by 8 incredible authors!

This anthology contains short stories ranging from romantic, action-packed, to HOT!

Filled with Vampires, shifters, demons, witches and more, this collection of fantasy romance stories will make you blush and have you begging for more.

Fans of dark fantasy, paranormal intrigue, and romance will devour these stories.

Buy it Here

My name is Luna.

I applied to a job ad that sounded too good to be true.

It was!

I'm being sent to an Alien Planet to marry an Alien guy with four-arms.

But now I'm here, I just found out I'm getting FIVE Alien husbands not one.

This was not what I applied for.

But one of the Alien guys broke my Translator and things are about to get messy.

Luna Touched is the first in a series of standalone books. This book is Reverse Harem. Sexy Aliens with four-arms and tails... what more could you want?

ACKNOWLEDGMENTS

Thank you Reader for taking a chance on Twice Bitten.

It truely means so much to me. This story has been waiting for a long time to be written. I love vampires and shifters, and what a better way then to have them both, together.

I know I have left you on a cliffhanger but it shouldn't be too long, Book Two will be late June/ early July and Book Three will be released early August.

If you have a chance, would you please consider leaving a review? All reviews, good and bad help other readers find their next book. And I am very grateful to all the reviews I have received.

I want to thank my amazing PA Andi Jeffree, you keep me on track and help me from going down the social media worm hole that are puppy videos. Thank you for all that you do.

I want to thank Patricia At, who was a great help with climate in Washington State, High School themes and every other silly question I asked you. You were so happy to answer and I thank you for that.

I want to thank my brand new editor, Meghan, you have fixed everything that went wrong. And all the stress I had been under after hiring the wrong person for the job the first time around. I am so glad to have you on my team. And looking forward to working with you more in the future.

I also want to thank the amazing and talented Author Sam Hall for her sanity saving messages and the amazing friendship we have. You are the best, and everyone should read your books!! (Hint Hint)

ABOUT THE AUTHOR

Belle is an Artist, Author, Wife and Mother.

She has an addiction to reading, notebooks, coloured pens and mint chocolate. She lives in the beautiful Australian bush, surrounded by wildlife and the smell of eucalyptus trees.

She also has a strong love for all 60's music, believes she was born in the wrong era and should have been at Woodstock.

If you would like to find out more about Belle, please come like and follow her:

Click Here to Like Belle's Facebook Page

Join Belle in her Facebook Group

www.authorbelleharper.com

Sign up to my Newsletter to keep up to date with my new Releases, Free Books and Giveaways.

https://www.subscribepage.com/belleharper

BELLE'S RECOMMENDED BOOKS

The Wolf At My Door

Buy It Here

All Jules wants is to get a job. The drought is causing work to dry up along with the land and she and her dog, Buddy are starting to get desperate. Then she spies an ad for an all-rounder at a remote place called Sanctuary, whatever that is.

Somehow Jules is the only applicant and it appears all her prayers have been answered. She now has food, board, a job and a whole lot more. It appears Sanctuary is the home of a huge pool of ridiculously good looking men who are 1. All vying for her attention and 2, expect her to choose to have relationships with multiples of them.

Just as Jules thinks she's Alice and she's fallen down the hole into Dickland, she starts to look past the guys who read romance novels to better understand women and the HR manuals written by kink practitioners and starts to wonder. What is behind the huge fence at the centre of Sanctuary? Why is everyone waiting for the full moon? What secrets are the staff hiding? Join Jules as she finds her answers to these questions and those she never thought to ask.

Author note: This is a super steamy, fast burn, but slow emotional burn reverse harem title. 18+ only. Does feature some MM and mind that cliff!